NO MORE
MISTER NICE GUY

Howard Jacobson was born in 1942 and educated at Cambridge University. He is also the author of *Coming From Behind*, *Peeping Tom*, *Redback*, *The Very Model of a Man*, *The Mighty Walzer*, which won the Everyman Wodehouse Award for comic writing, *Who's Sorry Now?*, which was longlisted for the Man Booker Prize, and four works of non-fiction.

ALSO BY HOWARD JACOBSON

Fiction

Coming From Behind
Peeping Tom
Redback
The Very Model of a Man
The Mighty Walzer
Who's Sorry Now?

Non-Fiction

Shakespeare's Magnanimity (with Wilbur Sanders)
In the Land of Oz
Roots Schmoots
Seriously Funny: An Argument for Comedy

Howard Jacobson

NO MORE MISTER NICE GUY

VINTAGE BOOKS

London

Published by Vintage 2003

4 6 8 10 9 7 5 3

First published in Great Britain in 1998 by
Jonathan Cape

First published in Vintage in 1999

Vintage
Random House, 20 Vauxhall Bridge Road,
London SW1V 2SA

The Random House Group Limited Reg. No. 954009

A CIP catalogue record for this book
is available from the British Library

ISBN 9780099274636

The Random House Group Limited supports The Forest Stewardship
Council (FSC), the leading international forest certification organisation.
All our titles that are printed on Greenpeace approved FSC certified paper
carry the FSC logo. Our paper procurement policy can be found at:
www.rbooks.co.uk/environment

Mixed Sources
Product group from well-managed
forests and other controlled sources
www.fsc.org   Cert no. TT-COC-2139
© 1996 Forest Stewardship Council
FSC

Printed and bound in Great Britain by
CPI Cox & Wyman, Reading, RG1 8EX

For Peter Fuller
1947—90

ONE

'GET OUT! JUST get out! Do it for yourself if you won't do it for me. Take a holiday. Go away for a month. Go away for a year. You've had the best of my life. Can't you find it in your heart to leave me to enjoy what little's left of it?'

But what man can believe in his heart that a woman will enjoy her life without him?

'Mel . . .'

'Get out! Get the fuck out!'

He feels he is being attacked from the air. Buzzards are after him. Lean, ill-balanced, scraggy throated scavengers with torn wings and bleeding eyes.

Serves him right. Teach him to have loved the bird in the woman.

He sits in his study, his head on his desk, protecting his eyesight, amid the machinery indispensable to the smooth running of his life. The phones, the fax machine, the computers, the screens, the printer, the scanner, the photo-copier, the batteries on charge, the tape recorder, the radio, the CD player, the strip-screen television, the laptop television, the VCRs, the manual typewriter in case of a power failure, the dictaphone in case of a manual failure.

Only twelve months ago he had an electrician in to give him more sockets. 'Enough to get me through to year fifteen of the new millennium.' By which time civilisation will have discovered an alternative to electricity? No. By which time he will be dead. 'Say two doubles on each wall?' 'Say three.' Making eighteen in all, one wall being nothing but books. But already he needs more. Today every socket is in use, three with adaptors. Twenty-one plugs all warm and whirring at the same time.

'Shut the fuck up or get the fuck out!'

The noise his room makes is part of the problem. He has the volume down on everything. The phones' ringers are off. His laser printer is the quietest money can buy. He oils his office chair. He has rugs on his carpets. Nothing bleeps. If he is in his room when a fax is arriving – and when isn't he in his room? – he throws a cushion over the machine to stifle the sound of the paper-cutter. He watches television all day. He can't not watch television. Watching television is his job. 'Wear fucking headphones, then!' And he does. He sits in a creakless chair watching television all day, wearing fucking headphones, the gaps between his ears and the pads stuffed with tissues so that not a sound, not a squeak or a throb, can leak out and distract her from what's left of her fucking life. If he could fit his halogen reading light with a silencer he would, God knows he would.

But the problem still isn't solved. He fears that the problem can't be solved. When she says he makes too much noise she means it ideologically. She can't think with him in the house. She can't think with him in her life. 'Let's face it,' he says to her, 'you can't think with me in the fucking universe.'

'Just try shutting your door,' she tells him.

'Ha!' He laughs. As if one little door could fix it.

Everything is stopping her from concentrating. He is just

part of the wider problem. It's not personal. He can see that. Every adult female of her acquaintance feels as she feels. They can none of them think above the ceaseless racket of a masculinist universe: the humming of the spheres; the sizzle of static; the mad bleepings of car alarms – the assertion of men's rights over men's things.

But why can't he just try shutting his door?

Ask him that and he'll tell you that he's keeping it open for her. So that she shouldn't feel rejected by him. The truth is, though, that he's the one who fears exclusion. He keeps his door open so that he can hear her moving about, hear her thinking, sighing. This isn't jealousy. He isn't straining his ears to catch her sighing for someone else. It's devotion. Love. He's fixated on her. He hears her breathe and he knows he's alive. Close the door and he's dead.

So that's something else that's preventing her from concentrating – the sound of him listening.

'Stop that!' she calls to him from her study.

'Stop what?'

'Stop listening to me!'

His point is that she couldn't hear him listening if she weren't so finely attuned herself. And by she he doesn't just mean her, Mel, he means her sex.

'You've turned yourselves into acoustic freaks,' he tells her. 'You've all got micro-hearing. You can hear yourselves fucking bleed . . .'

'Bleed? Shows the age of the company you keep when you're not at home. Women of my years don't bleed.'

'Doesn't stop you listening.'

'Frank, I'd leave the subject of blood if I were you.'

She's starting to use his name. That's how serious this is becoming.

'Mel, you're all out there tuning into the silent fucking

spring. You can hear the grass grow. If I wasn't here you'd be screaming at the fucking spiders for swallowing so loud.'

'You go, I'll deal with the spiders. I can tread on a spider.'

Go? Go where? Everything indispensable to the smooth running of his life is here.

She doesn't use machines. Doesn't hold with them. She writes her feministical-erotic novels long hand. When she's interviewed about a book, which is rarely – since she finishes a book rarely – she says that slowness is of the essence. As with love-making so with prose-making. You can tell when a novel's been written by mechanical means, she says. It lacks the pace of real life. The rhythm's all wrong.

Like him. His rhythm's all wrong. 'In fact,' she tells him, 'you have no rhythm.'

'You mean I don't share yours.'

'You don't share anybody's. When we first made love I used to wonder where you were. You seemed to be out there on your own, entirely solitary, going about your own private business.'

'And later?'

'What *later*?'

He doesn't say that her feministical-erotic heroines are all out there on *their* own, going about their private business, getting multiple orgasms as by right, without reference to whoever it is they're getting them with. Or through. Or by. Or on. He doesn't say that that's the only thing that distinguishes them from pre-feministical-erotic heroines, who squandered their sexuality (whatever that fucking word means) fretting about what men wanted. That and the amount of inter-orgasmic intellectualising they do – these Serenas and Cybeles with cunts they can call their own and the conversation of Wittgenstein. It isn't safe to talk about her work.

Just as it isn't safe to talk about his.

'What are you watching that crap all day for?'

He would like to say that it isn't crap. That he doesn't hold with snobbery about popular entertainment. But it is crap. And getting crappier. And he does hold with snobbery about popular entertainment. That's the other reason for not looking beyond the year fifteen of the new millennium – there will be nothing left worth staying alive for.

He would also like to remind her that it's his job. That he is the best television critic in the country. Or one of. That watching that crap all day is what pays the bills. That without his watching that crap all day she couldn't afford the luxury of writing a hundred words a month. But that would take them back to talking about her work. Which isn't safe. If he wasn't sitting there with his door open watching that crap all day and listening to her listening to him listening to her, her output would be more like the hundred *pages* a month she was capable of before she knew he existed.

Not safe to talk about the time before she knew he existed.

Nothing's safe. Now they are fighting over towels.

They have towel rings in their bathroom, one above the other, to save space. On these they hang the identical chaste white dimpled French table napkins she insists on calling bath-towels. 'What do you think it means,' she asks him, 'that in the twenty years I have known you I have always hung my bath-towel below yours?'

It is, of course, an ideological question. One that he knows better than even to attempt to answer.

She shakes her head, disgusted with herself, with her education, with her sex's long connivance in the rituals of deference. 'It's utterly humiliating,' she says. 'I can't assert myself sufficiently to put something of mine above something of yours.'

A string snaps in his brain. The buzzards have cut through a vein or an artery. He lurches past her, blood pouring out of his ears — blood *must* be pouring out of his ears; he can hear the rush — and pulls the towel from the higher ring. It is so light it floats like a rose petal before it lands. Even before it's settled he is jumping up and down on it, treading it into a rag, mopping the bathroom floor with it like a curler sooping the ice. 'OK?' he says. 'That better? That do? Or would you like to shit on it now?'

She wants to know why he is treating her towel like that.

'What do you mean *your* towel? How can it be *your* towel? You've just seen me take it from the top ring.'

'Exactly. That's where mine has been hanging since this morning. I've started to assert myself.'

'*Started* — !' But he is not able to finish. A fax is coming through and he has to fly down the stairs to suffocate it.

He sits among his startled, twitching machines, like a shepherd calming his flock after a thunderstorm, and wonders whether it will be towels that finally do for the relationship — whatever that fucking word means. He considers himself hard done by around towels. When he steps out of a shower he doesn't want to have to dab himself dry with a kitchen roll. Going from wet to dry should be a voluptuous experience. The towel he has always wanted wraps itself around you like a courtesan. In his mind's eye he sees the towel he would have were he allowed a choice in the matter; it is as voluminous as a sail; it is as soft as a cloud; ribbed like an acre of Santa Monica beach; fluffed up like a Playboy bunny's tail; the colour of a Pasadena sunset, all pouting carmines and molten golds . . .

'To go with the gold chains around your neck . . .'

'I don't wear gold chains around my neck . . .'.

But of course she means ideologically. Ideologically he is

gross. A used-car salesman. An *arriviste*. A crap-watcher. His taste in towels proves it.

As does his taste in bathrooms. He would have liked a sunken bath. A spa system. A star's dressing-room mirror, lit by a thousand winking bulbs. A Moorish tiled floor. Black silk blinds. And yes, yes, gold taps. What he gets is a Shaker chapel: plain white bath with its legs showing, hinges on the outside of the cupboards, tongue-and-groove walls, and communion cloths for towels.

But then he would have liked a penthouse or an apartment in a huddled mansion block to sink his Babylonian whirlpool in. Something with a Malibu terrace giving out on to the odours of the city, the fried food, the petrol fumes, the screams. Life. Life with a whiff of death in it. And what does he get instead? A whitewashed cottage on a village green in Dulwich. Dulwich! A garden. A wooden fence. Space. Death with a whiff of life in it.

So why doesn't he assert *himself*?

'Ha!' Ask her. She knows. 'You may not think it,' she tells him, 'but you are living, in every particular, the life you want. That's why you stay. It's what you understand. This is the domestic universe you were brought up in – you and the rest of your sex. A mad woman with an eating disorder hidden away in the bowels of the house, getting madder every minute, while you complain, bang your forehead, and get on with your work. You couldn't live any other way.'

Couldn't he?

Maybe he couldn't. Maybe his know-all painstaking feminist pornographer of a companion, Wittgenstein-the-Fucking-Wise, is right: this *is* the only life he understands. There's a deranged woman concealed in the attic, the bedroom, the kitchen, the scullery, the hen-house; there's a lunatic loose – wasn't that the terrible unspoken truth that the men in his family had passed down to him through the

7

generations? He remembers his grandfather smiting his forehead whenever his grandmother opened her mouth. And didn't his father do the same? Woman – mouth – speak; man – forehead – bang.

His father's father's brother, great-uncle Noam, used to rise from his rocking-chair, button up his waistcoat and leave the house the moment the mother of his children so much as gestured at him. As a young man he had enlisted to fight the Kaiser, took a wound in his knee and was photographed in gaiters. That gave him the right never to work again and never to be spoken to by a woman in his own home. Great-aunt Isadora was permitted to clean for him, screw the heads off the chickens for him, raise sons for him, but not otherwise make a sound. Only let her look as though she might be thinking of saying something and Noam would put up his hand to indicate the desirability of silence, touch his head to denote the presence of craziness, and be gone limping through the door. Where did he go to every night? No one knew. Some said he had another woman. But who? A mute? Others claimed they saw him going into the local pub, and that he was known to sit over a single half pint of ginger beer and water, talking to no one, until closing time. Wherever he went, he went there every night of his married life for close to fifty years. And when Isadora died – with her lips sealed – it broke his heart. A month later he was dead himself. He couldn't bear the loneliness.

Has he, Frank the crap-watcher, ever lived in a house, visited a house, heard of a house that doesn't have a mad woman – a Mrs Rochester from whom you have to keep the matches, a Lady Macbeth from whom you have to hide the knives – sequestered away in it somewhere? These days it's the keys to the drinks cabinet or the freezer you have to hide from them. The restaurant critic for his newspaper doesn't leave for work until he's marked the level of every bottle in the house with a hair plucked from his wrist, and even then he has to ring home from whichever eatery he's scoffing in at fifteen-minute intervals, just to boost morale. 'Hang on, sweetheart. Back soon. I don't know, soon. Soon! All right, but only halfway up. Good girl. Love you.' The books editor is herself a woman, never at home except at weekends. But she can do as much damage to herself on a Saturday morning in the kitchen before sun-up as any conventionally crazed Hausfrau can do in a week. Frank knows the hubby. Come Friday evening he has to remember to take the light bulb out of the fridge. 'It doesn't stop her,' he explains to Frank, 'but it slows her down.'

Woman – mouth – drink; man – forehead – bang. Alcohol, cigarettes, pills, penises, ice cream – if it fits into their mouth they're in trouble. What does Mel weigh right now? Six, seven stones? Fresh out of Belsen. Her friends all look the same. Big staring eyes. Sunken cheeks. Rickety, uncertain limbs. Down in Mel's kitchen, where they huddle, heroin-haggard, with their backs to the fridge, complaining about noise and shaking with hunger, it's like Battersea Dogs' Home. And last week they were all the size of Oliver Hardy.

He knows she is putting her finger down her throat again. The usual tell-tale signs. Blotches on her neck. Sinks clogging up. The liver-coloured nail polish on the finger in question corroding. But he doesn't crack on he's noticed. Live and let live is his philosophy. Which only underlines what she's been saying: a house with a woman going mad in it is a perfectly acceptable phenomenon to him. He couldn't live any other way.

And she's right about his work, too. The further back into his room he is pushed, the quieter he is required to be, the better his column gets. Coincident with the finger going in and out of Mel's throat, comes the award – Broadcasting Critic of the Year. Except that it's no coincidence.

But even a man who is living in every particular the life he wants can be pushed too far.

'Funny how engrossing a domestic brawl is,' he says to her, since they happen to have collided in the kitchen.

'You'd call this a domestic brawl, would you?'

He realises he has blundered. 'I use the phrase loosely.'

'What phrase would you use instead?'

'Forget it, Mel. I'm sorry I spoke.'

'No you're not. You've just said you're engrossed. You've just said it's funny how engrossed you are. What's funny about it, Frank? Show me the joke.'

'I didn't mean funny in that sense.'

'No. You never do mean funny in that sense. It's a long time since there's been any funny in that sense. I tell you, Frank, I don't mind that we don't fuck every morning. I don't mind that we can't talk to each other any more . . .'

'You like it that we don't talk.'

She breathes in. He's interrupting her again. 'I've just said, *I don't mind that we're not talking.* I don't mind that we're not fucking every morning. I don't mind that we don't have a friend or an interest left in common. What I do mind . . .'

'Is that I'm alive.'

'Shut the fuck up.'

'Stay calm, Mel.'

'It's perfectly calm around here as long as you keep your trap shut. You're offensive. You're an offensive individual.'

'Whom do I offend, Mel?'

'You offend me. Now will you shut the fuck up and be quiet. Will you shut your fucking trap when you're in my company.'

She waits for a response. Apparently she has asked him a question.

'Well?'

What can he say? *Yes, I will shut my fucking trap when I'm in your company*. For two pins he'd bang his fucking forehead and retire to the quiet of the local pub for the night. Supposing there to be such a thing left as a quiet local pub, one that's not a discotheque full of kids sucking Mexican beer through a lime wedge. For two pins, if there were somewhere to go, he'd be gone.

'What *do* you mind, Mel?'

'I mind that you're engrossed, as you call it. What are you doing being engrossed, Frank? Who do you think you are, a member of the fucking audience? Waiting to see what the mad woman is going to do next. What about you, Frank? What are you going to do next? What do *you* want?'

'I want to know what else you mind, Mel.'

'I mind that you don't know what you want. I mind that you're engrossed. I mind that you think it's funny. I mind that funny doesn't mean funny any more. When did funny last mean funny between us, Frank? That's what I mind most, that we don't play together any more, that there are no more jokes, that you've stopped making me laugh.'

Without any warning his eyes spring tears. His first instinct is to defend himself. Not make her laugh? Him? Broadcasting Critic of the Year for the very reason that he makes three-quarters of a million readers laugh – aloud, *aloud*, Mel – every Sunday. But he knows what she will say. 'That's work, Frank. That's what you do for a living. I'm talking about me. It's *me* you don't make laugh any more.' And he knows he will have no answer to that.

He wonders if his tears might melt her heart. Might affect the way she feels. But what can they change? The fact that he doesn't make her laugh any more? Can he cry her into finding him funny again?

'What's the matter with you?' she says. 'Upset that you're not appreciated?'

'I'm upset for you,' he says. And he is. How can he not be? She has attacked her hair with kitchen scissors this morning. Cropped herself like a penitent; jagged into that dense dangerous jungle of dark-plum ripe-fig purple mane, where once, given half a chance, he would go burrowing for days at a time, led by his love for the aroma of strange fruits. Not enough hair now to provide cover for an ant. Moreover, she appears to have shed another fourteen pounds. Her short slut-schoolgirl's skirt — into the likes of which, moons ago, it had also been his wont to vanish for long periods — soughs like an empty coal sack in the wind. You can irrigate a colon one too many times. She's leaving bits of herself, scrapings, coils of intestine, in clinics all over London. And helixes of body hair all over the house. Nothing sprouts under her arms any more. Nor between her legs. Although she's not a beach girl, never was a beach girl, she's taken to shaving her pubes down to a minimal vertical strip, like a furry elastoplast or an exclamation mark. Uncover Mel's once proliferous cunt today, and you find yourself staring into Hitler's moustache.

She can't stop plucking at her pores and clawing at her innards and hacking at her flesh. All because his jokes (he has nothing to say about her sentences — it's not safe talking about her sentences) have dried up. How can he not be upset for her?

Easy. Mel knows how. By being more upset for himself. 'You always were a sentimentalist when it comes to your sense of humour,' she says. 'All I have to do is tell you that you don't have one any more and I can have you blubbering like a baby.'

And that's what does it. After so many shut-the-fuck-ups and get-the-fuck-outs, this is all it takes to get him pulling out clothes from his wardrobe and stuffing them into a travelling-bag — her insinuation that he is incapable of feeling for another person, her accusation that the waning of his comic gifts matters to him more than anything else, her considered opinion that his comic gifts *have* waned. He's not a boy any more; he's looking down both barrels of fifty. What does he have left except the capacity to enter imaginatively into another's distress, and a sense of the ridiculous? If neither is in operation here, then he may as well be off.

Since the subject has come up, he also minds that she doesn't mind that they are not fucking every morning. But only since the subject has come up.

And his machines?

To hell with his machines. She's the silencer – let her keep them quiet.

TWO

H E'S OUT. FREE. Feeling fifteen, not fifty. Call me
Kerouac. The greatest ride in his life is about to come
up.

He's over the river and on the Shepherd's Bush flyover,
following the signs to Oxford, before he remembers that he
can make all the noise he likes, that he can have the soft roof
of his Saab down *and* his radio on loud. Where has he been
for the last half century? What has he been doing? His car's
ten years old and it's got four thousand miles on the
milometer. How many trips to Sainsbury's is that? Where's
he been? He's been at home, turning down the volume of his
life.

Somebody honks him for hogging the fast lane. He puts
up two fingers and goes slower. He'll hog the whole fucking
flyover if he feels like it.

A cargo of pimps and pushers in a beaten-up Mercedes
overtakes him on the inside, yelling and pointing at their
foreheads, just like his uncle Noam. 'Shoot me then,' he
shouts. 'Go on. A life for a lane. Go on – ram me!'

He's in heaven. With Mel in the car he has to turn a blind
eye to every automotive malfeasance, capitulate to every
taunting horn. She doesn't want to be taken out by some

drug-crazed road rager, thank you, just because his skin's worn thin. Today he's on his own and if there's any raging to be done he'll be the one to do it. He accelerates and pulls level with the Mercedes. Blows it a kiss. The driver takes one hand off his wheel and whacks off in the air. Miserable stumpy little spasmic strokes. A bleak working-class jerk off. Frank hits his automatic aerial button, telescopes his aerial down, zooms it up; it whines like a dentist's drill going into enamel, in out in out. Wanker? He'll show them that where he comes from even a wank can be lordly. Then, in a single convulsion of speed, he Saabs past them, punching the air with his fist. The lone rager.

Heaven. Except that heaven will never be so good. He's got cricket on the radio. He's got the sun on his face. He's got the west London early August holiday smell of malt biscuits in his nostrils. He's got that old truant sensation of release from homework in his heart. And he's got no one in his car.

He's never been happier.

And does he know yet where he's going? It's still looking like Oxford, but he's leaving it to the Saab to decide destinations. His fingers barely touch the wheel. Wherever the Saab fancies going, he'll go. All points of the compass look equally tempting to him. If it goes on being Oxford – and doesn't suddenly become Aylesbury or Warwick – so much the better. He has known good times in Oxford. There have been those in Oxford, long ago, who *would* have minded had he not been fucking them every morning, had they not been fucking him every morning, had they severally – to be democratic about it – not been fucking one another at all hours of the day.

But fucking is not an issue. Fucking is definitely not on the agenda.

In despite of what *she* thinks.

It isn't entirely true that he's got no one in his car. A part of Mel is in his glove compartment. Her talking spleen. 'Following our dick, are we?'

'No, Mel.'

'First thing we think of when we leave the house – where can we put it tonight.'

'I won't be putting it anywhere, Mel.'

'Liar.'

'You'll see.'

And in truth, his dick is the last thing on his mind. Twenty years ago, ten years ago, his dick would have been driving the car. The great consolation of being fifty, for all your other organs, is that they finally get to sit behind the wheel.

The Saab slows so that he can take a look at the royal-icing of the Hoover building. Now owned by Tesco. Tessa Cohen. What odds would you have given against Mr and Mrs Cohen succeeding, however long ago, when they hit upon that artless elision as a name for their wholesale food empire? Frank remembers staring into their garden from the upper deck of the school bus, trying to get a look at Tessa in her kitchen. It troubled him, imagining her life. Do you cook and clean when you're the Tes in Tesco, do you go shopping in your own shops, or do you just sit there, aloof like a stone statue? It seemed an important question at the time; it bore upon how you escape the ordinary. Once, he took Tesco's next-door neighbours' au pair to the pictures. Polish. The only Polish au pair in Manchester anyone had heard of. She did everything up close, whispered in both Frank's ears, blew in Frank's face, and danced her fingers at the entrance to her mouth when she spoke, as though not just helping her words on their way, but her breath and her spittle as well. He sat wet and entranced and up close while she flicked her fingers around in his pocket. Frank had never owned a pet but he guessed that this was what it was like to bring a white mouse to school in your trousers. Whenever the film reached an emotional climax the mouse nibbled on his dick. Yet the moment he tried a reciprocal nip at any part of her she wagged her free fingers at him and flicked his nose. You took whatever was offering in those days. And a dick gnawed black and blue in the pictures was still better than a night in on your own in front of the television.

Where is she now? Still au pairing on the Bury Old Road? And what's *she* like at fifty? Still up close? Might she still be willing to mouse around in his pocket? If he cuts diagonally across the country to Birmingham, and then picks up the M6, he can be in Manchester well before dark.

'Liar . . .'

He lets the road to Bury idle out of his mind. The Saab hesitates between the A40 and the M40. Oxford, either way. Slow or fast. The clock on his dashboard says four-thirty. If he takes the motorway he can be at the Trout Inn, drinking icy lagers over the river, before six. Fish in the waterfall. Peacock in the gardens. Crazy Jane in her Oxfam trilby and ratty fur coat, his first Oxford romance, his first girl with a mind, ordering pints in her Pete and Dud voice, passing him joints under the garden furniture. Where is she now? Mistress of a college was the last he heard.

Slow . . . slow might be better.

He's out of touch with the customs of the country, but some indestructible instinct tells him that fish and chip shops open at five. He would love to be eating fish and chips, in the heat, while he drives, with his roof down, with cricket on the radio, and no one to advise otherwise. The car refuses the motorway, pootles round the edges of a couple of forgettable Berkshire towns with their garden centres and their excitable Palladian function and conference hotels, their Beefeaters and Harvesters, and pulls up of its own, dead on the stroke of five, slap outside a half-timbered chip shop on the western extremity of Beaconsfield. Open! And frying tonight! If he's consented to be booted out of his home for no better reason than this – all the grease and batter his old heart desires, and fuck you with your nutritional censoriousness hanging retching over the bath – then he's consented wisely.

A chemist's shop is handily situated next door but one to the chippy. He goes in for a box of tissues, mansize, to protect the upholstery of his car from what he is about to dump on it. Double chips, he is thinking. And two fish. Maybe treble chips. Maybe one fish and two fishcakes. If they've got gherkins he'll have a couple. Ditto pickled eggs. Peas he'll skip. Or maybe he won't. Everyone in the shop looks up when he asks for the biggest box of tissues they've got. Man on his own, end of the day – they're bound to have their thoughts.

Because he's wearing unfamiliar trousers – holiday chinos, pants for starting a new life in – he has trouble finding loose change and scatters coins across the floor. Doubtless they think he's embarrassed. An old lady waiting for her prescription peers out at him from the alien world of the underprivileged. She has a small boy with her, hanging on to her hand. She nods and trembles, as much out of the perplexity of her class as the infirmity of her age, imparting the vibration to the boy, who nods and trembles along with her. He has a loose eye. Shaken out of its socket. Fucked, Frank thinks. Plebeianly fucked already. The kid'll either be a doormat or a criminal, but he won't ever know what any of it's been about, either way. Thanks, Grandma.

Thanks Ma.

Thanks Mel.

He's in the queue for his dinner when the old lady taps him in the small of his back. 'You dropped money,' she tells him. She gestures to the boy, standing looking at him with

his loose eye, obediently holding out his hand. 'He found it.'
A pound coin. They've come looking for him to return a
pound coin. That's less than the price of a syllable at current
Broadcasting Critic of the Year rates. All Frank has to do to
earn a pound coin is start to write the word crap. Whereas
who's to say that in Beaconsfield a pound coin doesn't
represent a day's labour. A week's labour for a kid. A week
up a chimney or down a pit; whatever they do in
Beaconsfield – a fortnight on the towpath pulling a barge. It
would be insulting in that case – wouldn't it? – to wave it
away, dismiss it, laugh the trivial amount back in their faces.
So he thanks the kid and takes the coin. Which royally
snafues his fish and chips. For the next half-hour, as he drives
into the dying sun with his roof up, separating batter from
paper with his free hand, he castigates himself for not setting
a moral example and saving a soul, for not demonstrating that
honesty can still be its own reward in this wicked wicked
world, for not blessing the child and telling him that the
pound he has found is now his to start a new life with.

He hasn't left all his machines behind. He has his portable
computer with him, and his Hitachi laptop television (having
still a column to write), and his mobile phone. He thinks
about ringing Mel and telling her about the pound coin.
Confessing. Even when they're fighting they have a tradition
of his confessing. 'I feel such a shit,' he says. 'You *are* such a
shit,' she tells him. It's the only thing they agree on. But they
are past fighting now. They have *fought*. Full stop. He keeps
his fingers off the winking phone. He's going to have to get
used to confessing to himself.

In sight of Oxford, he luxuriates in the thought of a night
at the Randolph. A third-floor corner room, if he can get
one, with views of the Martyrs' Memorial and the walls of
Balliol and the Apollonian urns on the roof of the

Ashmolean. Up among the heavenly choir. The Randolph's not what it was – let's face it, Oxford's not what it was – now that Inspector Morse has passed over and through it, like the angel of popular rigor mortis; but that's the business he's in himself: killing by commonness. England your England as seen on the telly. 'Welcome to Jane Austen country', a sign on the A3 promises as you cross into Hampshire. How many people have read Jane Austen since she died in 1817? But the sign didn't appear until they put her on the box. Soon the Department of Transport will cede its obligation to erect road signs to the *Radio Times*. Wildfell Hall, straight ahead. Vet's Dales, filter left. Throw a right for Brookside Close. There the Hovis Street. Here Frank's Column.

Did the Elizabethans do that? Guided tours round Falstaff's Eastcheap. Weekend for two, with dinner, in Dunsinane.

His ire is academic. The Randolph's full. So much the better. Who wants to be where everyone wants to be, anyway? Popular religion knows you can't have everybody crammed into one heaven; there has to be an elect. Popular culture has yet to sort that out. In the meantime its purveyors leave the mob to its milling and head for the Tuscan hills.

It's for the guest houses and bed and breakfasts of north Oxford that he's heading. Up the Banbury Road, with mounting misgivings, but no will to resist. He knows what's coming. At the Marston Ferry lights the retrospection gang jumps him, the heartbreak memory boys who have been waiting at this very intersection for his return, their fists in their mouths, for twenty years or more. Drive, they say. Stop, they say. Here, they say. No prizes for guessing where here is. The Dewdrop Inn in Summertown where, *ante* Mel, *ante* the melancholy and the maelstrom, he taught the girls from Wittenberg to drink deep.

He does as he's told and pulls into the kerb. Summertime in Summertown. The very time of the year and the very hour of the evening. If he sits here long enough he will see himself come and go, shoulders rolling, fag burning his fingers love-bite yellow, cord jacket pinched in at the waist, black leather tie, scrotum as tight as a bag of pennies. A sprig in the pink of post-graduation. A feather in any foreign student's cap. Which one will he have on his arm tonight? The Venetian on whose underclothes you could smell the lagoon? The Spaniard who would touch a man anywhere but only through the embroidered scented handkerchief she kept tucked in her conventual sleeve? Hard to be certain after all this time, but isn't it the Finnish screamer? Yes, yes, that is who it is, it's the Shrieker from Hameenlinna.

She fucked them all, the most famous of the language-school Finns, she fucked the principal, she fucked the social secretary, she fucked the head of studies, she fucked the tutors, she even fucked the school minibus driver – smoking throughout and screaming the whole of Oxford awake whenever she came and whoever she came with – but she fucked Frank better and longer than she fucked anybody. And once, sliding to the edge of a crowded bar stool, hooking her ankles under his knees, spurring him like horse, and with nobody able to believe that they were seeing what they were seeing, she fucked him in the Dewdrop.

He prided himself on how squeamish he wasn't. They passed her along, the way you could in the early seventies, with accompanying warnings about her cigarette habit, the foulness of her breath and the racket she made. He was the last to have her, being busy at the other end of the chain, preparing and passing on Greeks. Her mouth wasn't the problem to him it had been to the others. He stuffed whatever he could get of himself into it, and later kissed her deep and long.

She lit up and marvelled at him. 'Nobody before kiss me like that,' she said.

21

'Maybe you didn't give them time.'

'Hold my cigarette.'

He liked it that she screamed so loud. 'What you've all failed to see,' he told the others, talking their nights over in the minibus that drove them down the Banbury Road from where they slept to where they taught, 'is that it's a joke. She's taking the piss.'

'Finns don't make jokes.'

'Where you're wrong. It's you who don't *get* their jokes.'

'So who's she taking the piss out of?'

'Well, us for a start. But I reckon mainly herself. She thinks she's crazy wanting to fuck so much.'

'She is.'

'We fuck as much as she does. And she's got the excuse of being on a sort of holiday. We're supposed to be working.'

'Fucking *is* working.'

'Speak for yourself.'

'And at least we don't scream.'

'Speak for yourself.'

He'd started to scream with her. They egged each other on, like two cats. Coming and laughing and howling all at once. It beat gazing fondly. She didn't have the looks, or the shape, or the aura, to inspire adoration. She was built on classically Ugro-Finnic lines – thick neck, sparse hair, short legs, sandpaper skin, flat nose. 'Like fucking a platypus,' Josh Green reckoned, the morning after he'd taken his turn. He was the only qualified language teacher among them. Not that anyone cared about qualifications in this school. 'Like licking an aardvark.'

Nicholas Heywood, who affected fastidiousness and had no qualifications at all, was appalled. 'You mean you licked her?'

''Course I licked her. She's a visitor to this country. I'm paid to make her feel welcome.'

Frank licked her too. Fucked her, kissed her, licked her, screamed when she did. A platypus? So what, if that was how a platypus went about it. Why be anthropocentric? If anything, he rather liked her rough condition, the way her cunt spread all over the place, the way her mouth jerked about, the sudden appearance of one of her scaly legs under your arm or around your neck, no part of her ever where you expected it to be, nothing in repose. Being ill-favoured and disconnected enabled her to let herself go *and* take the piss. Beauties can't do that. Furthermore, it enabled him to feel he was making a contribution to her self-esteem. You can't do that with a beauty either. Beauties come to you as finished products. You may admire, but you are not expected to add or to subtract. Which is why no man likes fucking them, whatever they say to the contrary.

Or do to the contrary. The Swede, whose attention he first caught, as chance would have it, while the Finn was digging her heels into his femurs from the bar stool of the Dewdrop, was the age's abstract of the beautiful. Tall, but not too. Slender, but not too. Eyes the colour of a Hockney pool; hair that aureoled about her head in gold leaf, like the halo of a Byzantine saint. Beauty in a woman either has to have some boy in it or some baby. The Swede's beauty had both. She held herself like a cupbearer, straightbacked, waiting on men in order that she might soon take their place among them. But her mouth smelt of milk and her teeth looked brand new, as though they'd turned up in her mouth that very day. And of course heartbreak entered into it as well. 'The arse,' Josh Green moaned in the minibus, 'the arse on her!' He might have been delivering an elegy. Everyone felt the same, as though they were in mourning; and each of them mourned for his favourite part.

The knees. The glossy shins in which, once you were low enough, you could see your own sorrowing reflection. The ankles – oh the ankles, with their little continental tufts of winnowing amber down.

'I'm sorry,' burst in the Pakistani playboy Wasim, 'I don't know how you can go past the tits.'

'Depends which end you start from, Was. Some of us haven't *got* to the tits yet.'

'Well when you do you'll find me there.' Was was the only one among them who boasted. It was a cultural thing. He couldn't grasp the comedy of deprivation. He didn't understand that offering to do without, even when you hadn't actually done without, was a male-bonding device. 'In fact I'm there most nights.'

His voice was too deep, too heavy for him to carry. When he spoke he gave the impression of a man falling over himself.

'Has anyone noticed,' lamented Nick Heywood, bringing dolour back into the minibus, 'that they move separately when she walks?'

Everyone had. But everyone took time to review the heart-rending phenomenon again in their minds.

'I maintain there should be a law,' said Was, a lawyer himself, 'against tits moving like that.'

There should be a law against you, everybody thought. Was was social committee, not teaching staff. Strictly speaking he shouldn't have been in their minibus at all, screwing up their funeral.

What Frank liked best about the Swede was less specifically located. He liked what was between and around her: the space between her legs when she walked, her atmosphere and weather-sytem, her Arctic fuzz. You could say he was returning her to the abstract of beauty which, for three short weeks in August, she made flesh. So how could he ever have expected anything of the fuck? It was so much not the thing she wanted to be doing that she turned her head away and wept all through it.

It wasn't him. Or it wasn't *only* him. She'd wept all through the others as well.

But oh, the tragic adoration she induced. Frank mopped her tears with the corner of his pillow case, wiped her symmetrical nose, and let his eyes wander like hungry lambkins over her grassless slopes. Smooth thighs, flat belly, perfect self-righteous little cunt, labia crossed like a nun's wrists, thus far and no further, not a hair out of place. Refused the promised land, Moses would have gazed like this from Pisgah. Beautiful, beautiful, but never to be mine.

The knocking on his bedroom door seemed to be an event on another planet. She made the connection before he did. 'You have visitor,' she said.

'What?' He was still lost; alone on the mountain. 'What? Who?'

'Friend maybe,' she said. She was sitting up now. 'Shall I leave?' She couldn't wait to leave.

'There's no way out. Only the window, and we're three floors up.'

He realised that this was a tactless thing to say. She was a Swede. She could easily decide to jump.

He looked at his watch. A little after one in the morning. No one came calling at that time. But someone was definitely out there.

'Just cover yourself,' he said. It must have been the only time in her life she'd heard such a phrase. He threw on a dressing gown, put his ear to the door, then opened it fractionally. It was the Finn. He'd wriggled out of her tonight. Told her he had a headache and when she gave him aspirins told her he was washing his hair.

She'd known something was wrong. Some lousy self-annihilative Finnish impulse drove her to find out who.

'How's your head?' she asked.

'Better, thank you.'

She looked more than ever unfinished, raw, like an uncooked burger.

'It doesn't seem so clean.'

He touched his hair and shrugged at her disconsolately. He wanted her to feel that he respected her too much to lie to her. To lie to her *again*.

She lit up a cigarette, sat down on the landing outside his door and began to cry.

He wasn't sure what to do. That was two of them in tears, one inside, one out. He thought how ill the Finn's tears became her, compared to the Swede's. Whereas when it came to screaming, the Finn was without equal. He felt suddenly sad for her and for him and for the thing he'd betrayed. You can dishonour a fuck. But if he asked the Finn to come in, and asked the Swede to go home, and fucked the Finn, would he then feel he'd dishonoured the aesthetics of his feelings for the Swede? Not Solomon in all his wisdom could settle the dissension between the dick and heart. Polygamy, that was the only answer Solomon had been able to come up with for himself.

Frank leaned against the door frame, wondering how to act honourably, bearing in mind that he didn't like to wake up in an empty bed. Now he really did have a headache. He rubbed his temples and put his hands over his eyes. When he removed them he saw the Swede on her knees with her arms round the Finn. She was stroking her hair. The princess and the frog. Who was going to turn into what?

'Tea,' the Swede said at last. 'Can you make tea.'

'I have wine . . .' Wild thoughts of a party crossed his mind.

'Not wine. Tea.'

It meant going downstairs to the communal kitchen,

26

looking for kettles, gas taps, matches, tea-pots, stuff he didn't normally bother with in the daylight let alone in the dead of night, but he went anyway. The thing might sort itself out better without him. And it did. When he returned, bearing a tray of tea and chocolate biscuits – it behoved him, he believed, once he was down there, to go to some trouble – they were lying on his narrow bed together, as blameless as Hansel and Gretel; the Finn turned to the wall, the Swede stroking her thin hair and crooning to her in Norse. Frank poured them tea, put a biscuit in their saucers, turned off the light, and went to sleep in an armchair. When he woke in the morning they were both gone.

Neither of them spoke to him again. Worse than that, neither of them fucked him again.

Two days later he stood outside the school, across from the Dewdrop, and watched them climb aboard the bus chartered to take them all to Heathrow. The girls hadn't become friends, they weren't talking, they were back in their original parties, Finns here, Swedes there; but they were united in their heedlessness of him.

'Goodbye the loveliest little arse I'll ever see,' Josh Green lamented.

All the tutors were there, the principal, the head of studies, all the social committee, even the staff minibus driver, lined up to wave goodbye. The three weeks of acclimatisation to the idiom of English ways were over. The final morning had been a terrible ordeal. Knowing that they were taking leave of one another on the banks of the River of Eternal Separation, they had indulged one last reckless orgy of oath swearing and heart swapping. Addresses and phone numbers, photographs, rings and necklaces, items of apparel, books that told their story, records that played their music, objects that were themselves love-tokens from others, passed from hand to hand. So extensive and surreptitious had been the passing that sometimes you received your own offering back. But nothing took from the augustness of the ritual. It was like throwing gifts into a grave. Everyone promised never to forget. Some promised to leave their wives and abandon their children. For the space of a morning no earlier allegiance was secure. For the space of a morning at least a dozen innocent English children were fatherless.

They watched the bus pull away, the golden faces recede, then they returned in silence to the staff room. No one spoke for an hour. Just occasionally someone coughed. A fat summer fly buzzed in the pane. You could hear it cleaning its mandibles. Then the throb of a diesel engine and sounds of activity coming from the office told them that the new crop had arrived. They hurried out on to the pavement, swallowing easily again, craning to see into the sun-filled windows of the bus, impatient to get a look at what the next three weeks held in store for them.

The lawyer Wasim was the last to arrive on the scene. His booby-trapped voice rolled rudely into the road like the Indus flooding another insignificant village. 'OK, so what's worth fucking this time?' he wanted to know.

He wasn't to be trusted around anything solemn.

Has he made up his mind yet, after all this time, sitting shaking his head at the wheel of his Saab, whether it really is the Finn he'd like to see walking out of the Dewdrop again, or whether he'd prefer the Swede? Has he reached any adjudication as to the competing claims of the dick and the heart?

Some question. He's fifty years of age. When he talks of his heart today it's to a doctor. His heart is the thing that will eventually kill him. What lies heavy on his heart right now is not beauty, but cheese. As for the dick, he doesn't mind being the first to admit it – there are mornings when you're

28

fifty when you cannot be certain you have a dick. 'What's that?' Mel used to complain. Panic in her voice. 'What's that poking me in the back?' It was her contention that he deliberately woke her up with it. That the tyrannical reign of the dick had begun before she was even conscious. Had she not made it sound so punitive he'd have agreed with her. He wasn't awake himself yet. Having a dick was like having a dog that needed to be walked early. You got no peace with it. It wanted a walk, then it wanted a pat, then it wanted a game. Then. That was *then*. Now if he wants to get a look at his dick before breakfast he has to stand on a mirror.

But Nature must intend something by this, must She not? If he is free at last of the importunings of his dick, he must be free for some purpose. It's just a question of discovering what that purpose is.

The language school is gone. The times are against it. Once you take the fucking out of teaching, a school like the one to which Frank was devoted loses its rationale. That students learn less as a consequence — learn less *of* consequence — he is convinced. That teachers too were once happier when fucking their students was an allowable perk — in most cases their *only* perk — he doesn't doubt either. Show him a happy teacher today!

He knows better than to raise this matter in the company of any of the little Heloises of yesteryear who have columns on his paper. The times are the times. He isn't distressed by hypocrisy. It's important to own to a code of beliefs, whether you live by it or not. He just wishes more people would stand up for fucking as a teaching tool.

Where the language school was, there is now a guest house. Frank has no choice in the matter. This is where he will spend the night. Who knows, this may be where he will spend the rest of his life.

Nothing remains of the old interior. The builders have

been through. It was deceptively formal before, hinting at monasticism and scholarship; now it's snug and homey. For couples. Love in a cottage. Ceilings lowered. Creaking boards installed. Panelling ripped out for flowery wallpaper. And nautical junk everywhere. Why is the theme of every guest house, no matter where it's situated, the sea? Prints of wrecks. A polished diver's helmet on a little table. An onyx lighthouse on the reception desk. The breakfast room is where the common room used to be. It was here, in the first years of the school, before the social committee grew ambitious, that they held the discos. They played only one record. Heavy breathing, somebody whispering Je t'aime, somebody coming in a French accent. Round and round it went. The school anthem. It suited everyone's tastes. The Finn darted her sour tongue in and out of his mouth in time to it. Empurpled in the crossfire of the disco lights, the Swede dropped her beautiful cupbearer's head on to his shoulder and wept to it. Had anyone tried to put something else on the turntable there'd have been a riot.

Frank hasn't heard it, hasn't been anywhere he could have heard it for an eternity, but now he can't get it out of his head. He is relieved they give him a room in the new extension – no associational problems here at least. He hangs up his clothes and lays out his machines, remembering to put his batteries on charge. He would like to lay himself out for an hour or two, but he can't silence the Je t'aiming, not even in the shower. Out is the only place to be. But not out to the Dewdrop. He wonders whether to take his phone, decides against, and walks into town.

A reader of his column recognises him in the Broad and asks for his autograph. The usual: female, not in the first flush, hair going crazy, goldfish bowl spectacles, children grown up and gone away. Nothing much to do with herself now except go touring and recognising people with televisual connections. Her husband hangs back. Asking for an autograph, in Frank's book, is the same as asking for sex. He reaches for his fountain pen. 'What have you got for me to sign?'

The woman reddens, pats her person as though a couple of pale green leaves from an autograph album might flutter out of her, dithers, then remembers that she is carrying a bag, with three novels in it, from Blackwells.

'A book?'

Frank knows it can't be one of his. All his crap-watching collections are out of print. And the new one, with Broadcasting Critic of the Year on the cover and an old photo on the back, isn't published yet. 'I'm not sure I can sign a book I haven't written,' he says. He wonders if one of them might be by Mel. And what he would do then.

'Why not? Go on.' She risks boldness. 'You choose.' Behind her glasses her eyes flinch from her own temerity. In broad daylight, in a public place, she is opening a bag for a man she's never met before to look in.

The husband hangs back even further. Frank wonders why he doesn't quit the scene altogether. But that's naïve. A man has to be unusually lacking in masochistic curiosity not to want to grab a glimpse of a stranger fucking his wife in the middle of Oxford in broad daylight.

Frank inspects the contents of the bag. All telly books. Uppity telly books. An Inspector Morse mystery. A Commander Dalgliesh thriller. And *Middlemarch*. He chooses *Middlemarch*. Winner in category best provincial novel by woman over thirty not a lesbian. Had she been alive now, they say, George Eliot would undoubtedly have been writing for television. Oh yeah – just as Marquez and Llosa are, Roth, Kundera, Bellow, Grass, Gordimer, Updike. Can't keep any of 'em off the box. Frank knows he's in the wrong profession. He likes sentences more than he likes action. Thoughts more than he likes pictures. Nothing he can do about it, it's his age – he's a moral insight man. As for example, since *Middlemarch* is in question, that shrewd and poignant encapsulation of the motive force of men's long-suffering fidelity to their wives and mistresses – *He dreaded a future without affection.* He being Tertius Lydgate. But what's in a name? Tom, Dick, Tertius, Frank.

He inscribes it on the title page. And signs it as though it's his own.

She bows, drops a bead of perspiration on to his wrist, then stands beside him in a peculiarly artificial manner. It takes Frank much longer than it should to realise that her cuckold of a husband has his camera out and is snapping them. The pervert, Frank thinks. The weirdo. But in one corner of himself he is envious. With Mel, all deviant snapping had to stop.

Twenty minutes later Frank catches sight of the smutty pair walking slowly, shoulder to shoulder, down St Aldates, trying to figure out the meaning of his inscription. One of them looking for the compliment. The other looking for the pain.

Otherwise, Oxford isn't giving him whatever it is he's come for. The stones still exude the sickly mildew odour of collegiate privilege, enticing the morbid to imagine what they can never have. Even his own not so very old college with its kitsch bridge and far-from-secret gardens has sealed over in his absence and once again become a mystery he cannot hope to penetrate. Like the Swede's cunt. But the town, the town has become a mug and T-shirt bazaar run by bouncers. Heavies in black trousers and summer anoraks, striking aggressive attitudes and communicating through walkie-talkies outside genteel tea rooms and public houses, places of entertainment to which, in his day, you wouldn't have scrupled to take your mother and father . . . people the age he is now.

What explains the number of foreign bouncers is the number of foreign kids. He has always thought of himself as a man who likes crowds, but a crowd is evidently a relative concept. His tolerance level of kids in numbers was determined in more tranquil times, when the world's population was half what it is today. He finds himself stepping off the pavement to avoid them. Sometimes he doesn't see them coming. They don't know they're coming themselves. They gather involuntarily, inexplicably, like flocks of migrating birds darkening the sun, swoop in a body across the road or into a store, then just as inexplicably disperse. Would these be his students if he were back here doing his old language job, these hard-faced little consumers with writing on their clothes? Where are the lovable ones? Where are the fuckable ones, come to that? The girls are wearing skirts so short they might as well not be wearing skirts at all. But they're not dressed for pleasure. For *his* pleasure. They're actually in uniform, tunics of the puritan revolution; they might as well be Stalinist youth, kitted out for callisthenics, so stern are they in pursuit of . . . what? He doesn't have the word for it, but he has the word for what it isn't. Dialectical. The girls he used to know shortened their skirts in order to pursue a satiric dialogue on the nature of exposure. With these kids it's straight narrative: what it says is what it means.

What's done it? Communicable sexual disease? The women's movement? Is this why Mel and her consumptive chums are vomiting themselves to death, do they know that the next generation has got what they want and never can have – complete freedom from the desire to please?

Or joke. He's been away from home a half a day and already he is beginning to worry about his capacity for survival. How is he going to make it in a world where people wear what they mean and mean what they say; where the genitals are not a sort of joke about genitals; where there's no dissonance, no counterpoint, no dramatic irony?

Or is he missing their joke? Are they altogether too ironical for him?

He is in bed by ten. Flat on his back with his head on his fists, staring up at the whorled love-in-a-cottage ceiling with its oaky chandelier, trying not to hear the sounds of riot issuing from the Dewdrop. Not a position that flatters him physically or spiritually. He is at his best upright or on all fours. He needs to be busy. Prone, he is prey to passivity and mawkish sentiments. The pity of it, oh the pity of it, Iago. The pity of his unravelling sleeve of flesh. The pity of his dulling senses – remember how it used to be in a strange hotel room, how every sound was thick with promise; how the very doorknobs and window-catches, the swinging keys in the wardrobe, the slightest ripple of the unfamiliar drapes, gave shape to the unimaginable future. Where's the unimaginable future now?

Imagined. Imagined out.

And more pitiable still, most pitiable of all, the present. What a waste of himself it is, to be lying here in a bed – a bed! – as it were unattached, as it were unemployed, and no one to get the benefit. Of all life's squandered opportunities, this has always been the one that touches him deepest. A nameless night in a nameless room in a nameless town – going begging.

He made the mistake, once, in their early days, during a period that was meant to be experimentally adult, of trying to explain to Mel how it felt to be out of town and on his own in a begging bed.

'Even for just one night?'

'What do you mean, *just one night*?' Like telling someone they were to endure hell-fire, for just eternity.

'So how does it feel?'

He paused, to give it weight. 'It feels as though a great prince is languishing in prison,' he told her.

She rewarded his confidence with a raised-letter feministical-erotic satire – *The Great Prince*. His consolation was that it took her six years to write and didn't sell. Her readers didn't want satire. They wanted cunts, wet panties and Wittgenstein. And they were the bright ones.

He has to change his position; the French pair have begun Je t'aiming again in his head. At a pinch he could always knock himself out by whacking off, give his dick a treat if nothing else. But that would entail finding it. To say nothing of allowing Mel the satisfaction of being right again. 'Letting the prince out of prison, are we? And how many hours is that he's been incarcerated? Six? Seven?'

He can't face television. That too would be a capitulation to the predictable. Dick in his hand, crap on the box – Mel would love that. He props himself up on one elbow and tries the tourist literature provided for more easily amused guests – *What's On Around Oxford*, *Twelve One-Day Walks in the Cotswolds*. When he's done with those he flicks through an old hotel browsing copy of *Oxfordshire Life*. Sees a couple of Manor Houses he wouldn't mind owning, a chair he wouldn't mind rocking in, a life-style he wouldn't mind indulging – apartment in Rome, boat off Barbados, the gallery that funds it all in Woodstock. The Josh Green Gallery, specialising in Fine Paintings mainly British of the Nineteenth and Twentieth Centuries. *His* Josh Green? The arse connoisseur? A photograph of the owner in front of an Alma-Tadema Roman bath-house confirms it. The same owlish eyes, red cheeks, receding chin; the same somewhat drowning look. Greyer now, of course, but still just bobbing above the waves, the very Josh Green whose hand he hasn't grasped since the last bus of the summer pulled away from the Dewdrop in the year of the Finn. Frank remained a regular for several summers after that, partly because language teaching was his only source of income at the time, partly because he couldn't face not being there when the new bus pulled up. Josh only did it for one season. He was the one with the qualifications; English as a Foreign Language was his oyster. Frank had heard vague rumours that he'd gone to France, gone to Greece, gone to Turkey, then that he'd given up teaching altogether and opened a shop; but a gallery in Woodstock, Fine Paintings mainly British, apartments in Rome and the rest of it, all this is news to him.

Frank is unable to read an article in a magazine or a newspaper from beginning to end, consecutively. He has to skip, jump in at the middle, come out before it's finished. It's not personal or judgmental; he would read his own column this way had he not written it. It's habit. Consecutive reading is for special occasions. Like *Middlemarch*. So he has to jump back in again to know what else Josh is up to. Once a teacher blah blah. Runs gallery with wife Anna-Liisa blah blah. One daughter blah blah. Largest private gallery outside London blah blah. Finest collection . . . Frank hauls his eyes back up the page. Anna-Liisa? Was that the wife Frank remembers? Anna-Liisa . . . ? No, Josh Green's wife was Jean, no, Jill. Could have been his twin sister, owlish eyes, receding chin, air of drowning. They always looked as though they'd made a pact to go under together, but they haven't have they, quite the contrary, or at least *he* hasn't . . .

So what's become of Jill and why does he think he knows the name Anna-Liisa? His pores open suddenly; in a matter of seconds he goes from bone dry to wringing wet. Anna-Liisa was the name of the Swede! That was why Josh Green hadn't returned for another dip in the paradisal lake – the canny little bastard had hot-footed it to Sweden and *drunk* the paradisal lake!

Dewdrop din or not, it is necessary for him to throw open his windows. He paces the room, shaking his head. Perspiration continues to pour from him. He doesn't know why he is so disconcerted by what he has learnt. Who's Josh Green to him? Who's the Swede? Can he possibly begrudge Josh twenty-five years of having to mop up around those eyes after every fuck? Once was enough for everyone else. Anna-Liisa, oh lovely Anna-Liisa what ails thee so? Except . . . except that when he recalls embrocating her distress away he doesn't recall addressing her as Anna-Liisa. Frida, that was the Swede's name. Frida the Phenomenal.

So does this mean Josh Green hasn't, after all, married the Swede? And since it must do, why isn't Frank feeling any better? Why is he still pacing his room?

It's that name, Anna-Liisa. He knows he knows it. Anna-Liisa. Anna-Liisa. He rubs the back of his neck. A shaft of iron has entered his spine. Anna-Liisa. Anna-Liisa. Through the open window comes the sound of screams. Girls at play. Leaving the Dewdrop and getting into cars. Jesus Christ, don't tell me . . . It is, it is, that's who it is, it's the Finn! Josh Green didn't do the blindingly obvious thing and sneak to Sweden to marry the snivelling Swede, he snuck to Finland and married the fucking Finn!

If Frank goes on walking the carpet much longer he will walk through it. He thinks about another shower but knows he will come out of it stickier than when he went in. He is unaccountably upset. Forget disconcerted; he is discomforted, discomfited – spell it how you like. He is discommoded.

Viewed from the point of view of envy, it makes no sense. Frida was the prize. Frida was the beauty. But what if it's been the most terrific fun with Anna-Liisa? A half a lifetime chasing her fidgety cunt all over her body. 'Tis here, 'tis here, 'tis gone! A scream for them both. A co-operative of talents. Runs the gallery with the assistance of his wife Anna-Liisa blah blah blah. What if Josh Green, connoisseur of the lovely arse – which Anna-Liisa's definitely was not – made a supremely intelligent choice, abjured the aesthetics of the heart in favour of the dick and has been rewarded with a happy and successful life?

As opposed to, 'I mind that we don't play together any more – '

He climbs back into bed. If I'm going to make a go of this, he tells himself, I'm going to have to avoid comparisons. We can only live our own life. The trouble is, by imagining Josh Green first with the Swede and then with the Finn, he's given him two lives. And Frank can't decide which of them he must avoid comparing his own with.

He puts out the light. There'll be no sleep until he has mentally trampled on his day. The last-straw brawl, the greasy chips, the boy with the loose eye he's probably criminalised, the pathetic fan, the inane record . . . Serge somebody and Jane somebody, Jane with a Lawrentian surname, Chatterley, Brangwen, Birkin, Jane Birkin, that was it. Went to Paris and lived with a frog. What a waste of brain cells. Not living with a frog, remembering Jane Birkin. He drifts off, women of all nations coming and coming and coming in his head in pidgin French.

THREE

Y OU CAN'T JUST breeze into the Josh Green Gallery. It
isn't a shop. You have to ring a bell, wait, and then
suffer the scrutiny of a sort of chamberlain, a melancholy
gentleman of a gravity beyond his years dressed in an
undertaker's suit. Where there's art there has to be death.

Frank is asked whether he is looking for anything in
particular. He is quick to realise you don't say you'd just like
to have a little browse around if that's all right. On the off-
chance that a Holman Hunt might take your fancy.

'Mr Green is *who* I'm looking for. Though I have no
appointment. I'm an old friend of his. Frank Ritz.'

Now that he's here, Frank hopes that Josh isn't. The
reunions he always plans entail old friends marvelling at how
well *he*'s done. He might be Broadcasting Critic of the Year,
but that's not a hell of a lot to crow about to someone who
owns the National Gallery. Least of all when you've just been
booted out of your home – your only home – and are feeling
a lot less optimistic about that than you were the day before.
And it shows in ink and charcoal circles around your eyes.

Josh is bound to be away. It is August after all. Why would
you bother hanging around Woodstock in August when

39

you've got a boat off Barbados and an apartment in Rome to choose from?

But he can't be away, else Frank wouldn't be invited to wait in the front gallery while the undertaker announces his presence in an anterior room. Unless it's Mrs Green who hasn't gone away.

The Alma-Tadema Roman bath-house is on the wall. Alongside a Lord Leighton Grecian spring. And an Etty steamroom. So this is a themed gallery. Bathing and showering. Women bathing and showering. In rivers. Streams. Lakes. Ponds. Bagnios. Turkish baths. Russian baths. Finnish baths.

The women bathe and shower with their bodies on a twist, an aerobically difficult three-quarters turn that enables the sun to dry their breasts and their buttocks simultaneously. Josh Green always was an arse man. Frank wonders whether this is a sign that art and experience have mellowed him into a tit man to boot.

A door opens to an adjoining room. The Sickert Room, where Frank espies him closing a deal – a disconcertingly strange yet familiar figure, like the father of an old friend. He has a pop star with him, whom Frank vaguely recognises but refuses to fish for a name for, and with the pop star is an equally renowned black model who stands discounted to one side, restless but faithful, like a borzoi. Frank assumes that the pop star is buying a painting, but the scene is equally suggestive of his selling the model. Or putting up one in part-exchange for the other.

The undertaker interposes his body between Frank and the objects of his curiosity. 'I have told Mr Green you are here, sir.' In the meantime, he gestures, if you would care to look about you in *this* room, observing the feeling for flesh-tone which the great academicians brought to the painting of ladies' posteriors, you will be using your time wisely for once and, who knows, you may learn something.

However, he's too late. Josh has seen him and recognised him and waved. This is the advantage, or not, of having your photograph above your column. Your appearance comes as no surprise to anyone. He waves back; a self-deprecatory dumb-show – don't mind me, go on with what you're doing, business is business, a couple of million smackers don't come your way every day, whereas a friend –

Dumb all right. What if a couple of million smackers do come his way every day? His and Anna-Liisa's?

Once he's free – the short all-over-white pop star and his tall mahogany companion having made a sudden dash for it, darting out of a side entrance so as not to be spotted, and diving into the inconspicuousness of a thirty-foot limo – Josh proves to have changed little, on the exterior anyway, from the flushed owl-eyed familiar of those filthy minibus rides up and down the Banbury road. He is wearing a camel cardigan, not unlike the ones he used to teach in. And he is still estuarine in intonation. 'Hello matey,' he says. There are pink spots in his cheeks. 'Long time no see.'

They embrace in the new manner of men. Arms around each other, lips to throat. Frank is glad he has lived until the age he has for this, if for no other reason – he has lived to kiss and be kissed by men. After centuries of shaking hands like butlers, heads bowed, stomachs tucked in, groins well back, men have started to nuzzle one another like bears. Frank is surprised how readily he's taken to it; but now that nobody minds he's not fucking them, the musky entanglement of moustaches, the abrasion of rough cheeks, are just about all he's getting in the way of bodily love.

'Well?'

They offer to admire each other, look each other up and down.

'Well?'

Frank opens his arms wide, another of his dumb-shows meant to take in the enormity of Josh's universe, his walls of showering nymphs, his chamberlain, his clinking troglodyte clientele, his chunk of Woodstock. 'Terrific,' he says. 'This is terrific.'

Josh can't get rid of the pink in his cheeks. '*Was* terrific,' he says. 'Until John Major.'

'John Major?' It crosses Frank's mind that John Major has been buying Stanley Spencers and not paying for them.

'The recession, matey.'

They are standing in the Sickert room where, not that many minutes before, a deal of some magnitude was struck. You only have to look about you, at the alarm systems if not at the art, to see that there's no other sort of deal you can strike in this room. Josh Green reads his thoughts. 'He doesn't come in every day, you know.'

Frank doesn't know what to say. 'Must be handy when he does, though,' he tries.

'He pays off what's owing on my credit card. Do you know what it costs to run this place? Rates, insurance, staff, bank interest . . . ?'

Josh never was one to hold back on embarrassing personal details. But this is quick.

'. . . advertising, international fairs . . .'

'I can imagine it must cost to corner the market in Camden Town nudes,' Frank says. Wherever he looks, Camden Town nudes, Sickert's wonderful sticky suburban trollops wasting the riches of their flesh in dying light.

Josh corrects him. 'Mornington Crescent, most of them.'

'Even costlier, then.'

'You don't think I own all these.'

'Josh, I've got no idea what you own and what you don't.

But I can't believe you're not proud of what you've achieved, you two. Together.'

'Together?' Josh Green scratches flesh at the corner of his left eye. 'Who's together?'

Frank knows not to get too excited too soon. A man can be not together with a Finn but very much together with a Swede. 'I'm sorry,' he says.

'Not as sorry as I am. We had an apartment in Rome, she's got that. We had a boat, she's got that. She's even got the Ferrari. I'm having to get about in her Fiesta.'

'Is this recent?'

'Too recent. We should have done it years ago. The passion goes out of it, matey. And that's when you should call it a day, when the passion goes out of it.'

'Josh, we're middle aged. The passion is meant to go out of it.'

'You sound like my daughter. Act your age, she tells me. Well I appreciate that, I tell her, coming from someone I've always tried to treat like a friend. Precisely my complaint, she tells me; I don't want a friend, I want a father. Don't come to me, then, the next time you *do* want a friend, I tell her.'

'Do I remember a little girl from Oxford? Jeannie, was it?'

Josh pulls a face. Who cares what she's called.

'How's she doing, anyway? Married? Kids of her own?'

'Married? Joanne? Course not. She's gay. Lives with a bird in Lewisham. They run an electrical business together.'

Frank lowers his virginal eyes. A generational thing. 'Are you all right about that?' he risks.

'The electrical business?'

'No, no, the – ' Frank swallows air, like a fish hauled out of water.

'Just pulling your leg, matey. Yeah. We knew before she did. We were surprised it took her so long to find out. Anna-Liisa spotted it right away. You know how you notice things when it's not your own child. In a way she was closer to her than either Jill or I were. Perhaps because she couldn't have any of her own.'

'Jeannie?'

'Anna-Liisa.'

So how are we going so far, Frank asks himself. Business – in trouble. Marriage – kaput. Relations with offspring – deeply flawed. Prospects of grandchildren – zilch. Way of life – fallen into the sere, the yellow leaf. If he could bank on every visit to old friends going as well as this one, he'd do it more often.

He doesn't want to see Josh Green unhappy. He just wants to be certain that fifty's no good for anyone. Equality in dismay, that's all he's after.

'I can see what you're thinking,' Josh says. Some of the merriment that Frank remembers from their language school days has returned to his eyes. 'You're thinking I've got a bird myself.'

'Whereas you haven't.'

'Whereas I have.'

'And she's the reason you and Anna-Liisa broke up?'

'Not the reason. No. She was just someone I leaned on *while* we were breaking up. Her marriage was in trouble, too. We leaned on each other.'

'When you say leaned . . .'

Josh pulls a photograph out of his wallet. 'Look. What would you do?'

Frank holds his breath as the photograph comes into focus. Softly. Softly. But it's all right. Not anyone he knows. Not anyone he can't bear *not* to know. A squelchy blonde. Squinting in the sun, on the walkway of a marina. Wide apart eyes. Striped nautical jumper over good breasts. Slight blip below, where the belly is wanting to roll. Not so much a boat blonde as a boat blonde's mother. Navy sail-cloth skirt over deck shoes. Strong legs. Still. It's the still part that's upsetting. The defiance. The bravery. Death where is your sting-a-ling? Age where are your ravages? Frank has seen a painting in Josh's gallery he would buy if only he were a pop star – a Matthew Smith nude rolling in colour, falling through an everywhere of paint, the creamy bedclothes unravelling as she whirls, but bearing her up like a lavishly upholstered magic carpet of clouds, her flesh buoyed, protected from all harm, inexpugnably alive. But Sickert's truer. Forget space, time's the issue. It doesn't matter how voluptuously we turn a woman's body through its planes, the moment we become conscious of it in time – the moment *she* becomes conscious of it in time – not all the paint in Camden Town can cushion it against tragedy. But Frank's a sport. 'I'd lean on her, too,' he says, offering to return the photograph.

Josh isn't ready to take it back. He waits, hungry for more appreciation. 'So where did you meet her?' is all Frank can think of asking.

'Chicago Art Fair.'

'You do a lot of fairs?'

'Used to. Couldn't resist them. You know what they say an art fair is?'

Frank doesn't.

Josh Green the man is suddenly illuminated by Josh Green the boy. 'A cunt mine.'

Frank's too impressionable. He can't hear of a cunt mine without wanting to go down it. But that's all right by Josh. He waits, roseate with pride, for Frank, groggy with gas, to come back up.

'And now that you've mined your treasure – ' Frank starts to say. He means to turn a compliment, but he is anxious that his fidelity to the metaphor shouldn't lead him back into the cunt of a woman he can hardly be said to know.

But that too is all right by Josh. He's been waiting for Frank to open his eyes again only so that he can now close his own. Drowning momentarily was something he always did, Frank remembers, as a prelude to paying a sentimental compliment himself. When he surfaces he looks queerly transfigured, as though he's glimpsed God's face among the fishes. 'Oh, matey,' he says, 'you should see her from behind. You should see the lovely little bum on her.' He makes a mould of it with his hands for Frank's behoof, a pair of trembling palms like scales for a fairy.

'Josh, how old is she?'

'Forty-eight, forty-nine. But the bum's half that age. Peter Blake was going to use a photograph I'd taken of it for his Nine Prettiest Bottoms in the National Gallery . . .'

'But?'

'It isn't in the National Gallery.'

He goes over to a drawer and begins sorting through some papers. Frank wonders if he's going to bring out the photograph of the lovely little bum. Men do this. They confer publicly over photographs taken in the strictest and most solemn confidence. Frank has done it himself. Here you are boys, what think you of this? Nice, eh? Mine. Cunt mine. Mein Cunt. But not of Mel. Mel read him too well. Three weeks into their relationship she confiscated his camera. That was after confiscating all the photographs his camera had taken. He's not sure he's ever forgiven her. That you should destroy the previous lot in order to supplant them with poses of your own – that's only just. But to cut off the supply both ends – where's the fairness in that?

In fact what Josh removes from the drawer is a cutting from a not very recent *Tatler* showing his new love at an old ball, on a boat, shaking a leg with Onassis, circa 1970, about the time Frank was moving his own limbs preternaturally slowly to 'Je t'aime'. Sad. Frank isn't the only one stuck in the past.

'*Tatler* voted her one of the ten most beautiful women in England,' Josh says.

'I can see why.'

'What would you do if you were me?'

'I've told you. I'd enjoy myself.'

'What would you do if you couldn't enjoy yourself?'

'What do you mean?'

Josh hesitates. Even for him there are words you can't use without putting spaces round them. 'If you had trouble getting it up?'

'You can't get it up?'

Josh pulls back from the finality of that. 'Don't know about *can't*. Haven't so far. I think it was the fight with Anna-Liisa. You know what it's like: things get said. You lose your respect for yourself as a man.'

Know what it's like? Yeah, Frank knows what it's like, but he takes a moment to think about it, so that he can add to his list. Where was he? Marriage – kaput. Relations with offspring – deeply flawed. Dick – inoperative. Self regard – down the drain. 'Isn't it a question in the end,' he says, 'for . . . what is her name?'

'Sara.'

Sara with an ah. Not Sarah with an air.

'Isn't it a question in the end for Sara? What does she think you should do about it?'

'She doesn't know. It's never happened to her before. When you've been voted one of the ten most beautiful women in the country you're used to men being able to fuck you. The first time it happened she sat on my face and cried and cried.'

'And the second time?'

Josh tries to remember the second time. 'I think she struck me.'

'And even that didn't work?'

'Joke all you like, matey. It's hurtful to a beautiful woman. And she's just coming out of a painful marriage herself. On top of that she's got to go into hospital for an operation. Only minor, we think, but there'll be a scar. She's frightened that'll make it even harder for me.'

'And will it?'

Josh shrugs.

They fall silent. An operation has entered the room. You never know with operations. Sensible, maybe, to concentrate on the scar. Never mind whether my lifeblood is draining out through a plug in the theatre floor; what if my lover will be put off by a two and a half inch suture above my bikini line? This is a gallery. And Josh is a connoisseur. Aesthetics matter. Perfection is everything.

'Do you see a future with this woman?' Frank asks, once it is clear he must ask something.

'An erotic future?'

'I just meant a future. But I suppose eroticism enters into it.'

'I want five more years of erotic life. With Sara. I'd settle for that.'

Five years, Frank thinks, of Sara sitting on his face and crying. He could have got that with the Swede ages ago. Or with Mel, come to that, speaking figuratively.

Five years. We're into that phase. Just give us five more years. That was what his father reckoned he would have settled for at the end – just five more years. And he was seventy.

Frank wants to know something. Will there ever be a time when you are happy for it to be over? Not five more years or five more weeks or even five more minutes. Stop now! Case closed.

Silly question.

They walk to a Chinese restaurant, where Josh has a regular table. His own wine. His own won ton bowl. His own chopsticks. Frank imagines them being locked away in his absence like private snooker cues on a rack in a snooker club. They used to play together in Oxford when they weren't fucking. Now he has an image of Josh at full stretch over the table, trying to pot the pink with a ten-inch stick of ivory. 'Can you get extensions for those?' he asks.

Josh takes this to be an allusion to their earlier conversation. His chin recedes. 'You think an extension might be the answer?'

Their eyes meet in a sort of silent toast to old mirth. Unspoken between them is the realisation that if they let the same amount of time elapse before they meet again they will be seriously old men when they do. Older than Frank's father was when he died, wanting just five more years.

Josh orders them crispy Woodstock duck, over which he remembers to ask Frank what he's up to. But he starts to go sleepy, slide down in his seat, drown, as soon as Frank starts to tell him. Frank's own fault. He won't return the compliment. Won't open his heart. Won't say how much he earns. Won't say who he loves. Won't make a little floating picture of Mel's bum with his hands. Though Christ knows there's a good enough reason for that – Mel no longer has a bum.

They go back to the gallery for decanted port. Raise glasses. Exchange cards. Before Frank realises that there's not much point handing over a card with your address on when you don't have an address. 'Let me give you my mobile number instead,' he says. 'More reliable.'

49

He needs a new card, with only his mobile and his car registration numbers on it. Frank Ritz, gipsy.

Oh, and of course his e-mail. But for the bad dreams, Hamlet could have boarded happily in a nutshell. Why shouldn't Frank be bounded in a laptop and count himself a king of infinite space?

Before he goes he asks to have a last look at the Matthew Smiths. Take a bit of fleshly hope away with him. While he's looking and wishing, it occurs to him that the only paintings on the walls of Josh's gallery that don't show a nude on a bed show nudes in a bath.

'Josh,' he says, 'where are the landscapes?'

Josh smiles. A long melancholy smile that seems to go all the way back to the intense seriousness of boyhood. 'These *are* the landscapes, matey,' he says.

FOUR

So who's it to be next?

If this is what reunions with old friends are always like, he's ready for more. Wheel them on.

He's stayed away from old friends as a matter of principle since he became old enough to have old friends. As a matter of Mel's principle, that is. Other than when it comes to crap-watching, Frank has no principles. Principles are Mel's territory. Don't look backwards, she is always telling him. *Was* always telling him. It unsettles you. And you do it out of the worst of motives. There are only two reasons why you ever want to see an old friend: you either want to suffer or you want to crow.

Living with Mel has been like living with an Old Testament prophet. She denies him every pleasure.

And foresees only disasters.

Well, Mel too is now the past, an old friend as of five days ago. He has got through a working week. Had his laundry attended to in a farmhouse bed and breakfast on a stubbly field just outside Shipton-under-Wychwood, and faxed in his weekly column via laptop and modem from a country house hotel in Burford. So far, touch wood, he has eaten well, not got too drunk, and kept his dick in his pants. Not that, touch wood, anyone has invited him to take it out.

Touch wood.

He left Oxford after two nights in Summertown. Sleeping badly. The retrospection gang keeping him awake. Since then he has been trying to get into the Cotswolds proper but has been restricted to the margins by holiday crowds. On a rough calculation, he hasn't ventured more than five miles from the A40 since he was booted out of his home. Not his fault. Twice he has tried to find a hotel room in Bourton-on-the-Water, but everything is taken. August, the girls at the desk tell him, shaking their heads. He knows it's August, but what he doesn't know is why August should affect Bourton-on-the-Water. The Venice of the Cotswolds they call it, on the strength of a couple of man-made streams and a bridge. A sign points to a bird-park in Bourton-on-the-Water and another sign points to a place where you pay to see a model of the village you're already in, otherwise it's heritage and has-been shops. Has there been a sitcom set in Bourton-on-the-Water? Unable to park his Saab, unable to find anywhere to sit for lunch, unable to get a room, Frank stands in the middle of Bourton-on-the-Water and scratches his head. He is the only person not wearing shorts. Is there something wrong with him? Wherever there is a blade of grass someone wearing shorts is lying on it. The village is so crowded there are people wearing shorts lying on the road. What happened to the idea – prevalent when Frank was young – that you went to a beach if you wanted to lie down in the sun? What happened to driving to the coast, parking by the sea, eating sandwiches in your car and staring at your death in long trousers, as a way of spending August?

Such questions are driven by serious professional considerations. Already, and there are another three weeks of August still to be negotiated, he has come within a single advertisement break of missing an early-evening programme it was imperative he watched. Bourton-on-the-Water – no room at the inn. Lower Slaughter – no room at the inn. Stow-on-the-Wold, Moreton-in-Marsh, Bourton-on-the-Hill – forget it. 'I'll pay you,' he offered at last, 'just to let me sit on the edge of someone's bed and watch their telly for half an hour.' No go. He went so far as to count out money from his wallet, notes, the stuff itself, rubbing them together to release their irresistible odour the way you do when you're asking a bellhop to turn a blind eye in downtown Panama City. Money talks, sister. Not in Stourton-in-the-Mire it doesn't. 'What about the telly in the lounge?' Fine, so long as the programme he wants to watch is an Australian soap. They're in there as well, lying about in their shorts, watching Australians in *their* shorts. Is this where they get the idea from? Do they think they're in fucking Melbourne? In the end it was a lay-by on the A429 that saved him. Roof up on the Saab, Hitachi running on its batteries and his laptop plugged into the cigarette lighter. Not good reception, but at least a moving picture. And a fond old sensation of misbehaving in a motor.

So who *is* it to be next?

He tells himself he's taking time around the peripheries of the Cotswolds because they suit his temper. The yellow of the stone – the yellow of his dying sun. The misty distances of the slumbering hills – the story of his fitfully rumbling life. Their calm reserve – his extinguished fervor. But in truth he is slowly, inexorably, nudging towards Cheltenham.

Where there are ashes to stir. Who knows, maybe even coals to poke.

His heart is leaping in his chest. The bones of his cheeks ache like ice. His eyes sting. He can't speak. He can barely breathe. He opens his arms. Arms are opened to him. In he goes. All the way in, all the way back. Everything blackens and fades – his trespass, his sorrow, the years.

Kurt!

Frank!

He holds on. Is held.

Is she there?

The question that spoils it every time. Is *she* there?

Liz!

Frank!

He can't keep it just between the two of them. Never could. Neither of them could.

Try again.

Kurt!

Frank!

Hold still. Hold very still. The time before her. Boys. Boys on backs. Boys on backs in summer parks looking up at sky. Aeroplanes, one a day, maybe fewer, pure white in the clear heartbreak blue, like the future. Where will you be? Where will I be? Boys boating. Boys rowing, knee to knee, on creaking seats. Fingers skimming the water, gloves of seaweed, mermaid's oily tresses. Who's down there? Boys on lakes, boys in gardens, grounds of stately homes, ruined monasteries, abbeys, priories, castles, smelling time. What will you do? What will I do? Boys waiting.

Is it only about girls? Even when it's about chemistry sets and telescopes and chest-expanders and boxing-gloves and bikes and skates and buses to sites of ruination is the waiting only ever really about girls, birds, keife, nekaiveh, polones, call them what you like?

'I've been waiting to be in love all my life,' Kurt admits, on a train they have taken to Harrogate, to find love in the rose gardens.

They are fourteen and haven't found it yet.

Frank can't call it love. What he's been waiting for all his life is an affair. 'It's a shtup I've been after, Kurt.'

'But that's what love is, you berk,' Kurt corrects him. 'Love is a shtup.'

'Who's the berk? I'm talking about shtupping *outside* love. Cruelty and possession; the sacred terror – all that stuff. I'm talking a walk on the wild side, Kurt.'

'A walk on the wild side? Do me a favour. Where'd you get this shit?'

'Morecambe.'

'Morecambe! When were you in Morecambe?'

'When I was six. I was there on holidays with the deelos. We were stuck in a boarding house. It parneyed the whole time. There was nothing else to do, so we just sat around in the breakfast room all day, doing jigsaws. Four o'clock in the afternoon we were still scoffing corn flakes and sorting straight bits. There was this geezer staying there at the same time. A Spaniard or a Turk or something. He had a sort of semi-shvartzer keife with him. Thick lips, huge Hottentot aristotle, but totally shtumm. They'd come down for breakfast, then they'd go back to their room. Then they'd come down for more breakfast, then they'd go back to their room. All day, up and down. But whenever you saw them he'd have his hand on her Gregory Peck. Not on her shoulder but actually *round* her neck, pinching it between his thumb and his fingers. The only time he took his hand away was when he needed it to butter more toast, and then you could see the marks on her.'

'And she didn't object to this?'

'Of course she didn't object to it. That's how they do it over there.'

'In Morecambe?'

'In Africa, shmuck.'

'So what are you telling me? That you're looking for some

dumb shvartzer with a huge aris who'll let you pinch her black and blue?'

'I'm telling you that every time they came down into that breakfast room I felt my kishkes go klop . . .'

'Listen, boychick – stop moodying me. You were probably just hungry.'

'Hungry? I was eating six breakfasts a day. Lonely was what I was. Lonely and longing. I saw what the Turk had – I saw the look of devotion in the keife's mince pies – and I longed to be looked at like that.'

'And that's what you call the sacred terror?'

'Yep.'

'You're a sadist, Frank.'

Better to be a sadist, Frank thinks, than a shmuck. But he doesn't acknowledge this to Kurt. To Kurt he denies the charge. 'I was six. How can you be a sadist when you're six? I just knew I wouldn't be happy until I had a keife of my own to hold by the neck.'

'Only you couldn't find one.'

''Course I couldn't find one. I was fucking *six*, Kurt. If I'd found one I wouldn't have been able to reach the neck.'

'Because *you* wanted a big girl.'

'Like you don't, all of the sudden?'

In sight of Harrogate station, Kurt caves in. Sure, that's what he wants. That's what they've come to Harrogate for – to find a couple of big girls. Zwei shtarker keife. Big in the sense of grown-up. Grown-up in the sense of knowing that you go to a rose garden when you are looking for love.

And the miracle is – they find them!

It's Kurt who does the pulling. This has never been discussed between them but the assumption is that as Kurt has the looks of the hour – a sallow Elvis complexion, easily-hurt Elvis eyes, something Red Indian somewhere in the genes – he should be the one to bait the hook. Once the catch is landed, Frank gets his chance. Jokes, risks, nobbels, fannies, moodies, lunges – whatever it takes. Since they haven't done this many times before, they don't know what it takes.

One of the girls is exceedingly tall, one isn't – that's the first thing Frank notices. The second thing he notices is that Kurt has angled for himself the one that isn't.

'Thanks,' Frank whispers. 'So I still don't get to reach the neck.'

'Forget the neck,' Kurt whispers back. 'Just concentrate on the tits.'

But it's a moot point, as even Kurt concedes, whether Frank will be able to reach the tits either.

They sit on the grass and lie about their age. Kurt says he is in the army. Frank is reading psychology at Basle University. Soon he will explain their dreams to them. The girls are nurses. Soon they will make Kurt and Frank better.

Frank wonders whether the tall one might not even be a matron. She has an otherwise-engaged look about her. One eye on an imaginary drip. Whereas the short one is bleary, and looks dumbfounded. Lucky old Kurt. Dumbfounded equals performance – isn't that the received wisdom? You can be finished with the dumbfounded before they've realised that you've started.

Kurt hands around the snouts. Army supplies. 'An army marches on its lungs,' Frank says. First joke.

The girls pick snouts from the pack as though they're chocolates and it matters which they select.

Kurt has a steel lighter. The girls extend their pursed faces towards his flame. Kurt lightly touches their fingers, steadying their hands.

'You look like Elvis,' one of the girls tells Kurt. The tall one. Frank's. Frank feels as if someone has punched him in the stomach. Klop go his kishkes.

'Elvis who?' he says. Second joke.

That was what he was going to be had he not been a student of psychology at the University of Basle – a high court judge.

The girls know a quieter bit of park. Kurt and his put one arm around each other's shoulders and then lace themselves together by putting their second arm behind their backs and holding hands. Frank wonders where Kurt has learnt to do this. On the Rhine, presumably. Frank's leads him by the hand as though she is his mother. She has very large hands, dry, flat as spatulas, her fingers almost all the same length. It passes through Frank's mind – more as a disturbance than a thought, a sudden shock to the cerebral cortex – that while it would be with only the greatest difficulty that he could take possession of her Gregory Peck, it would be the simplest thing in the world for her to take possession of his.

He has read somewhere that when a woman scratches your palm she is signalling that she is hot for you. A Mexican or a Peruvian thing. But he can't believe the meaning isn't universal. He releases one of his fingers from her grip and runs his nail across the inside of her sapless hand.

'Ow!' she says.

'In Basle,' he explains, 'we say that pain is just another form of pleasure.'

'Well that's not what we say in Harrogate,' she tells him.

Considering how little she seems to like him he is surprised that they end up on the grass in the quieter bit of park, separated from Kurt and his only by the trunk of an ancient oak tree. In such a spot, under such a tree, Kurt and Frank have been stretching themselves out for a forever of boy-years, remarking on how sad tree trunks always are, how they resemble the feet of elephants, wondering whether it's true that elephants have long memories, wondering what the future has in store for them. Now they know.

Kurt!

Frank!

Hold the picture still.

Lying down, Frank's is far more agreeably quiescent than she was standing up. He wonders if this is always the way with girls. An alchemical thing. Vapours rising to the top of a heated horizontal body. Or merely physics. Sex spilling out of a woman when she's laid flat just as coffee runs out of an overturned coffee cup. If he could think of more things to do with her, he has the feeling that she would allow him to do them. But once he has rubbed her over a few times, like a window cleaner working at a stubbornly greasy pane, he is out of ideas. That she might let him *under* her clothes never so much as crosses his mind.

Of course he knows better than to make a grab for her neck. Do that to someone when they're flat out on the grass and it has another meaning. Even in Yorkshire.

The tree prevents him from seeing how Kurt is getting along with his. It obscures their middles. From their extremities he is able to draw no inference other than that they appear to be getting along.

It's kissing that comes as the real surprise to Frank. He has pecked at girls at parties before now, even banged teeth with them given half a chance, but nothing has prepared him for the sensation of swooning invasion that comes with making a black O of your mouth and allowing a thick viscid serpent of a tongue to maraud around in it at will. He closes his eyes and submits to the idea that man is nothing but a lightless honeycomb of leaking caverns; up into his palate the serpent goes, slick between his gums, blind behind his fillings, slow as torture or a sneer tracing the spongy pouches of his cheeks, then, in a sudden mocking writhe, quick past his uvula, brushing it aside like a bead curtain, and down down into his pharynx, where it might tickle his heart or stop his breath forever.

'Mine has to go,' Kurt tells him during an air break. The girls have gone to find a lavatory and to generally debrief. The boys use the bushes.

'How was it?' Frank asks.

Kurt rolls his eyes. 'Didn't you see? She touched it.'

'She *touched* it?'

'Didn't yours?'

Frank is ashamed to say he forgot to ask her to. 'We were too busy kissing,' he says. 'She's got a great tongue.'

'Yeah, and a big enough mouth to keep it in. She looks like a fucking camel.'

'Yours isn't so fair.'

'Don't start that. I like camels.' Kurt is agitated. Pacing up and down. You can't touch a boy of fourteen and not expect him to be agitated. 'So what are we going to do?' he says.

'I don't know. Get the train back?'

Wrong answer. 'Mine,' Kurt says, 'reckons that yours doesn't have to go.'

Frank thinks about it. He wouldn't mind more kissing. And he knows he really ought to ask her to touch it while he's got the chance. But he doesn't fancy the journey home on his own. 'No,' he says, 'I'll come back with you.'

'That isn't what I mean.'

Frank stares.

'Mine says she does it.'

'I thought you said she's going.'

'No, she says *yours* does it.'

Frank's eyes open. 'Toss off?'

'Better.'

'She performs?'

'Better.'

60

Frank shrugs. Can't think of anything better. Except kissing, and he's done that.

Kurt makes a sucking noise in Frank's ear. Slurp, slurp, swallow, gulp.

'Ligner!'

'I'm not. It's the emmes. Mine says definite.'

'Then I'll stay.'

'What about me?'

'What *about* you?'

'Mine says yours'll do two. Actually prefers two, she says.'

Stillness falls over Harrogate.

Boys. Boys on backs. Boys on backs in rose gardens with trousers round ankles. Looking up at the sky. What will you do? What will I do?

She is on her knees, dipping from one to the other, like a woodpecker.

Can't be clean, Frank thinks. Where had her tongue been immediately prior to its being down his throat? Can't be hygienic. Can't come.

Kurt neither. Not with Frank there.

Frank proposes a short walk.

'Go on, then.'

'Not me, you.'

'No, you,' the girl says.

'And make it a long walk,' Kurt tells him.

When he comes back they are kissing. 'My turn,' he says.

'Too late,' she tells him. 'You wouldn't come.'

'*He* wouldn't come either.'

'He has now.' She pokes her tongue out at him. That tongue. The tongue that once upon a time brushed his uvula aside. Out of her mouth – out of his mouth, come to that, and out of Kurt's – it's as flat as an egg-slice, like her hands. But not dry. Frank notices that her cardigan too is wet.

'This time I'll come right away,' he promises.

She shakes her head.

'Give me thirty seconds.'

No.

'Twenty.'

Still she shakes her head.

'I almost came before.'

'I know,' she says, 'and I like the taste of Kurt better.'

Me it sucked first, and now sucks thee,/And in this flea, our two bloods mingled be. Donne's Flea. Frank's favourite lyric poem. No flowers or mountains. Nature simply acting as a go-between for the sexes. So did Kurt and Frank commingle blood in Harrogate?

Not his fault, boychick, Kurt says on the train back. Free country. If someone likes the taste of his sperm better . . .

Frank looks out at the Pennines. He's never cared for them. Reservoirs and chimneys. And no sky. Rainbows in the smoke. God's apology. No, thank you; apology declined.

How long before Frank recovers his self-esteem, sperm-wise?

'I have heard,' he tells his doctor, 'that there is such a thing as a sperm test. I would like one.'

'How old are you?'

'Fifteen in a week.'

'And you would like a sperm test to ascertain what?'

'Taste,' Frank says.

A year later he is one of a party in a friend's parlour, parents away, whisky decanters emptying fast, seven of them sitting in a circle of ormolu chairs with their dicks out waiting for Marcia, a teamhander from Accrington, new in town, to gobble them up before they settle in to a night of poker.

Although she has already agreed to this, Marcia wants to lay down a few ground rules.

No touching.

OK, Marcia.

No coming out of my mouth until you're finished. This is a new blouse.

OK, Marcia.

Everyone only comes once.

OK, Marcia.

But she still isn't entirely happy. Teamhanders are like this. Punctilious. Protocol is everything with them.

I want a prize, she says.

Oh no. They all groan. If she's a brass they don't want to know. Absolutely not. Respectable boys don't go with prostitutes.

Fine by her, she'll just get back into her skirt and go then. What's in it for her? All she was going to suggest was that they blindfold her, change seats, and let her try to identify them by taste. Put the sperm to the boy. A tusheroon for every one she gets right.

It's Morris's house. He's prepared to double that to five shillings – a caser. He fetches one of his mother's favourite cut glass fruit bowls. That's the pot. Everyone puts in. OK? Bar flukes, Morris believes their money's safe. Sperm's sperm. All sperm tastes the same. Everyone agrees. Everyone except Kurt, who looks down.

And Frank, who walks out.

Later, he hears that Marcia screwed up. Only one she got right. Kurt's. 'I can taste something Red Indian,' she said. And then, ripping off the blindfold – 'You!' After which she reneged on all her own stipulations and went upstairs with him.

They are all shtupping on a regular basis now. A house only has to be empty of parents for half an hour and there are ten of them round. Up to the bedroom fast, and then down again, a swimming Durex in each fist, just like the polythene bags you are given at fairgrounds to carry away the goldfish you've won. Frank too. No more window-cleaning a girl over her cardigan. He can unbutton her with his teeth now. He can part her like a peach with his hands tied back his back. He can bring her off with his nose, with his chin, with an eye-lash. And as for the taste of his sperm – it is good to report that he has suffered no lasting aftermath of trauma in that regard: he comes into mouths all over Manchester without giving a single cause for complaint. Except –

Except when he is in the company of Kurt.

If Kurt's fucking in the same room he is, he can't come. If Kurt's fucking in the same house but in a different room he can come but the girl always spits him out. Kurt sours his sperm, that's what it comes to. Kurt curdles him.

They remain friends, catch the school bus together, go rooting around the second-hand book stalls on Shude Hill together, buy shirts in Halon together, go to the Hallé together, swot in the Central Library together, get told off in the Central Library for making too much noise together, but they can't pull keife together, can't share one, can't start from an end each and meet in the middle. Invidiousness has entered their friendship. *It's a free country, not Kurt's fault if someone prefers his sperm to Frank's . . .* but Frank knows that in his soul Kurt can't leave it at a free market; in his soul, and in relation to Frank, Kurt has come to think like a genetic supremacist: he believes that chromosome for chromosome he is the better man. Frank makes the better jokes, but he shoots the better spermatozoa. And it's not the joke that gets the girl, it's the jism.

Of course Kurt never *says* this to Frank. He loves Frank. Wouldn't hurt him for the world. But there's an unmistakable *noblesse oblige* about him now. When Frank is offered a place at Oxford Kurt is pleased for him in the way that one is pleased for a man with no arms who wins an egg and spoon race – it's not something he can begrudge him. Kurt himself goes to Birmingham. Only Birmingham. But then *he* doesn't have anything to prove, does he?

Frank doesn't like the way Kurt sits on his settee and looks about him whenever he comes to stay with him in Oxford; he has a way of making Frank feel that he is living in a doll's house. Cute. Dinky. Nice for him. Well done, Frank. Your secret's safe with me. Out in the college courtyard he pats Frank's bicycle seat. Springs, eh? Aren't you doing well! Kurt himself drives a sports car around Birmingham. Brrrrm brrrrm. But then that's to be expected. Tasty sperm, tasty car. He marries, too, after graduation. Meets her, impregnates her, marries her, boom. Brings her swollen-bellied to meet Frank, his best friend, presently fucking his life away in a language school in Summertown.

Liz — Frank.

Liz!

Frank!

Steady.

Not a qualm about sitting her in a corner of the disco where Frank is to be found Je t'aiming it in the psychedelic crossfire. God, that Frank! Kurt Je t'aimes it himself, just once, with a double-jointed Italian. Go on, Liz laughs. Go for it. Kurt doesn't look like Elvis any more. He looks like the Temptations. The lights pepper him purple and orange. Thank your lucky stars I'm into responsible husbanding these days, Frank. And yourself, do you mean to go on fucking much longer? Well, why not. Ssh! It's safe with me. Your secret.

And then the baby. Look what we've got, Frank. Go on, hold. Isn't she beautiful? But then that's to be expected. Tasty sperm, tasty baby.

And tasty wife? Yes. No. Frank can't make up his mind. Yes. Maybe. Narrow green eyes. Generous mouth. Goodish legs. Flat behind. Breasts nothing special either, but then she is feeding, and a tit with a baby on the end of it is *hors de combat* even for someone as omnivorous as he is.

Yes. No. Yes, tasty. It's the laugh. It's what happens to the green eyes when she laughs. It's how wide she opens her mouth. It's the amount of chest she gives it. It's her concentration on the thing you've said to make her laugh. It's her gift for exclusive attentiveness.

Frank!

How will her laugh be now?

She has another baby and loses a third. Frank writes a letter of condolence. Faulty sperm, Kurt? But tears it up. His own sperm is raging. Red hot emissions. In quantities that would put to shame a sperm whale. His bed is like the Atlantic. He is coming five times a day with a partner. Four times a day without. On days that begin without and end with that's nine, plus one more for the element of surprise.

And what am I worth as an element of surprise?

You, Liz? You're incalculable.

They have started to meet. Once a month, that's all. In restaurants. When she comes to London to see her gynaecologist. Frank has left Oxford. It hurt, but he's out. He has found a flat in Kilburn. North London is what you say. He is patching a living together with a bit of supply teaching and some GCE examining and occasional reviews for small magazines. Kurt and Liz are in Cheltenham. Kurt is already head of media studies in a teacher's college. He speaks in tongues and looks like Al Pacino. There are rumours that he has a mistress. A student. What other kind is there? Liz is having babies, losing babies, and coming to see him. He makes her laugh. Tells her about his adventures in the big smoke. Where he goes at night. Who he meets. How much sperm he's making. If it were oil, he tells her, I'd be rich, I'd be a Sheik. Her green eyes narrow to pricks of emerald light. She laughs and laughs. That's all.

They correspond. She writes to his flat. He writes to Gloria, poste restante, Cheltenham. Just to be on the safe side. When a partner moves in with him she writes to Errol, poste restante, Trafalgar Square. Also to be on the safe side.

Sometimes he tells her he has someone living with him when he hasn't, just so that he can go on collecting her letters from the post office. He loves the palpitating tube ride under London. Has she, hasn't she? Loves coming up out of the smoky underground, like Don Juan returned from hell. Bearing his exceptional secret through the crowded square. Joining the itching queue of aliens watching as the clerk goes through the mail. Striped envelopes worn thin with distance, queer brown paper packets done up with string and wax, the same ones there week after week after week, stale news from Kingston, Auckland, Izmir – *Ibrahim. War over. Come home* – Cape Town, Lima, Kabul, maybe Cheltenham, maybe not. The sting of disappointment. Another day of waiting.

For what? They no more than gossip to each other. Make jokes. Try out popular philosophy. Pass on hearsay, tidings, tittle-tattle. Films, books. What Kurt's up to. No reason not to mention Kurt, is there. Love, Liz. Love, Frank. Not even much love, or lots of, or all my, or undying. Or you. Love you.

One day he receives a letter in which she tells him of a dream. He knows this is the one. Last night I dreamt I.

Steady. Hold steady.

Normally he rips open her letters and reads them where he stands, stock still like a hare in the middle of the post office floor. Not this time. This time nothing is still. His hands do battle with his eyes. Last night I dreamt I . . . No, not yet. He snatches the page from his own scrutiny. Strikes his thigh with it. Anyone watching must assume he has received the most appalling news. *War raging. Family wiped out. Stay where you are.*

Should he have stayed where he was?

Liz!

He puts the paper back into its envelope and conveys it through the crowds into the great squirting square. Holds it tight against his chest, so that the pigeons can't steal it. But the pigeons don't come near him. They can sense his agitation. They can hear his heart. His kishkes going klop. He stands under a lion and reads. Skipping the preliminaries, the night, the moon, the poplars, the symbolism. He knows what he's looking for. Knows it's in there. And then I dreamt . . . It's here, this is it. And then I dreamt . . . He turns his head away, as though to look back down the corridor of his old life one last time. Then he plunges in.

And then I dreamt you fucked me.

Silently, all the Trafalgar Square pigeons converge on him.

Back in Kilburn he carefully folds the letter over and over until he has a little parcel, almost a cube, the uppermost face of which reads 'fucked'. The u of 'you' is just visible, as is the m of 'me', but they aren't distractions. 'Fucked' pure and simple is what he wants and 'fucked' pure and simple is what he gets. How long does he sit and stare at that single word? One hour. Two hours. He undresses. How many times does he come reading it? Three times. Four times.

What he feels is a mystery to him. He has wallowed in sperm for half his life. He has waded up to his eyes in cunt. What can a little word like fucked hold for him?

They decide against Kilburn as a sacred site. If they're going to do it, they're going to do it well. They arrange a long weekend in Paris. She tells Kurt she is going away with a girl friend. Needs a break. Kurt understands. More time with the mistress, Frank thinks. They stay in a hotel in Montmartre. Why shouldn't they? Are they not, in every sense of the word, tourists? Just visiting.

They don't wait to unpack. The view their room enjoys

of Paris is an intrusion of sexual outrage in itself, but they don't have eyes for it. They stretch out alongside each other on the bed, their toes touching, their bellies touching, their foreheads touching. How long have they known each other? Five, six years?

'Been worth waiting for?' she asks him.

'This,' Frank says, 'is the fleshly experience of my life.'

He means it. He can sense every particular hair on her body. Give him the time and he could count them with his eyes closed. There is a fibrous magnetic field between them. He feels he is floating a couple of centimetres above her, and she above him. Some rare phenomenon of temperature variation is also at work. Wherever they meet they are five degrees hotter or colder than each other.

'You know what I like,' he says. 'The way we don't meld.'

'Aren't we supposed to meld?'

'No. It's a fallacy. You can mix but you shouldn't meld. You don't want to feel that you're fucking yourself.'

'You've told me that you like fucking yourself.'

'Not in company, Liz. And not any more. I won't be fucking anyone any more who isn't you.'

He means it. He has never experienced a more exquisite penetration. One way or another, penetration itself is usually a let down. The word flatters the deed. Either it's a bruising struggle to enter or you are swept in like a salmon awash in a waterfall. Today it is like cutting into a gateau.

The moment he begins to cut she raises her hips to him, brings her feet up, and locks him into place with her ankles. That's how you know if you belong together – if the cake cuts and the ankles lock.

They walk hand in hand to a restaurant where a gypsy violinist plays to them and an Algerian sells them a rose. Why shouldn't they? Are they not tourists?

On the way back to the hotel he drapes his arm around her shoulder, then brings his hand up to her neck.

'Yes,' she says, 'I like that.'

He tightens his grip.

'Yes,' she says, 'do that.'

They walk along in silence, the wind blowing her skirt, her heels sparking the cobbles, her neck hot under his fingers. Everything smells foreign.

They go out on to their balcony to breathe in the view. The entire sighing city submissive to their contemplation. Submissive but not meek. She raises her skirt from behind. And inclines towards the city. He moves into position.

'No,' she says. 'Use something.'

He dithers. Use something? He hasn't used something since he was sixteen. No one uses them any more. And he has already come into her twice today without.

'In my bag,' she says. 'My hair brush.'

He finds her hair brush and returns with it. She is further forward than before, one hand on the the balcony rail, the other clawing at her buttocks, pulling herself open. She hasn't bothered to remove her pants. They're nothing. Not to be respected. Nothing is to be respected. In the distance he can hear Paris roaring. Closer to home, all is silent.

He eases the handle of the brush into her.

'Not the handle,' she says.

He wonders if he has it in him to go through with this. But he only wonders for a second. *You're a sadist, Frank.* He reverses the brush, bristles first, and pushes.

'Harder,' she says. 'Rougher. And hold my neck. Hurt it.'

She doesn't moan. Women only moan in Mel's novels. She grimaces. She bites her lip. She grunts, yips, coughs, makes a series of rasping sounds from the back of her throat.

'Harder?'

'Mm.'

'Harder what?'

'Harder please.'

'Please who?'

It doesn't come naturally to him. He isn't at his ease. But he's read the literature.

And so has she. 'Please sir.'

'Do you love me?' he says.

She falls quiet.

He pushes violently. Twists the brush. 'Answer me.'

'Yes,' she says. 'I love you.'

He could throw her off the balcony. She wouldn't stop him. He could replace the brush with himself, fuck her and throw her off. Does he want to do that? No. But it's academically interesting that he could. Academically interesting that she would let him. Who is she? What is she playing at? And another question: does she do this – *did* she do this – with Kurt?

And still another: is she in any sense that matters doing it with him?

'I want you inside,' he says.

She doesn't demur. He twists the brush out of her and leads her in by the neck.

'Kneel,' he says.

She kneels.

He pulls off his belt and ties her hands behind. He puts the handle of the brush in her mouth. 'Taste yourself,' he says.

He undresses and sits in the little pink velvet bedroom chair. A nice thought of the management's, a honeymoon touch. Like the pretty matching valance round the bed. Like the vase waiting for the single rose they would inevitably buy. Romantic. Strange they don't provide the brush that goes up the cunt as well.

'Come over here,' he says. 'On your knees, stay on your knees.'

She does as he tells her.

In reality, in *fairness*, he has been doing what she tells him. She was the one who lifted up her skirt. She was the one who said use something. For his part he would have been happy to go on floating on their magnetic field, cutting into gateau. But he's a grown man, a free agent – *it's a free country, Frank* – and he's not obliged to do anything he doesn't in his heart want to do. One day, when I'm old, he tells himself, I will look back on tonight and I will not forgive myself. But old is still a long way down the track. 'Now suck me,' he says.

She seems surprised that this is all he has in store for her. Her eyes quickly register the abstemiousness of his expectations. *Suck him*? She's come all the way to Paris with her husband's best friend and a bag full of spiky brushes just to suck him!

He grabs her hair as her mouth is about to descend on him. 'I think you should beg to suck me,' he says.

She begs. 'I beg you,' she says.

'Use my name.'

'I beg you, Frank.'

Frank!

He comes copiously. In silence. Fingers through her hair. Fingers round her neck. Holding her head still. So that she can swallow everything.

'Now I would like you to talk to me,' he says, 'about the taste of my sperm.'

And she does. At length. Omitting not a single detail, no matter how seemingly trivial. It isn't difficult to ascertain from her, at the last, that she would rather swallow him than anyone.

Than anyone, Liz?

Than anyone.

Kurt!

Frank!

What are the chances? Arms opening to him, pulling him in, closing around him, boys, boys with greying temples, boys looking at early retirement packages, boys who haven't spoken or heard from or alluded for a quarter of a century – what did you do? what did I? – what are the chances of a warm welcome?

Mel has never met Kurt. He was gone, stone cold out of the life, well before Mel got her turn. But she knows the story. Frank's version of the story. And she recognises the symptoms of the *herzschmertz* that seasonally seizes him, usually at the beginning of spring, which is also when the dreams start, as a consequence of his cleaning out drawers and coming upon old photographs, or worse still, old letters. These days she doesn't bother to wait for the wistful expressions of regret – 'Funny how after a certain age you don't make real friends again. It's true what they say: no pals like old pals. Et cetera.' 'It's just a tic,' she tells him, refusing to look at the photographs. 'If you'd wanted old pals you'd have worked harder at keeping them. You'd have respected the rules of palship more.' But the fever has to run its course. Mamet plays. Buddy movies. Hands of poker, just the two of them. The sound of him on the phone to directory enquiries – 'No, I don't have their address, but there can't be that many Brylls in Cheltenham.' Before the business of life carries him on to some new repining.

What are the chances of a warm welcome? 'I wouldn't touch it with a barge pole,' Mel warns. Ezekiel.

And she doesn't even know the whole story. She doesn't know that drunkenly one night after a GCE examiners' meeting – he must have been drunk, mustn't he? – Frank spills the beans to a fellow examiner, a Cheltenham colleague of Kurt's, and a fellow admirer of Kurt's wife's green eyes. Maybe it's the warmth of that particular admiration that sets him off. He hasn't seen Liz for months. And no longer collects letters from her from Trafalgar Square. What is there to write about now she has told him – willingly or under duress, he will never know; but it was duress of her own designing, he knows that much – that she prefers the taste of his sperm to that of any man living? You can pack too much into a single night. You can cover too much ground. The new admirer – Billy Yuill (and the name doesn't help his cause with Frank) – has the look of a man just starting out on the journey. But under serious misapprehensions as to the nature of the terrain. Like someone in flannels and a boater turning up at the foot of Kilimanjaro. 'You're dressed wrong for where you're going,' Frank wants to tell him. 'Get out of those picnic clothes. And wipe that starry expression off your face.' It's the mother in Liz that Billy is soft on. He likes to see her with her kids. He's been accompanying her to children's playgrounds. He's helped her put a sandpit in the back garden. You're a vicarious pervert, chum, Frank wants to tell him. You're a proxy paedophile. He's not only worried for the children, he is affronted on Kurt's behalf. Men who are smitten by a woman's wifely little ways, Billy Yuill, should leave her to perform her wifely little functions for her husband. And then there's the insult to Liz herself to consider. We're talking person here, Billy. Not mother, not shopper, not angel in the house. We're talking woman. We're talking laughter that tears you to tatters. We're talking fibrous magnetic fields. We're talking cunt that cuts like a gateau. We're talking hair brushes. We're talking cock-sucker.

So let's talk it.

Billy Yuill has a big meandering mouth. It goes all the way round his face. George Formby, Frank thinks. A mouth for standing hoping by a lamppost with. How he holds it together, while Frank talks to him about the view from Montmartre, the city spread out like a woman's body, the darkling fuzz of the Bois du Boulogne, the creamy domes of Sacré-Coeur, Frank doesn't know. But when Frank rings Kurt a week or two later and Kurt tells him never to phone or call or write or otherwise make contact again, not with him, not with Liz, not with their children, not with their children's children, not now, not ever, he has to face the fact that Billy Yuill's control over his meandering mouth was only temporary.

So *now* what are the chances?

There's champagne tasting at the Burford fine-food shop. It may be barely eleven in the morning and he may only just have polished off his bacon and eggs, packed his bags and paid his bill, but a wedge of pork pie and a gargle of bubbly are just the ticket for Frank. No one brings you Cotswold crusty pie, strong English mustard and French bubbly for elevenses when you're living at home cowering from the buzzards and nursing your machines.

Already in their shorts, the crap-watchers from Sutton Coldfield congregate outside the shop wondering whether the sign saying free champagne tasting can possibly apply to them. Through the window Frank shakes his head at them. They back away. Not knowing what to do next on their holiday, some of them think about lying down in the road.

You can lead a horse to the water, Frank thinks . . .

Fortified, he swings the car back on to the A40 and points it in the direction of Cheltenham. His roof is down. *Woman's Hour* is on the radio. Someone talking about the new strong eroticism of women's fiction. Mel's work is being discussed. Forgetting, not a little proud, turning to share the transport, Frank reaches for his phone to tell her to listen, then remembers that they no longer mingle vicissitudes. His morning courage begins to leak away. He thinks of going back to Burford for another thimbleful of bubbly. This time, the speaker explains to Jenni Murray, it's ourselves we're pleasing. Unlike when, Frank wonders, hitting the accelerator.

The pliant hills turn harsh on him, fold back to show an ancient, unrelenting topography. Barrows. Blank farms. Cold lanes. Surely this is well north of Hardy country, but he feels suddenly like Jude Fawley behind the wheel of the Saab, reading his inescapable obscurity in the landscape. He passes a sign to Windrush on his right, to Woeful Lake Farm on his left. Just out of Mill End he drives by Hangman's Stone. He drives on, looking straight ahead. So as not to see the gibbet where hung his ancestors in the next field.

He is changing his tune. He is not now going to Cheltenham expressly in order to do what he was originally going to Cheltenham expressly in order to do. He is going to Cheltenham because it's on his way. On his way where? All right, *in* his way. Point your car west on the A40 and you don't have much choice, do you? Eventually you get to the sea at Fishguard Bay, but some considerable distance before that you have to encounter Cheltenham. So while he's there he'll stay a bit, have a look round, find a hotel, do his laundry and his column. If he happens to bump into anyone he knows from the past, even if it's anyone Mel has warned him against touching with a barge pole, well he's not going to do any more than doff his cap, wish 'em well and go on his way, is he?

Every day he decides he can't go on spending quite so much money on hotel rooms, but every day has its own exceptional quality that can only be requited by a comfortable bed. And wherever else he is going to have to cut corners, he certainly isn't going to cut them in Cheltenham. He drives around the town a couple of times and settles for the Queens. It occurs to him to ask for a suite with a balcony. But sees himself on his own in it, wandering from room to room, watching *Friends* on television. He is trying to stay rational. He is trying to convince himself that he has not come to Cheltenham in order to fall into Kurt's arms, beg his forgiveness, weep at his feet, and then sneak his wife back to his hotel again. He is trying to tell himself he is not that insane. But he isn't succeeding.

He knows where Kurt lives. He has his telephone number. It wasn't all that hard to find in the end. Kurt's college has become a university and Kurt a professor. Any fool can track down a professor.

In fact, Frank has been carrying Kurt's number, written on a corner of his driving licence, where the prophet Mel won't find it, for a year or more. He has always carried some arrangement of numerals relevant to Kurt about his person – scrawled in the back of a chequebook, pencilled into his passport. And not only relevant to Kurt, come to that. His wallet is an atomic scientist's notebook of curious forgotten formulae and ciphers, e-mails and codes and extension lines and house numbers taken down at parties and screenings and walks in the park, of no practicable use that he can see at the time, but who's to say what the future will bring. Notations for a rainy day. Which at last fade into mementoes of things you never did anything about. By the time you are Frank's age your life is a teeming saga of things you never did anything about. But now that he is a bachelor again, a man with no house to go home to and no one to fuck him when he wakes and no sperm left to speak of anyway, he believes himself to be perfectly within his rights to wonder whether the rainy day in question hasn't at last dawned.

He showers, puts on a bath robe, turns on the television – it's a calmative in the afternoons, restores him to his routines

– pulls his driving licence out of his wallet and stabs the numbers into the phone. Then he hangs up.

FIVE

IT'S LIKE LOURDES outside the little Arts Theatre. Apart from himself, everyone is overweight and hobbling. Apart from himself, everyone is a woman in need. If one's going to be literal about it, that last is not entirely true. There are other men in the throng, supportive men, ministering men, men who have entered imaginatively into the whys of their womenfolk's fatness and even accepted, no doubt, their agency in its ineluctable progress. But there are no men as Frank understands the term. Meaning, men whose function it is to put the other case. Life is argument; Frank believes that he performs a near-Darwinian function in relation to women – he quarrels their vital spark into flame. In this sense he is the best friend any woman could ever have. And in this sense there are no men like himself queuing to get into the theatre to see the fat stand-up comedian (no one says comedienne any more) whose stage-name derives from the size of the cups into which she lowers her ungovernable breasts – D.

'You fat bastard! You fat bastard!' The audience holler for D who informs them over the speaker system that she won't come out until they shut the fuck up.

The invective, in the mouth of a woman, makes Frank

temporarily homesick. *Shut the fuck up!* How long since he's heard that? Eight days? Ten days? An eternity? If he's not careful he will cry. As if he isn't already conspicuous enough, just three rows from the front.

D rolls on to the stage. Drink in one hand, fag in the other. Demoniacally slothful. Wearing a gross floral maternity frock over Doc Martens. A joke they all get. This is what you're expected to wear, this is all you *can* wear, if you're the size they are. So why aren't you all putting your fingers down your throats, Frank wonders. If you don't like the way you have to look, why aren't you all hanging over the bath in the time-honoured fashion?

You could fit Mel and all her friends into the frock D's wearing. One in each sleeve; four in the bodice. Tie the neck and you could shake another dozen down into it like dolly mixtures in a paper bag. Fling it over your shoulder – a sack of stray cats – carry it to the river and toss it in. Put them out of their misery.

'Cheltenham, eh!' D crosses her arms over her sloppy chest and squeezes her lips together. The audience laughs. In Cheltenham, Cheltenham is a funny word. She stumps to the front of the stage, coughing ('Fucking lungs'), breathing hard. 'Always wondered what it was like in Cheltenham. Applied for a job here once . . . headmistress of the Ladies' College. I had to fill in this form. Name, age, sex, previous experience . . .' One eye arches. 'So I wrote, "lots of shagging, but still not as much as I'd have liked" . . .'

On Frank's left a fat woman holds her stomach from sliding down between her knees. Tears spring from her eyes. The act hasn't got going yet but already she's beside herself. Lourdes. The miracle cure. Say fuck. Say shag. Own up to it: even though you're fat you fuck. Own up to it: even though you're fat you don't fuck anything like as often as you'd like to fuck. Only it's not fucking that you do and would like to do more – it's shagging. Shagging is fucking reclaimed by women. Fat women. Say it. Shag. Enjoy the comicality of it. Shag. Shag. Shag.

Rhymes with sag. Rhymes with bag. Slag. Hag. Fag. Rag. Everything disobedient. Everything out of control. Abundant. Riotous. Thin girls screw (if you're lucky). A cold steely wheedling little function. Fat girls shag. They spill. They bring the bed down.

Is this where Frank's gone wrong? Would his mornings be busier if he were shacked up with a fat fiancée instead of an emaciated one?

It suddenly occurs to him to wonder whether Liz is in the audience. Could that be her, splitting her sides, next to him? Could she have blown up over the years? Is she too getting about in a floral maternity frock, aged fifty, heaving her breasts whenever she hears the words shag and fuck?

And then I dreamt you fucked me.

He'd postponed thinking about her; put the phone down before either she or Kurt could pick it up, and strode out to see what Cheltenham was offering in the way of cultivated entertainment. He'd have preferred something clean and bracing. A J. B. Priestley or a Terence Rattigan. A single-issue play. A chamber concert. A convocation of inter-faith charismatics. Partly he's still proving Mel wrong – No, I wasn't following my dick, as chance would have it; I was at the theatre. Partly he's trying to prove to himself that he can lead a normal healthy life even though he's on his own. Sitting listening to shagging stories in a room full of weltering fat ladies proves nothing either way.

After the comedian he goes in search of a bar. Not a good idea to drink in the theatre; he doesn't want to be there when the miracle cure wears off and the fat ladies start to turn nasty. But then again, he doesn't want to be wandering around Cheltenham where anyone might see him. He chooses something at the boulevard end of town, in Montpellier – which has its reverberations – and orders a bottle of something red. Fleurie or some such. It has, of course, to be French.

He is halfway through it, absorbed in his thoughts, looking out over Paris, sightless, his elbows on the table, his fists propping his chin, when a hand sweeps the back of his neck. A cuffing action, symbolically rather than actually concussive, a blow from somebody with only half a grievance. Somebody who is more hurt than hostile.

Kurt?

Liz?

Mel, even? Come to find him? Come to take him home? Somebody who loves him. Loved him.

He jumps, but doesn't dare look round.

'It is you, you bastard, isn't it? I've often thought about what I'd do if I met you one night in a dark alley. Well here we are.'

He recognises the voice. He'd be a bit of a shmendrick if he didn't. He's been listening to her telling shagging stories for the last hour and a half. He also knows why she's been thinking about meeting him in dark alleys. This isn't the first time his loose tongue has landed him in trouble. You don't get to be Broadcasting Critic of the Year without upsetting a few broadcasters. Give them a bad review, give them only a half good review, and they're dreaming of slicing your ears off in an underpass.

D, he remembers, he once characterised as a pussy cat masquerading as a tigress. Threatens your balls with her claws but in reality only wants to jump up into your lap and lick your neck. It was just a passing notice. Part of a larger survey of the new telly stand-ups. Were they called alternative comedians in those days? That's how long ago the review was written. But time, he has learnt, doesn't enter into it. They are like elephants. As to memory, not as to skin.

He turns around, smiles and slowly rises. Go courtly, that's the received wisdom. Extend your hand. Look pleased to make or renew the acquaintance. Try to keep the colour in your cheeks even. Don't let them smell fear. And nothing extenuate. Get into apologies the way his paper's grizzling book reviewers are always doing when they meet a victim face to face at the Christmas party – I'll read it again, I promise I'll read it with more care the next time – and your bacon's cooked.

'This is hardly a dark alley,' he says. The bar is well-lit, broad-windowed, white-wickered. It is also full, the drinkers distracted, their drinks fouled, their relations with one another agitated and fractured, by the presence of someone they recognise from telly. Their upset is palpable, viral, catching; it rattles the glasses in their hands, sends a fevered tremor through the wicker furniture, makes the windows screech. Frank can feel it coming up from the tiled floor. Celebrity-palsy.

Famously extruding her lips, she pats his cheek. Stubby fingers. Schoolgirl's nails. 'It'll do just as well,' she says. She looks the tiniest bit drunk. Maybe that wasn't cold tea she was drinking on stage. She blows smoke in his eyes. Is this a prelude to something gentler? He is not at home in the world of fat stand-up female comedians. He is the habitué of thin female tragedians, where nothing comes of nothing. What will he do, he wonders, if she suddenly asks him for a shag.

'Buy us a drink, then,' she says. *Then*. As though to say she is now content with the way their old quarrel has been patched up. She punches his arm companionably, crumpling herself down in the chair next to his like an accordion at the end of a folk evening. Does she think he has made her an apology? She accepts it, anyway, whether he has made it or not. But then it never was that bad a review.

She is not on her own. She has a stringy boy with her. A roadie or a minder or something. Scots, Frank reckons. Wearing a white vest under a leather jacket. It's a warm night – August in Montpellier – but he seems to have a shiver going. Like a snail, he carries his home on his back; wherever he is, it is forever Glasgow. He has a stud in his lip and a sort of eternity ring through his eyebrow. Frank's mother bought him his first ring; a gold shield with his initials intertwined upon it. *FR*. Frank Ritz. A great looping monogram such as a drunken gentleperson might, in a bygone era, have employed to sign a dud cheque. A present for his sixteenth birthday. And strictly for wearing on his finger. What do mothers do now? Pay for the perforations? They are going round, some of these kids, so Frank has read, with rings through their prepuces. Is that something else you expect your mother to splash out on? First the Gameboy, then the dick ring.

No wonder they shiver, Frank thinks, if they've got that many holes in themselves.

The boy doesn't look at him. He seems to be in a pet with Cheltenham for being prosperous, with the bar for being full, with the furniture for being comfortable, with the night for being warm, with the sky for being above. Fuckin shite.

He isn't real; he's come out of a book. Frank doesn't know which book, only that it's one of those exercises in unaccommodated north of the border demotic and that it's dumped the fuckin bairn off the fuckin page.

If he were to bother being curious as to anything about him, aside from whether he's wearing jewelry in his penis, Frank would be curious about his age. Eighteen? Twenty-eight? This is a lost decade for Frank. He can't discern any of the subtle distinctions. Soon it will be eighteen to thirty-

84

eight that bamboozles him. Then eight to forty-eight. It's an impercipience he bears with equanimity. He looks forward, what is more, to the day when he will apprehend even less. What else is the wisdom of age but a condition of perfect indifference to the lineaments and paraphernalia of youth. That apply to the lineaments and paraphernalia of young women as well, Frank? I mean it to, Mel. I mean it to.

'White or red?' he asks the comedian.

'Come again, cock.'

'What are you drinking?'

'I'll have red beer if you strongly recommend it. Otherwise, the usual colour.'

Of course, ale with the boys. She's political, Frank recalls. When she's not encouraging fat ladies to fuck more she's pointing up social injustice.

'So it'll be bitter?'

'What do you think?'

'Pint?'

'What do you think?'

A pint of bitter. In a wine bar! Frank feels quite light-headed. When did he last order a pint of bitter? Twenty, twenty-five years ago? Probably at the Dewdrop. If not for the Finn, for one of her successors. After which, shagging ensued.

He wonders . . .

He turns to the boy. 'And for you?'

The boy hugs himself and rocks to and fro. Dumb insolence this used to be called in the days when men wore their rings on their fingers. Punishable by being sent to your room. Or detention. And now? Frank would favour the death penalty himself, but others, he acknowledges, reckon a stint in a detoxification centre should be tried first. Or a week's mountaineering in North Wales. Or a month's snorkelling off Tobago . . . Now that he's fifty, Frank finds that he's in possession of thousands of examples of indulgence meted out to young thugs. Is that how you die, mentally leafing through the holiday brochures of the undeserving?

'No beer? No wine?'

No yes. No no. No please. No thank you. No nothing.

'Orange juice? Mineral water? Cocaine? Speed?'

There is movement under the boy's vest. A heartbeat? Laughter, dying inside? Has something kickstarted his frozen engine into life, and is that something the farcical spectacle of an old geezer stumbling through the pharmacopoeia of the young?

Frank is susceptible to the criticism. He is of the aspirin generation. When he says heroin he over-bites the O, purses his lips around it the way an older and even more innocent generation of men fill their mouths with the Os in homosexual. He's susceptible but also fiercely proud. Don't tell *him* about addiction. The difference is — and here Frank's pride swells into the sort of fervour you associate with campaigning environmentalists — the substance he was addicted to was entirely natural. Cunt, that was his narcotic. He snorted cunt. One sniff and he was hooked. To tell the truth, it began even earlier than that; cunt was mentioned — that's how he got started. He heard the word cunt in the schoolyard and on the instant he became a cunthead. The taste itself only confirmed everything he'd already imagined for himself. He had friends who couldn't keep their faces out of their girlfriends' anuses; they'd start on the cunt and then nose their way rumpwards — girls didn't like you to come at the anus straightaway, that was the reason for the surreptitiousness: you had to creep up on them, edge silently along the perineum like a soldier bellying under a wire fence, and then break cover all at once in a sudden bayonetting of tongues — but in his judgment, though of course he tried in time everything organic that womanhood could manufacture, for viscosity and perfume, for being fried alive in Mother Nature's gumbo, there was no getting past the cunt. Not the bee in all its promiscuous drunkenness, not the worm gorking in the rankness of a writhing rick of compost, ever tripped as Frank tripped. So don't tell *him* about bombing out!

A waiter goes by, collecting used glasses. 'Got anything for young people, other than spiked lemonade?' Frank asks him. He can't resist. Let the little bastard laugh under his skinny vest. He'll flatten his Os and nail him. 'Heroin? Opium? Phenos? Mesc? Shmeck? Shmack? Es? Fuckin Es?' He turns his eyes, cold, on the juddering Scotsboy. 'What do you say, Hamish, to a penneth of crack, maybe?'

The boy pushes himself up from the table. It is impossible to tell whether he is sneering or in pain. He points a white attenuated finger at Frank. 'A cat can look at a king,' he says. Then he goes crashing out of the bar.

'Gnomic people, aren't they, the Scots,' Frank says.

'He doesn't sound Scots to me,' D says.

'What is he then?'

'How should I know? Cheltenham, I wouldn't be surprised.'

'Are you saying he wasn't with you?'

'Never seen him in my life. I thought he was yours.'

'My what?'

'I don't know – friend, driver, dealer, catamite, son . . . I don't know. What do telly critics have? Had he been your driver I'd have asked you to lend him to me.'

'What about if he'd been my catamite?'

'No, thank you. Do I get my drink now?'

'So what did he want with us, the wee rat?' Frank wonders aloud, on his way to the bar.

When he returns, D is squeeze-boxing her face into an

expression of mischief. 'You aren't by any chance prejudiced against Scottish people, are you?' she asks him. 'What have they done to you?'

'Not Scottish people, just Glaswegians. But you're the comedian. Isn't everyone prejudiced against everyone? Wouldn't you be out of work if we weren't.'

She swigs at her beer. Gives him a sideways look, lips mashed into a damson purée. 'We might start prejudiced but we don't have to stay that way.'

'So you see yourself as a reforming comic?'

'I don't see myself as a *con*forming comic.'

'You'll tell me next that you refuse the stereotypes.'

'I refuse the stereotypes.'

'And you think that's why they laugh at you – because you refuse the stereotypes?'

'I think they like a change.'

'I don't. I've just watched you. I think they like as little change as possible. I think they like you to tell them that it's OK being just as they are.'

'Which means bigoted, in your book.'

'No, not bigoted. Just not pervious to everything. Still capable of laughing at what's different to them. Still keen on derision.'

'Which you think is a good thing.'

'Fucking right. A good thing because it's good for them.'

She throws him another of her squelchy purple smiles. 'And you're still the same spunky little bastard you always were, aren't you? Is that how you like to think of yourself – ballsy? Do you think women like ballsy little blokes?'

He wonders if she's going to start tickling him. Would he know how to handle himself in a bar in Cheltenham, with everybody watching, if she were suddenly to make a grab between his legs? Is he even ticklish any more? Is there any feeling left in that sad old sac of his?

'I don't know what women like,' he says. 'I used to, but I've forgotten.'

'You think it might have changed? You've just told me people like as little change as possible.'

'I was talking about laughter.'

'Well, that's what women still like. Make us laugh. Or have you forgotten how to do that as well?'

Frank stares into the middle distance. Mel's territory. Will he say, according to the woman I once loved I have? Will he say, I have of late, whereof I know not, lost all my mirth-making faculties? Will he confide to her that they have gone the way of his dick? Will he have a little cry?

No. Surprise surprise. It seems he still believes sufficiently in the future to think it's worth keeping a few things to himself. 'You're the comedian,' he says again. 'You make *me* laugh.'

She's too smart to rise to that. 'What are you doing here, anyway?' she asks him, after a moment's reflection. 'Don't tell me you live in Cheltenham.'

'Do I look as though I live in Cheltenham?'

She surveys him. His soft unused skin. His travelling Italian linens. His Rolex. The invisible gold chain around his neck. 'Yeah,' she says, still considering. 'Or Essex.'

I don't live anywhere, he wants to tell her. Where my caravan stops, that's where I lay out my stall. But he sees that that might be an Essex thing to say. 'I'm here to see your show,' he says instead.

'You don't have to come to Cheltenham to do that. What else are you here to see? Or should I say, who else are you here to see?'

The question takes Frank's breath away. It is as if someone has just made off with his maidenhead. 'That's a mite personal,' he says.

She accordions her neck, puffles up her pudsy lips.

'Bollocks,' she says. 'A girl needs to know with whom she's drinking. You married?'

'I'm not.'

'You're blushing. How old fashioned.'

'Not as old fashioned as asking someone if they're *married*. How many *married* people do you know?'

'OK, are you' – she dances her fingers in the air like puppets, little fat Japanese puppets bowing to one another – '*with someone?*'

He hesitates. Once upon a time he was never *with someone* even when he was. Once upon a time the no was on his lips before the question had left hers. But then a lie always did come easier than the truth. Always did, always does. Which is why it takes him so long to admit, 'I'm not.'

'So what's a nice young man like you doing' – up come the puffing fingers again – '*without someone?*'

'Booted out.' This, for some reason, he can say. This, for some reason, he likes saying.

'For an even nicer younger man?'

Frank almost chokes into his wine glass. Until this moment it has never once occurred to him that Mel might have wanted to be shot of his ideological noise because she is in love with someone else's. Another man? Mel? Not likely. Why take on another man when you hold all men to be a plague? When she booted him out she booted out the whole sex, half the entire species. It was on that understanding that he consented to go. As a representative, an emissary. Not for himself personally, but for all men is he wandering the earth. The one thing he hasn't consented to is another man (forget the nicer younger, *another* is enough to be going on with) sneaking his fax machine into his office, hanging his towel above Mel's . . .

He entertains a futurable indignation. Falls into the righteousness of the future conditionally wronged. Will he his dick have kept decorously sheathed in honour of one who may turn out to have dishonoured him?

Ensnared in the treasonable grammar of sex, his imagination rackets between the tenses. She did, would she! He will, has he!

And between the senses. He can hear what he can picture. Mel's flesh rounding out again. Mel's penitential hair re-sprouting. Gone, the Hitler moustache. Already, to please the newer, nicer, younger man, a cunt as overgrown as Castro's beard. Hush, listen! Bristle, bristle. Now it's his turn not to be able to bear the din.

From what may yet prove to be the case he reverts to what may already have eventuated. 'Did you say something earlier about a driver?' he asks, inconsequently. But only *apparently* inconsequently.

'Did I say that you've been booted out in favour of an even nicer younger driver? No. But have you?'

'Did you say you were short of a driver?'

'I said I wouldn't have minded borrowing your young Scot, had a driver he turned out to be. Why?'

Fanned by provisional jealousy and heated by wine, a mad thought is catching in Frank's mind. Short of a review a week, which he's now proved to himself he can knock off in any old layby, he's got nothing on. Maybe nothing on for life. D employs no props that he can remember. Other than a carton of fags. And never changes her costume. Provided he can fit her in the Saab, there should be no problem with what goes with her. Why not? She isn't his kind of woman, but isn't it time he found another kind of woman anyway? And she has éclat. Where she goes she causes wine glasses to rattle and windows to screech. Add that to the mini-tremble he can set off in a room of ageing broadsheet readers and they become a pretty formidable pair. Who knows, she may even be prepared to do his laundry.

'Just an idea I had. Are you on the road for long?'

'Another thirty days.'

'Where do you have to be next?'

'I can never remember. Bristol, I think.'

'And after that?'

'Oh, I don't know. Cardiff, Swansea, Exeter, Torquay, somewhere down there. Don't ask me.'

'And you're short of a driver?'

'I will be after Bristol.' Her face is making concertina music again. She lays it on his shoulder, in parody of a woman waiting to learn her matrimonial fate. Will he or won't he? 'Why? Do you know one?'

'I'll drive you.'

She looks up at him, her face cocked like a parrot's, her eyes puckered into little ruches of sardonic fat. 'Is this a roundabout way,' she asks, 'of trying to get into my knickers?'

He rises abruptly from the table. Minutes ago she'd caught him out in a blush. Now he is quite white. 'Excuse me,' he says. He is distracted, unable to look at her, his hands reaching uncertainly for his wallet, has he paid, hasn't he paid. 'I'm so sorry,' he says. He is ghostly, like a man who has seen a ghost. And then he is gone, out of the wine bar, into the street, running.

The palsied at the next table go on staring, squinting at D through their drinks, wondering what, as a telly celebrity, she will do to amuse and enrage them next. She turns to them, giving them her fat shagger's shrug. 'Funny response to the word knickers,' she says.

Speaking conditionally, she isn't all that wide of the mark. It *could* have been the word knickers that did it. It is not a word Frank likes. If that's fastidiousness, it's fastidiousness about language not about sex. A man who has passed so much of his life with his head between women's legs is hardly going to have an attitude to their pants, looked at libidinally. He can take them or leave them. In so far as he has preferences they are the universal ones – for the exiguous over the voluminous, for the fresh over the feculent. Otherwise they don't matter to him. As decorations they have their place; as obstructions they are easily whiffled away. It isn't what knickers are and what they do that upsets him – it's how they sound. It's their jocularity. They insist a culture of buffoonery and clumsiness. They intrude an ugliness he has never, for his own part, experienced.

Never? Well, seldom.

There is another reason, not quite so impeccably linguistic, for Frank's distaste. Knickers are what fat women wear. Even when a thin woman talks about her knickers Frank immediately imagines her wearing what a fat woman wears. So when D, starting from a mountainous base, talks about hers – what's more talks about *getting into* hers: a manoeuvre, an act of breathless clambering, a negotiation of hazards analogous to potholing – Frank's imagination is stretched to its limits.

He has had fat girlfriends. In the beginning, when, like every other boy (except Kurt) he took whatever he could get, all his girlfriends were fat. Fat Susan. Fat Heather. Fat Reeny. Very fat Fiona. The rule was that you were allowed them – to practise on, as it were, like rough paper – so long as you weren't seen with them. You met them inside the pictures at the other end of town. You called on them at midnight and walked them in the park. *Their* park, where nobody, except the previous fat girl, was likely to recognise you. Rainy nights were good because you could hide them under an umbrella. Fog was very good. Blackouts would have been best of all but he was born too late for them. His parents' friends, his friends' parents, were always talking about what they had got up to under cover of a blackout. Those must have been paradisal times for fat girls. How their podgy hearts must have raced when the doodlebugs came over and the sirens began to scream.

The big mistake of Frank's fat period was to get caught with one.

They'd rented themselves a gaff, a talf, a deelo-free empty lettee, he and his wide-boy sexual argot-naut chums, for the Christmas season. A festive shtuppenhaus in Wythenshaw, over a newsagent's. They each had a key cut, agreed a rough timetable, decorated the place with balloons and streamers, stole sheets and pillowcases from home and shared in a carton of Durex, wholesale. The timetable reserved Saturday nights and all day Sunday for communal shtupping, teamhanders, persuadable au pairs, serial cocksuckers like Marcia, poker – whatever was going. Otherwise, they each had their own night. If they hadn't pulled that night they could swap with someone else who had, in return for a piece of the action, or not. Whatever. They were cool about it. United in a common cause. All for one and one for all. They might fall out over other things but they were not going to fall out over nekaiveh. The point of all the pulling and the shtupping – the whole point of keife, Kurt – was that it brought you together, not drove you apart.

Frank's night was Tuesday. A good night. The behavioural model on which they worked showed that girls from the social classes they routinely raided were contrite by Monday morning, were washing their hair on Monday night, and were hungry to rave again by Tuesday. Wednesday they were contrite again. Thursday they were saving their energy for the weekend. Friday they went out with one another. Saturday and Sunday they were dredged up anyway by the communal nets Frank and his chinas threw over the side. So for one-to-one shtupping, with time for a bit of a smooch before and a snout each afterwards – romance, in other words – you couldn't do better than Tuesday.

On this particular Tuesday Frank pulled from the baby-food counter in Boots on Corporation Street. They all used Boots. He'd ducked in to see if Rita or Mona in photography had anything doing – they all used Rita and Mona – and walked slap into Dilys stacking shelves. She was new. New to Boots and new to Manchester. New to Manchester was always an added inducement. In an immodest age it approximated to modesty. If you were new to Manchester there was a fair chance you hadn't yet met and fallen in love with Kurt.

Taken all round, Dilys wasn't strictly one to snap up, new or not. There was a snagged look about her. She made you think of holes and breakages. And spillage. Shagging had not yet been reinstated. Its grand comicality was still to be reaffirmed. Dilys was a shagger in the earlier sense; a shlump of a girl with a Bath bun face and heavy legs, a shlong-puller out of dreary necessity, not high-spirits. On any other day Frank might well have kept on walking to the photography counter and let her pick up her own spilt cans of powdered milk. But this was Tuesday; an empty bed yawned; Wednesdays belonged to Morris and Morris wouldn't let it go unremarked if he turned up for his shift and didn't find at least two knotted sacs of asphyxiated semen floating in the toilet bowl. What also encouraged Frank to press his suit was the fact of Dilys living in Wythenshaw, a hop skip and a jump from the shtuppenhaus. He could pick her up at the other end of town, take her for a drink at the other end of town, walk her to the scene of her coming despoliation at the other end of town, and even walk her home – all unremarked. The gods could hardly have dealt fairer with him than that. It was even threatening rain. Only an air raid could have served him better.

They began kissing on the stairs. She had a soft, sweet mouth. Not a trace of the usual Babycham and Woodbine vomit. What a mystery girls were. You just never knew what you were going to find. No wonder there were some men who never stopped. Every Saturday morning Frank went to the Kardomah in Market Street to observe them, the hoarse-voiced grandpas in their camel coats and toupees, Poles, Czechs, Hungarians, men in their fifties, sixties, God knows maybe even in their seventies, sitting watchful as spiders over their Russian teas and cappuccinos, still hungry for the dollies, more to the point still capable of opening their jaws and snaffling them up. Frank thought that he was one of those who would never stop. Fifty years later you'd find him in the Kardomah – the KD, as they called it, the Keife-Drome – his voice box worn out with all the chatting up, his putz worked to a frazzle, but not yet come to the end of his curiosity, not yet done marvelling that a face like this can come with a cunt like that, and vice versa. Take this Dilys, a nebbish with a ponim like an idiot Polak's, fat fall-away tits, a sloppy belly, legs like the Parthenon, laddered stockings, bad skin, zero conversation – who could ever have guessed that such a meerskeit would have a wine gum mouth, a tongue as subtle as Satan floating on a breath as odoriferous as an angel's. So what else is he going to find? There is not – there never was, there never will be – art to find the cunt's construction in the face. I will be at the KD till I'm a hundred, Frank thinks, plucking at her skirt.

They fall into the living room of the empty lettee, bringing down a Christmas streamer. Frank can't find the light switch, but Dilys wants it to stay dark anyway. She is self-conscious about her breasts. Feeling his way around her, under the blouse she won't let him remove, Frank under-stands why. She has vanishing nipples, inverts, retards, agoraphobics. No sooner does he suck one out than it pops back in again. If he's not mistaken, she has large aureoles too, like a nursing mother. So the dark's OK by him.

She is easier about her skirt coming off, her stockings, her girdle. The catch of his watch-strap snags in her pants. 'Mind me knickers,' she says.

He kisses her, to remind himself that there is an upside to all this.

He drops to his knees. What are the chances of her being ambrosial down there as well? He finds himself in a dense coppice of snarling bristles. Good. Where there's hair there's hope. He takes them, Frank the venereal flosser, one at a time, between his teeth. Savours their dry curling resilience. Enjoys their resistance to his bite, the way they spring back when he releases them, scratching the inside of his mouth, pricking his gums. Until he finds one that has a pearl of moisture, not of his making, too bitter-sweet for his making, upon it. And then another, and another. Like a dog in a desert he sniffs his way towards the source, pulling her down on top of him so that not a bead should roll anywhere but down the funnel of his throat.

'In my mouth, Dilys,' he tells her.

'What?'

'Come in my mouth.'

She can't hear him. 'What?' She's impatient with him. How is she supposed to hear him when she's got her cunt in his face. 'Eh? What?' She raises herself slightly. Which isn't what *he* wants.

'What's the matter?' he asks.

'Can't hear you.'

'I said, what's the matter.'

'Before. I couldn't hear you *before*.'

So he shouts it this time. 'Come in my mouth, Dilys.'

And that is when the lights go on.

They are all there. All his chinas. One for all and all for

one. Neville, Gerald, Morris, Ian, Kurt. Laughing. Holding their stomachs. Rolling on the carpet. They are all there, where they've been throughout, waiting, listening, hiding in the darkness with their fists in their mouths. They've got keife with them. Rita and Mona. Also beside themselves with mirth. That was how his chinas knew what was afoot: Rita and Mona had blabbed, Rita and Mona had seen him that morning in Boots and sent out the encyclical — to keep him company on his Tuesday night at the shtuppenhaus Frank Ritz was bringing back the dog to end dogs. One for all and all for one, provided you don't drop below a certain standard. Meerskeit — fine. Fat meerskeit — also fine. You do the deed of darkness *in* the darkness — you're business. Anything left over we'll have. If not, not. But in the case of Dilys, it seemed, all bets were off. Dilys was a class Z shtup too far. Dilys belonged to comedy, not to sex, and comedy was communal. Callous? Blame Rita and Mona. They were the ones who'd made the pronouncement: See Dilys and die.

Die laughing.

Frank knows not to say that Dilys has hidden depths; that despite every appearance to the contrary she kisses like an angel. And that she has a knish too, if they'd only have let him finish, that promised to be worth the eating. He knows his friends. He knows what amuses them, what would amuse him if he were them.

He lies where he is, burning with shame. His eyes are closed. His mouth is closed. His dick, out of his pants, looks as though it's been shot by a sniper. Dilys has had the presence of mind to raise her rump from his face, but hasn't had the presence of mind to do anything else. She stands above him wearing only her crumpled blouse, snail tracks of Frank's saliva on her inordinate thighs, her belly slack, her buttocks loose, on her dim steamrollered face the ghost of an attempt to find the situation funny herself, to join in the laughter. Which is more than Frank attempts at least.

How long do they go on rocking with laughter? A week, Frank reckons. A month. A year. You want to know the secret of perpetual motion? Begin with Frank Ritz asking a dog to come in his mouth.

In the end it's the dog herself who silences them. She takes them upstairs, individually, Neville, Gerald, Morris, Ian, Kurt, and gives them one. One each. And why don't they say no, since she was considered to be beyond the pale, an untouchable, the ne plus ultra of fat toerags, a joke, an anathema, dreck, only a half an hour before? Maybe they see it as an act of redemption all round.

How Frank sees it, reduced, betrayed, mortified, interrupted, and shtupless on his own Tuesday night to boot, only time will tell.

When he gets home he discovers he has Dilys's pants in his jacket pocket. Did he stuff them there when he was undressing her? His way of minding them? Or did his chinas plant them on him, while he lay like a dead man on the floor? Did she? Something to remember her by.

A fat girl's knickers.

So it *could* have been the word that did it. Pity the poor comedian. How could she have known what an associational minefield she was stepping into when she winningly puréed up her lips and questioned Frank's intentions as to her underwear? D for Dilys. D for displeasure. Disinclination. Disgust. Distemper. Death.

(Unless, of course, distemper was the very effect she was going for, she being a comedian, and he being a man and all.)

But in fact – and whether or not – the reason for Frank's abrupt and somewhat rude departure lay elsewhere. He rose from the table, white as a ghost, as though he'd seen a ghost, because he had. The ghost he'd seen was Liz.

He saw her through the window, standing on the street, looking in. Then he saw her coming through the door and pushing her way into the bar. Then he saw her seeing him. Then he saw her go.

There can be no doubt that it is her. The eyes may be twenty-five years more tired than they were when he last leapt into them, ablaze in Montmartre, but they are the same electric green. The discontented brackets that qualify her mouth are also unmistakable. She always did look sour and cheated. That those brackets could be coaxed into quite other configurations, that she could be amused into an eruption of laughter lines and carefree creases, had much to do with her appeal for Frank. He loved changing the geography of her face. He could do it still. In the fraction of a second that is given him to learn what has become of her he sees that she hasn't once and for all given up expecting to be diverted. Not bad for a woman of fifty. And a summons to him, if ever he saw one.

So the fat comedian's feelings, frankly, don't come into it. There goes Liz, and he is up and after her.

He thinks he sees her hurrying down Montpellier. But it isn't her. He has the hair wrong. He can't be expected to have noticed what colour her hair is now. Or what clothes she is wearing. A suit, he thinks. Grey, like a man's. She used to buy her suits from Jaeger. Now, presumably, with Kurt a media professor and no doubt an Eco man, she'll have turned to the Italians herself. Armani. Versace. He follows a loose-woven grey jacket into a would-be Irish pub with a fatuous name but he is wrong again. He goes back out into the street and looks about him. Should he recover his car from the car-park and go after her on wheels? If she did see him and she is fleeing she'll be long gone by the time he gets his car out. He runs his hands through his hair. What to do? He has her address in his wallet; he could get the car out, drive to where she lives and, assuming she is not driving herself (which is not a safe assumption), wait for her to come home. And then what? A scene outside the house? Children screaming. Neighbours coming to their windows. Kurt enraged. His hand raised. Haven't you been warned? Not to call, not to write, not now, not tomorrow, not ever.

Is this the slow subtle reconciliation – *Frank! Kurt!* – he's been planning?

But what if Liz *isn't* fleeing from him? Because he saw and recognised her in a flash, he's taking it for granted that she must have seen and recognised him instantaneously too. But they aren't equally placed, are they. He knows he's here, she doesn't. In a manner of speaking, he's been expecting to see her. But she can't have been expecting to see him. Unless . . . Unless he'd been spotted earlier in the day. Unless she'd got wind of him. Unless Kurt has had him under surveillance for the last quarter of a century, and today, at last, has known the hour for sacrifice has come – 'He's here. Go to him!' Like the mountie releasing Rose Marie to the irreducible wildness of the mountains. So was she coming to him? If she was coming *to* him, why was she running *from* him? Dumb question, Frank. What if she wasn't running from him at all, but leading him? But then again, if she was leading him why had she lost him? There is only one answer to that. She supposes that he'll know where to find her. There is such a thing as the secret language of love; lovers know what each other is thinking; they presume on their shared history; what they did yesterday, where they went yesterday, is inscribed on their hearts. So where did Frank and Liz go yesterday? France? Was that as long ago as yesterday? Well, he for his part has already honoured France in his heart by going to Montpellier and drinking Fleurie. And she for her part has read him aright by coming to Montpellier to find him. So far, so faithful. His turn. Where else? Narrow it down. France, Paris, Montmartre, balcony, bed . . . Bed! She's gone to the Queens! She's found out where he's staying, she's shown him her face, she's fled in the night and now she's waiting for him in the foyer of his hotel. He can hear the lisping of her stockings as she crosses and uncrosses her legs. No she isn't; she's waiting for him face down on his bed. The sound he hears is the squeaking of his sheets.

And how long has he been standing in the street combing his fingers through his hair? He starts to run towards the hotel. What if she *was* waiting for him face down on his bed, but has given up on him? What if Kurt is expecting her back; what if he has said you can have one last hour with him, not a minute more? The Fleurie is now a pool of acid in his stomach. He feels as sick as a jilted boy.

She is not in the foyer. He sees several sets of legs crossed in wing chairs, but Liz is not on the end of any of them. He can't wait for the lift. He dashes up the stairs, round and round the rectangular lightwell. The carpet is smudged crimson, the colour of his gut. He turns the key in the lock, breathes in, breathes out, and proceeds inside.

She isn't there.

SIX

'I KNOW,' FRANK TELLS himself, 'what I must not do now.'
This is one of the advantages of age. You know so
much. You know what you owe to yourself. You know
how to protect your peace of mind. You know consequences. Outcomes. You see the end in the beginning. You
know how you feel in the morning.

He sits on the edge of his bed and makes a list of what he
must not do.

He must not order another bottle of red wine from room
service.

He must not ring Kurt. Tell him he loves him. Tell him
he's sorry. Then ask to speak to Liz.

He must not ring Kurt full stop.

He must not go back to the wine bar to find D.

He must not ring Mel.

He must not think of Mel bearding some other man.

He must not get into his car and go looking for whores.
(Whores in Cheltenham? There are whores everywhere.
And if there aren't whores in Cheltenham there'll certainly
be whores in Gloucester. He must not get into his car and go
looking for whores in either place.)

Once having made this comprehensive list of what he

must not in any circumstances do, Frank feels altogether better about getting up off the bed and going ahead and doing them.

Of course not all of them.

He doesn't, for instance, ring Mel.

By the time he is out of the shower, his third that day, room service has rustled him up a bottle of red.

He pours himself a glass and throws aside his towel. He dries naturally, in his own heat, from the inside out. It's a hot thing to be doing, getting ready to go out in the Cotswolds at a quarter to midnight.

He has already transcribed Kurt's number on to the pad beside the telephone. Now it's just a matter of stabbing it in.

Does he have misgivings? He is nothing but misgivings. But what else is heroism if not the courage to say yes when every part of you is saying no? What else is sin?

A male voice that is not Kurt's voice answers. No hello, no number, no telephone manners, just a low incurious end-of-the-tether 'Yeah.'

Frank apologises for the lateness of his call but says he would like to speak urgently to Professor Kurt Bryll.

'My father's in America.'

Over the beating of his heart, Frank is listening hard. *My father.* Which one is this? I have held you in my arms, Frank thinks. The plump round tasty fruit of your father's plump round tasty sperm. I have tossed you in the air. But he isn't going to waste time on introductions. Kurt might be back from America any minute. 'May I speak to your mother?' he asks.

'My mother doesn't live here.'

Klop go the kishkes.

'Look, I'm an old friend of your parents. Do you have a number for your mother?'

'A *very* old friend of my parents. They've been divorced for more than twenty years.'

If he weren't drunk, if he weren't in a hurry, if he weren't given over to sinning, Frank would be devastated by this news. Devastated for them and desolated for himself. Kurt and Liz have been a stable point in his life. Tell him that Kurt and Liz haven't existed and you're telling him he's been living a lie all this time. If he weren't in a dash to perdition, Frank would be vexed with his old friends for letting him down like this. Then he would break down and cry.

'Do you have a number for her?'

'She wouldn't want to hear from you.'

Something catches in Frank's chest. He tries to laugh it up. 'How do you know she doesn't want to hear from her old friends.'

'I know she doesn't want to hear from *you*.'

Which one is this, Frank wonders. He never paid any attention to Kurt and Liz's kids. He threw them in the air and then got on with shtupping their mother. Is this their revenge?

'Which of Liz's children are you?' Frank asks.

'You won't remember.'

'But you think you remember who I am?'

'I know I remember who you are. I know you're in Cheltenham right now. I know what you're wearing. I know what you've been drinking. I know where you've been drinking.'

'How do you know?'

The boy doesn't answer. Unless a faint snort of self-satisfaction is an answer.

Egged on by befuddlement, desolation mounts on Frank. Some people are energised by mystery. Frank is saddened and weakened by it. What's going on here? If this were a girl on the other end of the line he would be better able to see

105

his way clear. A young Liz, spat out of her mother's mouth – that's who he saw through the window of the wine bar, and that's who saw him. Not the mother but the daughter. And he seeing not with the eyes of now but the eyes of then. Time plays these tricks. As for how come she recognised him – easy: either the portrait of him mummy keeps on her bedside table, or the picture at the head of his column. No doubt the latter. These days every columnist has a famous face. Oh look, there's Frank Ritz the telly critic. Wasn't he one of daddy's friends? That's how the girl knew him. Knew what he was drinking. Knew what he was wearing. The trouble is he isn't speaking to a girl. So that's that theory junked.

And since he isn't speaking to a girl – and as he now remembers, Kurt and Liz had nothing but girls – who is he speaking to?

'I don't get any of this,' he says. 'But I'd dearly love to talk to your mother. I saw her by chance tonight and I'd love to chat to her again. If you don't want to give me her number I understand. I'll give you mine. Just ask her to ring me.'

'You couldn't have seen her tonight. She doesn't live in Cheltenham. She doesn't live anywhere near Cheltenham. And she doesn't want to speak to you. I doubt that her husband wants her to speak to you either.'

'She has another husband?'

'She's had another husband for a long time.'

Unbidden, Billy Yuill's big meandering George Formby mouth conjures itself up, flashing its hopeful lamppost smile. Frank doesn't need to ask. Some things you just know. Billy stood his street corner. Until at last the certain little lady came by.

'What about your father – does he have another wife?'

The boy laughs his death-rattle laugh. 'My father collects

wives. He's marrying another round about now in America. I'm surprised you've not been invited to the wedding.'

Unbidden, a seminarful of beautiful dutiful media student mouths conjures itself up for Frank's displeasure. He doesn't need to ask. Some things you just know.

The other way of being fifty. Pretending you haven't noticed. Good old heedless unobservant Kurt. Knight of the Delectable Sperm.

'And you?' the boy continues. 'How many wives have you had?'

'I'm not the marrying kind.'

'Children?'

'I'm not the fathering kind, either.'

'No,' says the boy. Or is it, 'No?'

'So what's your name?' Frank asks.

'My name?' There is a long silence. Then, 'Ha! My name's Hamish.'

Then he puts the phone down.

Frank sits on the edge of his bed and adds to his list of what he must not do.

He must not think.

He pours himself another glass of wine and contracts the muscles of his face. If he can compress his head, making a steel helmet of his skull, closing down every sensory and cognitive access to his brain, he can keep out thought.

And if you can keep out thought you can keep out grief. Remorse. And dread.

He consults his watch. It is now well into the next day. Is there any chance D will still be sitting in the wine bar waiting for him to return? None whatsoever. Then it will do no harm, will it, if he goes back to look for her.

He puts on his linen jacket.

Montpellier has fallen quiet. A molten summer moon has

exerted its magnetic influence and drawn everyone off the streets. The wine bar is closed. Inside, the staff are tilling up, smoking, putting chairs on tables. Fun's over. A brute asseveration of anti-climax Frank is unwilling to accept. He knocks on the window. They wave him away, making kaput signs with their hands. He knocks again, making emergency signs with his. A waiter comes to the window. The new non-subservient kind, wearing a tablecloth for a skirt. 'Did you see which way D went?' Frank shouts.

The waiter puts his ear to the window. 'Who?'

'D.'

'D who?'

'D D. The comedian.'

The waiter shrugs his shoulders. He can't be bothered with any of this. D D the comedian. Coco the clown. Not at this time of night.

Frank stands on the street and runs his fingers through his hair. I'm repeating myself, he thinks. Groundhog Day. The price you pay for being a cynic: you forgo surprise, you turn every day into an exact replica of every other. Very well then; in for a penny, in for a pound. He should have thought of it before. Where else in Cheltenham is D going to be staying but the Queens? Probably in the room next to his. He sets into a modest trot. If he's quick she might not yet have turned over and gone to sleep. The thought of her turning over, heaving her bulk, listing, careening, slows him down. But only a little. There is red wine flowing through his body. His veins are vines.

He asks reception for her room number. Reception is afflicted with falling inflexions. Reception informs him that it doesn't give out room numbers. Even though he's a guest at the hotel himself? Makes no difference. Even though he and the lady in question are friends? Still makes no difference. So how is the lady ever to know when someone is calling on her? Reception rings her from the desk. So ring her! It is, he is reminded, rather late. Reception has difficulty pronouncing its Ts. Rather late comes out rather laid. Rather laid! Isn't this a Five Star hotel? Isn't a Five Star hotel accustomed to the sort of hours kept by people who are not native to Cheltenham? The lady, he can assure reception, is expecting him. Is even awaiting him. In her knickers, his tone would have them know. Very well, and what is the lady's name again? The lady's name is D. D? Is that her surname or her Christian name? He doesn't know. How the hell does he know. Just D. D D. The comedian.

'Bear with me.' Someone has been paid to teach reception to say bear with me. As though there is grief and suffering behind the desk which the client must perforce help to shoulder. Frank does as he's bid and patiently buoys up reception in its tribulations. Reception goes on tapping into its computer. 'We are very sorry, sir,' reception says at last, 'there is no one of that name staying in this hotel. Could you have the day wrong?'

So what does that leave, Frank wonders.

'I'd be very grateful,' he says, 'if someone could get me my car.'

What it leaves are the whores.

Wherever he has lived Frank has known where the whores are. Call it instinct; like a squirrel knowing the whereabouts of emergency rations. As for employing whores, he came to that at a relatively mature age. Nineteen he was, back in Manchester from Oxford for a long weekend, driving home in his father's car from a game of poker with the boys. He had won and was feeling affable, so the sight of a woman his mother's age standing at the kerbside at midnight in shabby respectable Cheetham Hill, nodding her head at him, aroused his compassion. She was either a friend of his parents who recognised the car and wanted a lift home, or she was a person in trouble, too well-brought up to signal her distress with anything more demonstrative than a nod of her head. He pulled up a few yards ahead of her, reversed, wound down the window, and smiled.

'Business?' she asked.

'No,' he said. 'I'm on vacation from university.'

They sorted their misunderstanding out quickly enough. He could go back to her place for ten shillings. He could have full sex in the back of the car for seven-and-six. But what she recommended, given the time of night and his hesitancy, was a gam in the front seat for half a crown. Frank had never heard the word gam before. In his world you were sucked off, or you were plated, or you were given head. There were syllables involved; the operation required skill: co-ordination, sensitivity, patience; it partook of the civilised arts. Gam, in its flat unevocativeness, its unceremonial gummy functionality, its promise to be over before it had begun, opened up a stratum of society he had never before plumbed. Common he'd tried. But this was lower and more desperate than common. This was nothingness. This was life without meaning. For the price of your first bet on a lowly poker hand, for a mere tusheroon, you could stop your car by the kerbside, wind down your window, and pop your dick in a complete stranger's mouth. Frank was electrified.

'Take a right,' the woman told him. 'Take another right. Now take a left.'

She was neither old nor young. She was neither handsome nor ugly. She wasn't anything. Frank was struck by how few concessions she made to the idea of glamour. Even pauperised glamour. No boots, no high heels, no stockings, no plunging neckline, not even lipstick. If she was dressed for anything it was housework. Had the idea of opening her mouth for passing motorists to pop their dicks into suddenly come to her while she was cleaning out her cupboards? A mere spur of the moment whim, like making a cup of tea or nibbling on a Nice biscuit. I know, I'll go out and gam for half an hour. Was she not even driven by necessity?

'Now right again. See that gate? Turn in there, reverse, and switch your lights off.'

Frank is shocked to see that she has directed him into the playground of his old primary school.

She holds her hand out for the money. Frank's pockets are full of tusheroons, his poker winnings. She hears them clinking. 'Tell you what,' she says. 'Why don't you make it five bob and I'll take my teeth out.'

On the last day of every summer term at Frank's old primary school the year's batch of leavers would hokey cokey in and out of the classrooms in a ritual goodbye to those they were leaving behind. Every year the same mocking valedictory song:

> Standard one, standard two,
> Standard cockadoodledoo.
> Standard three, standard four,
> Someone's knocking at my door.

Frank too sang it when it was his turn to leave. Full of tears, but full of expectancy as well. Who would be knocking at his door?

Now he knows. Now here he is, back. Parked under the wall against which he used to flick cigarette packets, weighing up the pros and cons of having a drab gam him with her teeth out.

He fights against all the obvious sensations. Is he a soldier of sex or isn't he? Any old person, positioned as he is, might choose to wind down the window and throw up. Wouldn't it be a more intelligent response to feel privileged? An hour ago he was scooping up his friends' loose change. What did that teach him about the world? Now he is being educated in the ways of people who have hitherto been as closed to him as a tribe of pygmies. Think of it: such indomitableness, such capacity to turn deprivation to advantage. Teeth fallen out eating crisps and candy bars for supper – all the better to gam you with, my dear.

The things they know, the northern industrial poor. The consolations they mine.

Frank hands her a second half a crown.

'Right then,' she says. 'Where's Fred?'

Fred, Frank gathers, is his penis. He ought to be taking notes. If he were back in Oxford at a C. S. Lewis lecture he'd have a pen and paper out. And he wouldn't be learning that Fred is the name for a penis from C. S. Lewis.

So where is Fred? Frank reclines the driver's seat, unzips himself, and fishes about in his trousers.

'Come on,' the woman says, 'I haven't got all night,'

This is Frank's first experience of the love talk of the English whore.

By some profoundly mysterious law of inverse eroticism, that which is by no means arousing arouses Fred. In one flowing movement the woman coughs her teeth into her hand and drops her head on to his lap. Frank lies back in the seat and closes his eyes.

Sea-anemones pluck at him. Porpoise nudge him with their snouts. Loofah'd, jellied, suckered, he submits to the snuffling pull of the ocean, loses all sensation of weight and bone, comes apart in the arms of the water. Until the warm silent pullulating sea-bed claims his remains.

The things they know, the industrial poor.

Thereafter, Frank was an *aficionado* of street whores. He could smell them out. Dump him in any town at midnight and he could have driven you blindfold to where they congregated. He had a feeling for their landscape. Something in him answered to their self-effacement. The blighted streets they idled on, the dispirited wastegrounds of the senses they half-heartedly haunted, nodding their mechanical siren invitations – what were these but the sites he'd been visiting in his imagination since he was a child, the shtupping fields outside the perimeter fence, where a man might do any ugliness he pleased?

Out of the blue he became a more affectionate son than he'd been in years, whipping up from Oxford to see his parents every couple of weeks or so, borrowing their car, putting five shillings in his pocket, and going in search of the woman who'd initiated him. Time works differently, he noticed, when you're looking for whores. He could drive up and down the same street for hours on end, observing the subtlest changes in the shadows, slowing if so much as a sweet wrapper blew out of a boarded doorway. It was never boring. There was always the prospect of one more whore turning up on one more corner. He got to know the other whoremongers who worked the area. He recognised their vehicles, became familiar with their driving habits and patterns of concentration, what combination of hour, traffic and fishnet would induce them suddenly to slap on their brakes. There was no freemasonry of whoring; in an obvious sense you were competitors, like men with metal detectors combing the same small strip of beach; but there was some quiet comfort in such unanimity of purpose. And that could keep you going during the long hours when the streets inexplicably emptied and not a whore stirred.

He never did find the one he was looking for, the one who had started him off. Whoever she was, she had vanished like a mermaid into the deep proletarian sea. It pleased Frank to think that maybe she had just nipped out of her house on a whim that night, fed up with the housework, short of a few

113

bob and who knows, in the mood for a gam and a gobble herself. What if he were her first and only client? And if so, what contribution had he made to *her* understanding of society? Did she now suppose that no Oxford-educated gentleman would dream of popping his dick into a lady's mouth until she'd taken out her teeth?

Back in Oxford he was carless and therefore, as far as the street went, whoreless; but he sometimes cycled late into the underworld of Cowley, just to keep his eye in.

Looking, anyway, was always mainly what it was about. There and back and round and round they drove, these Flying Dutchmen of the cobbled stews, often with no intention of ever stopping. You stopped when you were finally persuaded you wanted sex. But sex wasn't the compulsion that united Frank and his fellow obsessionals — members of the skilled or spiritual professions, most of them, thinkers, carers, healers, teachers — as they swung and circled, stalled, juddered, peered, hovered, maybe even haggled, then swung again. Close shaves, that's what they were after. Nearly-sex.

And nearly-seen. Eyes you think you know through whoremonger-misted windscreens thinking they know you. That your doctor? That your patient? That your wife's father wondering that my daughter's husband? Nearly-seen and nearly-caught. So who needs the sex?

They were in it for the money. Even more than the whores were in it for the money, the punters were in it for the money. Up until he'd been gammed for five shillings in the playground of his old primary school, Frank had toed the line in the matter of paying for sex. Who me? That'll be the day! When I have to pay for sex I'll be too old to want sex. But once hand over the cash and you know you'll never want it free again. What pay for sex, me? Maybe not, since sex, strictly, is not the commodity you're paying for. Shame, that's what you get for your pair of tusheroons. Yourself disprized. Which is where the driving round and round and never stopping comes in. Four hours up and down the same unlit street then home with nothing but an empty petrol tank to show enables a man to disprize himself without going seriously into overdraft.

All the same, Frank was grateful for his bike. No whore was going to gam him on the sprung seat of his bicycle. Whereas, if he took a car to Cowley he knew he'd blow his whole student grant there in a single term. Not because the whores of Cowley looked particularly good. But because they didn't.

English whores have always understood the subtle seductiveness of dressing down. Where the whores of Italy get themselves up in promises of grotesquery beyond the invention of Boccaccio or Fellini, and the whores of France put on pearls and court shoes so that Frenchmen might realise their fantasy of sleeping with their uncles' wives, or their brother's daughters, the whores of England reach for the first items in their wardrobes, confident that as long as they are turned out more frumpishly than the women their punters live with they won't go home empty handed. A shrewd comprehension of the nexus of sex, money and necessary dissatisfaction is at work here. And the whores of the West Midlands, taking that to be the carpet slipper of country bounded by the the M5, the M4 and the A40, comprehend it better than any. Let loose in Cowley, Frank would have pauperised himself in a matter of weeks, trying to figure out why he wanted to finger the fur of women who reminded him of dinner ladies.

Late as it is by the time he has his car back, the motor of insurgency that is now driving him decides not even to try trolloping it in Cheltenham but to rev straight for Gloucester.

It's ten miles to Gloucester and he isn't sober. But Frank can't be sure he'd have got it right in Cheltenham. He's out of practice. No whores since Mel's been in his life. Honour, partly. Love, partly. But mainly no need of them. Why go to whores to have himself disprized when he's got Mel?

It's also more difficult now than it was in his heyday to be certain that the nodding dolly propping up a lamppost with a fag between her fingers is in fact on the job. There's every chance that she's a company director just slipped out of a strictly non-smoking office to have a puff. Go anywhere you like in the West End during business hours and you see them, loitering on street corners and in doorways, one leg up behind, sucking hard on a Marlboro, and nodding with the stress of the job – whores for all the world. As always, it's morality that makes for harlotry. True, there's little likelihood of his hitting on a company director out smoking in a doorway in Cheltenham at one in the morning, but better to be safe than sorry. Gloucester has a meaner reputation. You can't come to grief in Gloucester. That's to say you can come to grief in Gloucester.

Besides, there's a cathedral there.

'Gloucester, Gloucester, Gloucester.' It took an Italian prince, as imagined by an American novelist, to grasp the sissing loucheness of English cathedral cities. Until he read *The Golden Bowl*, Frank thought he was alone in associating infidelity with cloisters and tombs and towers. It was a joke at the Oxford language school that as soon as Frank fell for one of his charges he whisked her away for the weekend to Wells or Winchester. Before she threw in her lot with the Finn, the Swede had been earmarked for Salisbury. Before he met the Swede, he had the Finn's name down for Lichfield. But these were just a young man's trial runs. The simple sex that is a prelude to the more serious business of betrayal. Later, when the golden bowl is cracked, you get the point of cathedral cities. Wives and lovers, other men's wives and lovers, those are the ones with whom you do the gargoyles; best friends, best friends of *your* lovers, those are the ones you take to evensong. Had Liz not wanted Paris, she'd have got Gloucester. 'Gloucester, Gloucester, Gloucester' – like an old song, the prince's unholy mistress marvels. In Gloucester he lost her. Except, in the case of the prince, he didn't. In Gloucester he tossed her. It was only later that he lost her. But let's not spoil the story.

Frank knows he shouldn't be drinking and driving. But the part of him that cares what he should and shouldn't be doing has been inoperative most of the evening. Even Mel's talking spleen, still in the Saab's glove compartment, gets short shrift. Fuck off, Mel. A man's dick's his own. And anyway, isn't driving good for drunks? He has his roof down. The night fans him. The moon sucks the poisons from his system. The convention of having to stay roughly on his side of the road – to say nothing of having to stay on the road at all – keeps his eyes open. If he's not careful, by the time he gets to Gloucester he'll be stone cold sober.

Although his nose tells him that he should skirt the city and make for the Bristol end, a sign for the cathedral lures him into the centre. He doesn't get out of the car. Under the moon, spotlit and scaffolded, the cathedral nods at him like a giant whore. He looks her up and down, decides against, and drives off. A one-way system carries him in a direction he doesn't want to go, then dumps him at the gates of Her Majesty's Prison. He stops the car. He's been outside this penitentiary before. How many years ago was that? Crazy Jane, his first girlfriend with a mind, brought him here, stoned, on a train from Oxford. She wanted to stand outside the prison all night. A vigil. At first she told him it was for her brother, who was languishing in a cell on a trumped-up embezzlement charge. Hugo, the darling of the family. Hugo the golden boy, who'd fenced for England in the Olympics until he lost an eye in a shooting accident on their uncle's estate. He'd gone to the bad after that, accumulating gambling debts, losing the hand of the second daughter of the present Duke of Gloucester and shortly after that losing his membership at White's. There wasn't much he hadn't lost in his short life, young Hugo. But he hadn't so far lost his head as to diddle Rothschild's out of a million. No, he would never have done that. Not Hugo. She'd cried, cataloguing her favourite brother's misfortunes, and Frank had put his arm around her as they circled the prison, trying to see over the wall, trying to guess which window might have been his. But at about three in the morning she confessed she had no brother Hugo and that the person she was invigilating was in fact an old school friend called Franklin.

'Same name as mine, sort of,' Frank observed.

Crazy Jane kept her eye on the prison ramparts. 'Yes, the name's similar,' she agreed.

'And what is he inside for?' Frank wondered.

'Do you think that could be his window?' Crazy Jane wondered in her turn.

'No idea. What's he inside for?'

'Receiving stolen property,' Crazy Jane said, distracted.

An hour later she confessed that Fanklin wasn't so much an old school friend as an old lover. And an hour after that she confessed he wasn't so much an old lover as a recent one, and that the offence he was inside for wasn't so much receiving stolen property as grievous bodily harm. She was carrying an article about him which she asked Frank to retrieve, since he was curious, from the inside pocket of her ratty Oxfam fur coat. They were standing in a light drizzle with their arms around each other; Frank with his back to the prison so that Crazy Jane could rest her head upon his shoulder and go on looking up. He'd had his hands inside her coat most of the night, comforting her by rolling her breasts around and sliding his fingers into the waistband of her jeans, so it was no imposition to be asked to retrieve the article. It was torn from a local newspaper and described how it took eight police officers to restrain Franklin D. Smith, a Jamaican-born musician and drug dealer, when they broke into his flat after a neighbour had reported hearing a woman screaming. 'That was me,' Crazy Jane told him. 'It's all my fault.'

'You were the neighbour?'

'I was the screamer.'

Now it was Frank's turn to cry. 'Have you been seeing him while you've been seeing me?' he wanted to know.

'It was only a physical thing,' Crazy Jane assured him.

'Has he been hitting you while you've been seeing me?'

'Not all the time. And anyway, you don't hit me.'

Was that an accusation? Did Frank have his shortcomings as a lover?

Frank remembers pushing his hands all the way down the front of her jeans — the back of his hands against her skin, so that she didn't have to turn around and lose her view of the prison — and sobbing like a baby. How they used to make him cry, those girls. What a blubberer they turned him into. Looked back on, from this vantage point, is that the essential story of his life? Here lies Frank Ritz: he cried over girls and felt their cunts. Usually at the same time.

Unless it's, Here lies Frank Ritz: he wasn't man enough to give a woman a good thrashing. Except when it came to his best friend's wife. But that was in another country, and besides . . .

Seeing Frank cry, and feeling the backs of his hands knuckling into her, Crazy Jane started up again on her own account. Blub, blub, they went, he into her neck, she into his. Until she freed herself to blow her nose, adjust her trilby, and pour them coffee from a flask she'd had the forethought to prepare. Then she unwrapped a little parcel of silver paper and rolled them a joint. Forethought again. Then she assumed her original position with her arms round his back and her head on his shoulder and went on staring into the cells. And that was how the dawn found them outside Gloucester Gaol, stoned, snivelling, glued to each other with rheum, frozen to the bone.

Had Franklin been watching from the window he'd have counted himself fortunate to be inside.

Warmer now at the wheel of his Saab, Frank looks up at the prison and wonders whether Franklin's still in there. In the good old Count of Monte Cristo days people were locked away and forgotten. Now telly can get you out provided you're photogenic enough. It ought to make him prouder of his profession. What an honour to be associated with a medium that is so jealously watchful of our freedoms. Prises the innocent out of their dungeons where they were pursuing law degrees and releases them into the privileges of police-dramas and pop awards. Frank wishes he had his laptop with him. He could have knocked off next week's column right here, in the shadow of the walls, on the very spot where Crazy Jane shattered the last of his illusions.

As for Crazy Jane herself, well, she went into penal sociology, married a murderer and became the mistress of a college.

A police car passes and slows. Frank realises he must look as though he's masterminding a getaway. A notice at the prison gate warns that it is an offence under the Prison Act of 1952 for any person to help an inmate to escape. Although it doesn't say so anywhere, Frank knows that it is also an offence to be pissed at the wheel of a Saab. If they stop and breathalyse him he's sunk. How can he survive without his driving licence now he doesn't have a home to go to? He will have to plead indigency to the court. He can no more do without his car than a gipsy can do without his caravan. He sits up very straight, trying to remember what muscles a face employs when it's sober.

The police car turns around and comes alongside him. Is everything all right with him?

He thanks the officers. He is in some distress, he tells them. But nothing they can relieve. He has a brother who is serving time. Embezzlement. He comes and sits here quietly sometimes. To be close. Just something he needs to do. He doesn't know whether they will understand that.

They do. They have experience of the ways prison can affect a family. But they ask to see his licence, even so. What they don't say is bear with us while we check you out on our computer. One day, of course, they will. One day every policeman will have to say bear with me before he squirts aerosol in your face. They notice that he is some distance from his permanent address. He doesn't say he has no permanent address. He says he is on business in Cheltenham. They recommend that he takes himself back there now and gets some sleep. He thanks them for their understanding. He doesn't ask them, though they are the very people *to* ask, where the whores are. Whores he can find himself.

He is not driven by desire. He is driven by recklessness. Whatever the opposite is of compunction. Before it becomes moral, compunction is a physical sensation, a pricking at the heart. The opposite of compunction is physical too. Frank feels it as a duodenal sinking. His stomach lurches, empties, then floods with pancreatic juices. These are the juices that prompt a man to act against the urgings of his reason. It is unreasonable to pursue whores in the dead of night when you feel no desire, but the pancreatic juices insist on it.

In no time he is in whore-hell. What does it take? A scrub of common. A council estate. A few sulphurous street lights. The odd alley dark enough for pimps to park in. And a lot of imagination on Frank's part.

A cluster of girls standing outside a phone box clock the speed of his car and simultaneously give him the nod. It pleases him to see it again, he realises he's missed it, the old St Vitus twitch. One of the girls is black and shows some shiny cleavage, otherwise they are all more modestly dressed than any secretary turning up for work at a building society. Frank accelerates past them, then has to slow again for a speed bump. Traffic calmers. Why don't they just pay the whores to lie in the middle of the road?

Ahead of him, Frank sees a Datsun disgorging a girl. You don't really want one that someone else has just had, on the other hand it can be useful, when you can't make your mind up, to have a second opinion. He tries to see from the way the Datsun drives off whether the whore has given satisfaction. He decides she hasn't. The girl spits on the car. The driver shows her his finger. Love! He slows to get a better look at the girl. She is wearing a navy anorak but apparently no skirt. She has bare, streaked vermilion legs. Her white stilettos are held together with sellotape. She doesn't appear to have a figure at all. She is younger than Frank remembers whores being. If he were to be moral or legalistic about it he would say she is too young; but this isn't about morals or the law, it's about pancreatic juices.

His are flowing now. He drives round and around the same couple of blocks. If his Saab were the blade of a saw he'd have taken a circle of real estate the size of Wembley Stadium out of working-class Gloucester. Not that there'd be anywhere for it to fall to. This is as low as it gets, Frank reflects, meaning this is as low as he gets. He is enjoying being back. He has been round so many times the girls have learnt to recognise and ignore him. He doesn't know himself whether he is going to stop and pick one of them out; forces well outside his control will decide that. In the end it's a black woman he hasn't seen before, sitting alone in shadow on someone's garden wall, eating a hamburger, who applies the brakes to his Saab. What attracts Frank to her is her long face. She reminds him of the French comedian, Fernandel. And what is so desirable to Frank about the French comedian Fernandel? Don't ask him. Maybe it's because she looks older than the others. Maybe it's because she looks experienced. Maybe it's because she looks like a man.

She drags herself off the wall and comes over to the car. She is extremely tall, like an Ethiopian, and wears an ankle-length grey skirt with many slits in it through which Frank sees that she has long thin Ethiopian famine legs.

'You look like a jumper,' Frank says.

'I'll do anything so long as you pay me,' she says.

She doesn't wait to agree a price. She climbs in over the passenger door, still eating her hamburger. Along with the onions Frank smells cloves and cinnamon.

'Take a left,' she says.

Yes, Frank thinks, it's good to be back all right.

On the way to wherever they're going they pass the under-age girl in the sellotaped stilettos. She waves at the Ethiopian. 'Can you give my friend a lift?' the Ethiopian asks.

'Depends where,' Frank says.

'She just wants to be with me. It's all right. She'll get out when we're doing it.'

Frank stops for the Ethiopian's friend. He can hear his pancreatic juices sluicing about in his stomach. The girl gets into the back seat. She doesn't introduce herself. But then she is seriously not of age; she may not yet have learnt to speak.

They park in the forecourt to some wooden garages. The girl gets out and takes herself a few yards off. She stands absently against a garage door, like a little girl in a schoolyard, memorising her ten-times-tables.

'So what do you want?' the Ethiopian asks. Frank sees that she has removed a condom from her bag and is about to open the packet with her teeth.

'Not that,' he says.

'I don't do sex without a condom.'

'I don't want sex. How much for a hand job?'

'Twenty.'

'Twenty?' Frank whistles through his teeth. 'It's gone up a bit,' he says.

She shrugs. He remembers Fernandel shrugging identically in *The Sheep has Five Legs*. 'Gone up since when?' she asks.

She has a point. Gone up since 1970. He takes out his wallet and hands her over the twenty.

'Why don't you give me another ten,' she says, 'and I'll suck your balls.'

Money, money, money. But how long is it since anybody sucked his balls? He hands her over a ten.

'OK,' she says, 'lean back.'

He notes that she doesn't ask where Fred is. He wondered how they'd get round that in Gloucester.

She is impatient with him immediately. 'Spunk!' she orders him. She is tossing him back-handed, as though she's slipping a doorman a tip, her long lugubrious face turned in the opposite direction, his dick barely out of the recumbent position, and she is expecting him to spunk. After ten seconds!

'You said you were going to suck my balls,' he reminds her.

'Don't dictate to me,' she says.

'Who's dictating? I'm just reminding you what I paid for.'

'I'll suck them when you start spunking.'

'There won't be any spunking,' Frank tells her, 'until you suck them.'

She sighs, dips her head into his lap, and for all Frank is able to feel to the contrary, sucks the dye out of the car upholstery. Ten more seconds later she is back up, expecting miracles. 'That's it,' she says, 'that's it, spunk for mama. Think of my black pussy. Ooh, yes. Yes. Imagine you're putting your big cock in my black pussy.'

She's so unconvincing that Frank wonders how come they have a population explosion in Africa. Is it possible she's a man after all? No. A man would have a better idea of what might be conducive to that big cock she's been talking about. If nothing else, a man would have a better idea of where another man's balls hang out.

'It's no good,' Frank says. He knows what he ought to do. He ought to call it a night. He ought to pack the little one in the back of the car and drive them both back to where he found them. He doesn't have to force spunk out of his testicles. And spunk is a bit of a flatteringly messy name anyway for the miserable dry spurtle he's likely to squeeze out at best. But he also knows what he will do if he leaves these garages without an emission of some sort – he will start on the obsessional Flying Dutchman pilgrimage again. One thing he can't do, if he is finally to sleep tonight and not brood over Kurt and Liz, to say nothing of young Hamish who he's now decided is definitely a child he fathered on Liz in Paris, is drive back to Cheltenham unspent.

'Give me another ten and I'll suck you off with a rubber,' the Ethiopian suggests.

Frank has a better idea. 'Call the girl back in,' he says.

They settle on a price. What does it matter? Another ten, another twenty, another hundred. The Ethiopian fiddles ill-temperedly with her clothing and brings out a long empty

125

rubbery tit, more blue than black. Such a sight never did much for Frank in the pages of the *National Geographic* and it does even less for him now. But he's not doing it for him. He's doing it for his pancreas.

On the back seat the girl with the sellotaped stilettos opens her legs and shows him what she has between them. It is not quite as criminal an act as he'd feared. At least there's hair there. 'Spread yourself wider,' he says. She wriggles in the seat and with her small bitten fingers pulls herself apart. Not *as* criminal, but a crime none the less. Fifteen years I could get for this, Frank thinks. Fifteen years minimum. With no remission. I'll be an old man when I come out. Except I won't be coming out. There'll be no exposés on the box on my behalf. No *Panorama* or *Rough Justice*. Who'd campaign for the release of a television critic? I'll be locked in a cell with Franklin for the rest of my life.

He re-arranges himself into a lying position at a three-quarters twist, so that he can put his mouth to the Ethiopian's tit while still being able to see the little furry pink-nosed gerbil the girl keeps between her legs. He has his dick in his hand. And on his dick he has spittle which the Ethiopian has sold him for a fiver. Thus positioned, he finally comes.

But only after imagining that he is on his back on the stage of the London Palladium and that D the fat comedian is pissing in his mouth.

SEVEN

He isn't well.

Mel kept him well. Maybe Mel made him well.

She found him, originally, wearing a three-piece Mafia suit, looking yellow and eating all the wrong foods at a conference on the televisual arts in Birmingham. He was doing television previews as opposed to *reviews* then, along with general media reporting, so he was there snaffling up tidbits and hearsay, and she was on a panel discussing, as you could tell from what *she* was wearing, the portrayal of women on television. They took an instant dislike to each other. That's to say she tried to have him ejected from her discussion group for hectoring, and he tried to fuck her.

'Why would I want to fuck you?' she asked him at the conference farewell party where he was re-doubling his efforts to make her aware of him. 'You're shorter than I am. You dress like a secondary-school hit-man. And you eat like a pig.'

'I could buy Cuban heels,' he told her.

'You're already wearing Cuban heels.'

'No, these are Sicilian heels. Cuban heels slope, and they're higher, and they're generally made of cow leather, unlike these which are part crocodile, part snake, part 9 carat

127

gold. You can tell Cubans from Sicilians because they're altogether less subtle. I'll show you.'

And he did. First thing the very next morning he purchased a pair of tooled cowboy boots with three-and-a-half-inch sloping heels from a shop that looked like a wild-west saloon – not difficult to find in Birmingham, where a five-foot man is considered tall – and towered over her in the sandwich queue on the train back to London. Make 'em laugh. That's always the way to do it.

In return for which she made him well. She got him out of his Brioni two-tone suits. She threw away his Stefano Ricci shirts with their mobster collars. She cut him down from seven curries a night to one curry a fortnight. She reduced his wine intake. She told him that what he was previewing for a living was crap but if he was going to do it he should do it in style. She pulled his hair out of his eyes and tied it in a pigtail. She taught him how to do stubble. She bought him a decent watch. And she refused to be mechanically fucked by him.

Every morning, before either of them was properly awake, he prodded her with his dick. His dick, at least, didn't need to be built up. On mornings when she pretended not to notice what was doing the poking he insisted on showing it to her. 'Look, Mel.'

'Why do I have to see your dick, why do I have to acknowledge your dick, why do I have to have your dick inside me every morning?' she wanted to know.

'Because it's there,' he told her.

She punished him by making him fuck her day and night. On the stairs. In the kitchen. On the bathroom floor. In the garden. In the back of a taxi. In the washrooms of a Chinese restaurant. Bang in the middle of Blackheath, with Sunday traffic hooting at them. 'OK, big boy, give it me now.' She wore him out. She had him begging for mercy. She reduced his manhood to a bleeding stump. And still she went at him. 'That's it, you hot fucker, ram it up!' Until he had to hide. Lock himself into the toilet for hours at an end, while she stood outside on the landing with her skirt up, describing what she was doing to herself and what she would be expecting him to do to her the minute he came out.

She made him well.

'Enough?' she asked him at last.

'Enough,' he conceded.

'Well that's tough because it's not enough for me. Here, suck on my tit.'

This was another of their disagreements. He thought she had perfect breasts and that the only way he could adequately attest to their perfection was to put them in his mouth. For her part she found the sight of a grown man suckling her grotesque.

'Go on,' she ordered him. 'Guzzle me. Get those lips around. Go on, suck. Suck like a baby.' She made him do it in front of a mirror so that he could see what he looked like. He agreed with her. The spectacle was unedifying. It made him look like a retard. He didn't say that that was the whole point, that you did it in order to *feel* like a retard. He was going along with the treatment. He was taking the medicine.

She drove him out into the country, blindfolded like O, a mystery tour, down a lane, up a lane, off the beaten, on to corrugations, along a logger's track (was it?) deep into a forest (was it?) the light dappling and dying through his blindfold, the trees at one another's throats, his heart swinging like the shafts of sun – was she bringing him here to kill him? 'Out,' she said, when the track finally came to an end. She led him along warm gravel, foliage nudging at him, lime the only smell, the only sound leaves breathing. She took off his blindfold. 'Strip,' she said. She produced a camera. His camera. The old Brownie box camera with which he'd won the school junior photography prize, for a series of studies of the Manchester Ship Canal in winter. The same Brownie box camera he thought she'd confiscated after he'd tried to snap her climbing out of the bath. 'But don't take everything off,' she told him. 'Nudity is always heightened, wouldn't you agree, if something is left to the imagination. Keep your socks on.' She draped him around a tree. She sat him on a stump and got him to put a finger in his mouth. 'Not your thumb, your forefinger.' She arranged him on the forest floor like a stricken nymph, with everything akimbo. 'Lovely,' she said, 'now moisten your lips.' He knew he had to take it like a man. He didn't have a leg to stand on. She'd found his photograph collection. She'd seen what he could do, compositionally, with a camera. She got him to crouch on all fours and then pout at her, upside down between his knees. 'One for the mantelpiece, that,' she said. He heard the clop of a tennis ball, saw through the trees a pair of lovers on a tandem. Suddenly he knew where he was. 'Jesus Christ, Mel, this is Dulwich Park! We live here!' 'So don't draw attention to yourself,' she said. 'Now reach for your member. Make as if you're picking a flower. You're a creature of the woods, don't forget. Wild and untameable, yet curiously innocent.'

He couldn't.

'Enough?'

'Enough.'

But it wasn't enough for her. 'Just a couple with your legs up around your ears then, and we'll call it a day. And try to look as if you're at home in nature more.'

She made him well. She showed him that he was suffering from a common compulsive order known as man – M.A.N. – and that contrary to popular belief there was a cure.

'And how will I know when I'm better?' he asked her.

'You'll know that you're *getting* better when you wake up

in the morning and your first thought isn't a fuck or a photo.'

Now he knows that there's another cure. They could have just waited till he was fifty.

But of course his hard-on was only the tip of the polluted iceberg that was his nature. 'I wouldn't mind if your appetites were cheerful,' she told him. 'But you don't fuck to feel good, you fuck to feel bad. You drink to feel bad, too. You watch crap all day on the television to feel bad. You even eat to feel bad. That's why you want a curry every night, so that you can punish your stomach and feel like shit in the morning.'

He took this hard. When all else was said and done, he considered himself to be a Rabelaisian man. He drank, he fornicated, he pigged out, he belched, he farted, he slept, he rose on the arched dolphin back of his dick, ready to breast the wild waves of existence all over again. He was a force of nature, wasn't he. He was the functions disporting themselves. 'According to the great Russian critic Mikhail Bakhtin,' he told her, 'no meal can be sad.'

'Well it can in your case,' she said. 'In your case no meal is ever anything but sad.'

He couldn't deny it. If he feasted at midnight he woke with a broken heart. Whatever he did upset him, and whatever upset him, he did.

She came home earlier than expected from a meeting with her publishers one afternoon and found him bending over the ironing-board, spitting on his shirt.

'How can you do that?' she cried.

He explained that his shirt was badly creased but that he couldn't be bothered with the palaver of setting the iron to steam.

'Why can't you treat your things with some respect,' she

asked. 'Why can't you take time over yourself? Why do you have to spit on your own life?'

She made him well. She taught him self-regard. She showed him how everything didn't have to be a hurry or a hurt, how he could make a ceremony out of eating, ironing, sex. She even showed him how to take some small pleasures in the crap he watched all day on telly. OK, Oprah might not have been to his taste, but she addressed the feelings, didn't she? And she was warm – that was called warmth, Frank. And sure, the conversation of those Cockneys who made all their important life-decisions in the pub wasn't of the sort that Frank and Mel may have recognised as penetrating, but it gave pleasure to others, and where would the world be if it only contained the sort of people whose conversation Mel and Frank found penetrating? Besides, she explained, disliking everything he saw and did was making him ill.· Bad heartedness was not just a figure of speech. Thinking and feeling badly actually made the heart bad. Weakened it. Predisposed it to disease. He would have a heart attack from attacking. When they cut him open they would see the scars made by all the intemperate attacks he'd launched on others and on himself. She calmed him; she soothed him; she talked to him as though he were an imbecile, she made him see that the universe was a plenteous place, roomy enough for diversity, and unlikely to run out of food and drink and girls, so Frank didn't have to gobble it all up at once and make himself feel poorly afterwards. She couldn't have succoured him better had she left him to guzzle on her tit.

It cost her in the end. Making someone else well always does. She expended so much energy on the reparation of his self-esteem that she had none left for the maintenance of her own. He was meant to do the same for her now. Massage her heart; talk to her as though she were an imbecile. But he couldn't ever make the sentences sound right. 'Get your finger out of your fucking throat!' he yelled at her. 'Is that meant to help me?' she asked. 'Is that your way of being calming?' But what was he supposed to do? He was a man; he suffered from M.A.N.; and men don't have tits.

Even when she'd given up on him and closed her ears against the noise he made, she kept him well by virtue of her brute presence. The mere fact of her being there – even if he didn't touch her, even if he didn't see her – was enough to stop him going whoring whenever the fancy took him. Whoever invented the idea of the stable relationship understood the necessity for anchorage. A cold line extended from Frank's keel to the icy ocean bed of habituation. Friend or foe, Mel was there, a mooring, a tether, an ever-present weight that prevented him floating out into the uncertain immensity of the night.

Then he became fifty and no longer felt the want of an anchor.

Was that why he consented to be booted out of his house? Did he know that he didn't need Mel any more? Did he understand that he was finally old enough to be trusted with the captaincy of his own bark?

Well he got that wrong, didn't he.

He isn't well. Even allowing for bad hotel lights and unflattering hotel mirrors, he can see he doesn't look well. There's no life in his skin. He's eating crap again. Watching it *and* swallowing it. His teeth feel loose. His heart's bad. Mel was right. You get a bad heart from having bad feelings. And he's been having bad feelings for a lifetime. And now he's having bad dreams.

Disaster dreams. Two on the run, both involving Mel. In the first, he was standing on a verandah looking out into a garden where Mel was sitting reading under a tented

133

umbrella. Her legs were crossed and her hair was blowing. It was their garden in Dulwich, but the light was Italian. In the dream, Frank felt Italian himself. He was back in a mobster shirt, having Italian thoughts, sucking in the light as though he were an Italian vegetable, a melanzana or a zucchino, absorbing what was rightfully his. Suddenly the ground began to open in front of Mel, then behind her, great fiery cracking fissures in the lawn, as though the great boulders on which the earth was founded had finally split. Mel took no notice. Her book was far more interesting to her. Frank screamed and screamed to get her attention but she couldn't be bothered listening. Merely Frank making noise again. He wanted to run to her but he couldn't move. He was growing in a terracotta pot on the verandah. A melanzana can't just leap out of the soil and scale a verandah wall when the fancy takes it. He woke as Mel was disappearing obliviously into the ground.

In the second, it was not just the end of the garden, it was the end of the world. Planes were coming at the house on revolving cylindrical clouds of black smoke, and in the distance the sky was broken and falling apart. The sun was hideously disfigured. The entire universe was shredding itself. Frank himself was hiding under the piano. Under the piano was the one safe place anywhere. But he couldn't persuade Mel to join him. He realised it was too late now. She was going to die along with everything else. 'I love you,' Frank called. He wanted her to know that their life together had had meaning. He loved her. It was his last and only chance to tell her. Ever ever ever. He shouted it out – 'I love you, Mel. I have always loved you.' But she couldn't hear him over the roar of the planes which were now alight and plunging into the roof of their house.

He woke with tears on his face.

That's when he knows he isn't well: when he starts the day blubbering.

He stays in bed in the Queens Hotel for twenty-four hours while all his clothes are being laundered. Then he stays in bed for a second twenty-four hours in order to catch the new Robert Hughes series on American art. Then he stays in bed for a third twenty-four hours in order to write his review. The box is never more gripping, he argues, than when you see someone thinking on it. He loathes the phrase 'good television', but he uses it. Good television is no different from good life: it's the sight of somebody thinking. No thought, no life, no life no television. All television should be arts television, that's the conclusion he comes to in his review. Except that 'the arts' is another phrase he loathes. He stays in bed for a fourth twenty-four hours trying to sort out his argument.

Counting phone calls and room-service and laundry, and throwing in the cost of the Gloucester whores, his bill for five days in Cheltenham is a small token of appreciation short of a thousand pounds. That's the better part of two thousand since he left home less than a fortnight ago. Call that four and a half thousand a month. Which comes to in excess of fifty grand a year. And he still hasn't had what a reasonable person would call a tolerably pleasurable evening.

There are reasons for going back to London. He has mail to collect. He has people to see. He has changes to make to his wardrobe. He has his monthly appointment with his hairdresser. Eventually he knows he will have to return and find himself a room; but he can't go back yet, not light two thousand quid and absolutely nothing achieved. Unless you call a stain of jism the size of a flattened mosquito on the inside of his windscreen, an achievement.

In a queer sort of way he feels he has let Mel down, being booted out of the house and not managing to find anything better to do with himself than he has found so far. He has to stay away if only to have one or two more interesting stories to tell Mel, should she ever ask him to come back, which of course she won't, now she has another man, which she hasn't, has she?

He takes the M5 going south. This has several advantages, none of which he gives a name to. He won't be making that mistake again. But loosely clinking about at the back of his brain are such place names as Watchet, Porlock, Lynton, Exeter, Little Cleverley. Watchet because he likes the drive to Porlock. Porlock because he likes the drive from Watchet. Lynton, he just likes. Unless it's Lynmouth he just likes. Whichever is the one that flooded. And then there's a dim memory he has of Billy Yuill telling him that he'd inherited a place, a holiday cottage, in one or other of them. He's only remembered that because he's thought about it every time he's driven through. Hm, Billy Yuill's holiday residence. Let's hope the fucking place floods again while he's in it. Not that he's going to Lynton or Lynmouth for any Yuill-related reason. If Liz is now happily Mrs Billy, summering in Somerset, she won't be wanting Frank Ritz of Kilburn and Paris rapping on her little cottage door, as somebody's son Hamish, whatever his real name is, so smartly pointed out. No. He's drunk the dregs of that one. Nor does Exeter being on his list of possibles have a ghost of a connection to Exeter being on D the comedian's list of engagements. That too is a non-starter. He's had his dick out, that'll do. As for Little Cleverley, well, well, time will tell, and if he does make it that far down the coast, he will be doing it, in a manner of speaking, for Mel. Given that Mel got into Clarice's pants before he did. Not by much, it's true, but a whisker is a whisker in Little Cleverley.

All the service facilities on the motorway are full. The cars spill back out on to the slip road. Frank is bemused by this until he remembers that it's still August. He is surprised that the summer hasn't frittered itself away while he's been in Cheltenham getting pale. No such luck. The proletarian crap-watchers are as hell bent on getting into their holiday togs as they were when he last paid attention to them back in Little Venice-on-the-Runnel. They queue, belly to buttock, smelling of burning car upholstery, at the all-day breakfast counter, counting the beans on one another's plates. They're suffering from Frank's disease. A pity Mel isn't here to put them right. They're attacking themselves with food. Abusing their spouses with fried bread. Knocking their kids out with chips. We're banning handguns, Frank thinks, but we're keeping motorway food. He has tomato soup himself, which he spoons from a giant witch's cauldron. Hot soup and croutons, just the ticket when it's eighty-five degrees in the shade. Hot soup and croutons and tea, for which he hands over a ten pound note and from which he gets no change to speak of. Frank can never get over how expensive it is to be poor. How the poor can afford to be poor beats him. But there they are again, paying for their petrol and crisps and make that a roll of scratch-cards while you're at it, duck. When Frank was a boy he used to play abstract noun I-spy in the back of his parents' car. That was before he borrowed it to ferry whores in. I spy with my little eye something beginning with C . . . Conundrum – I win! Now, in-car entertainment for kids is a roll of scratch-cards and a coin. They are our Damien, just shut ya trap and see if you can win us a hundred grand. Frank sees them rubbing and scratching in toddler-seats, their baby fingers smeared with silver, all the way down the motorway. No wonder, he thinks, that the whores of today are so mercenary.

He comes off the motorway at Bridgwater and pootles reflectively into Nether Stowey. Welcome to Coleridge country. How long before *Biographia Literaria* makes it on to the box? In his own way he is as sentimental a journeyer as any pilgrim to Coronation Street. He too likes to plug into the presiding genius of the place. For many years he has meant to come and stay in the Quantocks, put on red socks and walking boots and follow the paths that Coleridge and the Wordsworths took, tracking the course of streams, listening to rivers, recording starlight, reciting poetry in echoing groves. He communicated this desire to Mel in their early days. 'Think of it,' he said, 'no car, just you and me and the ghosts of Wordsworth and Coleridge, lost among the deep romantic chasms. We could walk all day among the waterfalls, not see a single soul, fall into a pub for dinner, drink honey-dew, then stumble into bed under a waning moon, listening to the big sea.'

'So let's do it,' Mel said.

She was so prompt then. So spirited and agreeable. Up for anything.

They bought each other woolly walking pullovers and marbled notebooks, sharpened a dozen pencils, took a room in a guest house a hundred yards from Coleridge's cottage and never got out of bed. It was too soon in their connection. The only deep romantic chasms that Frank had time for in those days belonged to Mel.

When they finally did get to walk in the west country it was at Mel's instigation, and it was Daphne du Maurier's west country, not Coleridge's. Impatience had entered into it by then. Mel didn't buy the cottage in Little Cleverley to celebrate their passion but to find an alternative to it. Frank was already making too much noise for her to take. 'If you're going to come down to Little Cleverley with me,' she warned him, 'you'd better be prepared to have quiet thoughts. No running around looking for curries. No yelling at the telly. No London stuff.' Among the hippy bits and pieces left behind by the previous sitting tenants was a parchment scroll on which was transcribed that once inescapable consolation ode of the culturally damaged – GO PLACIDLY AMID THE DIN etcetera. Mel ripped off the etcetera and posted the words GO PLACIDLY above Frank's side of the bed.

Now would be a good time for him to dump the car and walk the Quantocks, but he is too restless. He accepts that he will never do it. He blames the heat, the tourists, his commitments, but the truth is that he cannot face being alone in nature. How many bound notebooks has he bought in his life, for the purpose of recording his fortnight's solitary expedition to Brontë country, Hardy country, Lawrence country? There they all sit, in a neat pile on the top of one of his bookcases, labelled, dated, paginated – addressed even, with the promise of a small reward should anyone find them forgotten under an ash tree by a fairy stream – but otherwise quite empty. Get wisdom? No, thank you. Frank's got it and all that means is that he's wise to himself. No more notebooks. No point. He'll never fill them. He'll never stay in a Quantock valley and walk the hills until his legs give out. He'd rather sit on the edge of a bed and watch crap on the box all day. Mel made him feel well but she never cured him. He still does what he hates, and hates what he does. Of course, if there were some girl who'd like to go hiking through the Quantocks with him, walk all day among the waterfalls, drink honey-dew, then stumble into bed under a waning moon . . . But this fantasy too can no longer survive the penetrating gaze of wisdom. He's wise to himself. He don't want no girl. He thinks he wants a girl because he's been wanting one since he was six. It's a long-time tic. What you've been wanting for as long as you've been conscious you can't suddenly unwant. But when Frank puts his ear to the growling of his appetites he hears no clamour for a girl. Girls he's had. So now what? What does wisdom have to say today on the question of what a man who has been booted out of his house is supposed to do with himself if he has no appetite for a girl? A long-time tic has lots going for it. It points you in the direction of what to do next. Frank's long-time tic used to tell him that it was once again time to go and fuck a girl. If he no longer wants a girl, then what is he to fuck? He knows the answer to that, too. He isn't to fuck anything. But he's a man; the only truly passionate pursuit of his life has been fucking. There's a mathematical necessity involved in this. M.A.N. = F.U.C.K. If he's now to believe that a man of his age isn't for fucking, then what the fuck is a man of his age for?

Do the sums. Show him the equation. M.A.N. = what?

He knows the danger. There's no end to what you know once you become wise. He knows that he might end up following his long-time tic for the simple reason that he can't come up with anything else to follow.

This is not something philosophers of society have adequately addressed or foretold. They've been too preoccupied with the economic and psychological consequences of redundancy and geriatric longevity. No one has come along and said we have a massive sociopathic crisis in the making here: a generation of men is about to enter middle age with no passion left for fucking who have not been schooled in any other purposeful activity. Frank can only speak as he finds; it would have been better for him, as a man suddenly booted out of a stable surrogate-for-fucking home situation, had he known of some re-training programme he could have entered.

Back up on the high road the country he has just left gets up to its old beguiling tricks. If you could only descend into those deep-bosomed hills, slip silently into that arboreous cleft, all would be well. The wispy woods would take care of your body, and the smoky churches would take care of your soul. To his right the big sea slopes away from him, too blue to bear. It is always a shock to him to look at the map and be reminded that this is still only the Bristol Channel and that that is only Wales on the other side of the water. That should be Peru over there. Or Troy. Or Xanadu.

He drops down into Porlock for afternoon tea and finds a film crew painting the town into period picturesqueness. The all-singing, all-dancing late eighteenth century. Maybe they *are* doing *Biographia Literaria* for telly.

'It is not every man that is likely to be improved by a country life,' declaims Colin Firth Coleridge in a white knotted muffler, while the children whip their hoops along the cobbles and the costermongers bawl their wares. 'Education, or original sensibility, or both, must pre-exist, if the changes, forms, and incidents of nature are to prove a sufficient stimulant. And where these are not sufficient, the mind contracts and hardens by want of stimulants: and the man becomes selfish, sensual, gross, and hard-hearted – '

Cut to opium den.

The BAFTA, Frank warrants, is already in the bag.

Meanwhile, although there is nothing to look at except a few men in overalls painting the doors of houses, the ill-educated and the insensible cluster in their gross contracted summer shorts and wait for the stars to arrive. Who will be Dorothy? Who will be Hazlitt?

'I think I'll wait to see it on the box,' Frank tells an insufficiently stimulated family from Wolverhampton who think that the whole thing is going to start and finish the minute the paint dries.

'Isn't eet loive?' the head of the family asks.

Out of instinctual politeness, Frank offers to think about it. 'Unlikely,' he says. 'But you could ask one of the cameramen when he arrives.'

'When will that boi?'

'In about a fortnight,' Frank guesses.

He gets back into his Saab and climbs and then drops into the twin towns on the Lyn. Welcome to Yuill country.

This time he doesn't go looking for the best hotel. Anything will do. Anything will have to do given that he's running out of readies and the Lyns are running out of rooms. He takes an attic with a gable window that gives him the sea. Then goes in search of the tea he didn't get in Porlock.

A sign outside the only café that isn't full entices him in with its promise of a VERY SPECIAL TEA CAKE OFFER.

'What is that?' he asks the waitress.

'I'll just ask,' she says, disappearing into the kitchen. Half a minute later she is back. 'It's a tea cake,' she says.

'And the very special part?'

She hesitates, as though it might come to her if she can temporarily quieten everything else that is happening in her brain. There is something airy and ballooning about her. Unlocated. She wears a little frilly maid-of-all-work apron over black jeans and running shoes. It's not her fault, Frank thinks. She is unimproved by country life.

'I'll just ask,' she says. Half a minute later she is back. 'It comes with tea,' she says.

'I'll have it,' Frank says.

He pulls a face to himself, meaning all I want is a quiet life. But all he really wants is crap.

And he gets it.

How can you crappify a tea cake?

You can, that's all. A rural thing. After which, he has a further sensual errand to attend to. One of his machines needs to be replaced. His hair drier. Along with much else he finds it hard to be without, the old one blew up in Cheltenham. Ever since Mel got him out of his Palermo suits and taught him how to imprison his hair in a pony tail, and then, when times changed and men were expected to look more like minstrels than their mothers, to free it from a pony tail and coif it down over his eyes and ears in dreadlock-like corkscrews, he has gone nowhere without a drier. The moment he takes his drier out of his luggage, Mel is with him. Now, like the golden bowl of virtue, it's broken.

As is the heart of the woman who runs the only electrical shop he can find. She sits behind the counter in her coat, with her head down, staring at the linoleum floor, unmoved by the appearance of a customer. There is no light on in the shop. But then there is nothing in the shop you'd want to see. In a matter of seconds Frank is able to do a complete stock check. One iron, one kettle, two toasters, one set of curling tongs, a box of fuse wire, a dozen lightbulbs in dented cartons, three jars of locally made runner-bean chutney, and a hair drier. Since a hair drier is all he wants, enough is a feast. He hands the woman a twenty pound note. She gasps, thinks about holding the note to the light, remembers that she doesn't know what to look for and that she doesn't care anyway, and then gasps again when she sees she has no change. Her fingers hover like little starving birds over the empty chambers of the till. 'Oh,' she says. Frank finds her the right money. 'Oh,' she says again. She doesn't once raise her eyes to Frank. She is his age. And once would have been pretty, in the crushed-petal-under-the-heel-of-an-infantry-officer style. Being cast away in a dead shop, Frank thinks, is the same as being marooned in a body you don't want to employ for fucking any more. Neither of us has anything to sell. Neither of us wants customers. Re-training – that's all we require.

As he's closing the door behind him, he hears the woman say, 'Oh, I must – ' But she doesn't bother to finish.

After dumping his new drier back at the hotel and pausing to watch Oprah talking to grannies in filmy frocks who mean to fuck till they drop, he takes the cliff railway down to Lynmouth – that's assuming he's been in Lynton – where there's a sea wall with lines of grannies on it, puffing hard, showing their bloomers and eating pasties in the heat. He takes the cliff railway back up again and wonders whether to risk the Valley of the Rocks where, according to Hazlitt, Coleridge ran out bareheaded in a thunderstorm 'to enjoy the commotion of the elements'.

Does Frank need any more commotion just this minute? The sea roars and froths at the edges, otherwise it's a millpond; there is not a cloud in the sky, not a whiffle of wind; if you jumped from the cliff you could determine the precise parabola of your descent, and not make a mark on the imperturbable surface of the water. No thunderstorm looks likely on this benign Gulf-stream-touched day. So Frank decides to give it a go. What he hasn't calculated is the effect the benches are going to have on him. The North Walk is not a demanding ascent, but this is retirement country and retirees like to know there's going to be a bench to sit on every couple of yards. He's not averse to a comfortable sea-view bench himself. But on the third or fourth he tries he notices a brass plaque. These are memorial benches. To the memory of George and Mabel Wonnacott. To Ron Creacombe from his sister Alice. In loving memory of Lucy Pomeroy (1948–1983) who loved the sea, from her darling husband Frank.

He has nothing but respect for the memory of Mr and Mrs Wonnacott, and for Ron Creacombe come to that, but it's Lucy Pomeroy who finds him. She died when she was only thirty-five. A child. She was born the same year Mel was born. She loved the sea, Mel loves the sea. She had a darling husband Frank, Mel has – But what does Mel have?

He sits on Lucy Pomeroy's bench and grieves for them both, Mel and Lucy. What a touching thing it is, to name a bench after someone you love, to heave it up on to the cliffs, and to leave it there forever. Does he come here, then, Frank Pomeroy? Does he put on his suit and buy a bunch of flowers and come to visit her? Does he stretch himself out upon her and sob his heart out? Or is it comfort enough to know that she is always here, where she loved to be, bareheaded in the commotion of the elements?

And another question. Has Frank Pomeroy got over it? Do you ever?

He's been having disaster dreams. Every time his head hits the pillow he imagines Mel on fire or being swallowed up by her own garden. *'O mercy!' to myself I cried, 'If Lucy should be dead!'* He knows what Mel would say. If only Lucy *would* be dead! – that's the way to understand the emotional grammar of *that* poem. It's written in the wishful subjunctive, just as your dreams are. You're only imagining me consumed by the elements because that's what you secretly want to happen. Nothing's changed. You've been murdering me in your head ever since you met me.

Is that what he's doing? Is he sitting here visualising a bench in her name because he wants nothing but her name to be left of her? Her name and a few bleached slats of oak. Is this a murderer's grief he's feeling?

He'd be within his rights to want to murder her, lover or no lover. You can't go on telling a man to shut the fuck up and not expect him to murder you eventually. But he sees it from her point of view as well; it's precisely because he is a man – an M.A.N. with a D.I.C.K. – that she is so provoked by him. (*Was* so provoked by him. She is, of course, nothinged by him any more.) Her accusations were just: he did make a din. The racket of his dissatisfactions undermined her. Even when he kept his dick in his pants – which was often, which was most of the time if she was prepared to be fair about it – the sense he gave of a man jealous of his rights to a dick-led life of picaresque adventures (whether he went on those adventures or not) could only destabilise her. So if he'd be within his rights to want to murder her, she surely was within her rights to have wanted to murder him. But all that's water under the bridge. He doesn't want to murder her. He has never wanted to murder her. He reveres her and misses her and imagines erecting a bench to her memory looking out over the Valley of the Rocks. *In celebration of the life of Melissa Paul, who preferred the commotion of the elements to the commotion of a man.* He sees himself coming here every year, a foolish bent-backed old dodderer, drenched in tears. He is drenched in tears now. Heartbreak-blue late summer afternoons overlooking the sea do this to him. So do benches dedicated to dead women.

He trudges gravely back to Lynton, or is it Lynmouth, the high one anyway, where he finds a dark pub with a dark corner to sob in. He is quickly drunk. Salty tears drizzled into cheap red Italian screwtop wine on a hot day always increases the alcoholic content. Don't ask him how: he's a man of feelings, not a chemist. When he stumbles out he doesn't recognise the world. Which way to turn? And where is he making for anyway? He turns right, past a garden in which children are hitting one another with balloons, past another pub outside which a man is throwing beer mats for a dog to catch, past the open door of a centre for shiatsu which he thought was a form of gentle therapy but in this part of the United Kingdom seems to entail bowing and falling on a mat, and walks slap into Liz.

There is no mistake this time. He has not been looking for her, he has not been thinking about her, he has not conjured her out of the vapours of his expectation. And even if he'd known for sure that she was Mrs Billy Yuill, that Billy Yuill for sure still kept a holiday cottage here, and that Liz would, for sure, be in it, he would not have been on the watch for someone in a belted white oriental combat outfit.

'Liz!'

Her face falls into a mesh of distress lines. She looks away. If she can, she will walk on. Even run. She is fit. She throws people over her hip. She could outrun him.

He holds his ground. 'Liz, it's Frank. Frank Ritz.'

She raises her green eyes to him. The person he walked into was outside herself, free of time, cheerfully vacant after exercise. Now she is cruelly brought back to the dull oppression of interiority, memory, experience, bitterness. Thanks, Frank. He realises that he has done to her exactly what he has done so often to Mel – flung himself, like a brick through a screen, into the quiet blank of her attention when she was off happily with the fairies. Fuck the fairies, notice me!

'I know who you are,' Liz says. 'I'm not likely to forget.'

'You look good,' he says.

'Well, I was feeling good.'

She doesn't tell him that he looks good himself. But then he doesn't. He's been unwell. And he's just been blubbering on the cliffs. And mixing tears and booze. He must have red eyes. He must even have a red nose.

He touches the sleeve of her jacket. 'How long have you been doing this shiatsu stuff?' he asks.

'It's not shiatsu. It's tai chi.'

'Whatever. So are you good at it?'

'Tai chi is not a competitive sport, Frank,' she says.

'Unlike friendship,' is what he wants to say; but he is not such a fool as that. Instead he asks her to have a drink with him.

She shakes her head.

'Just one.'

'No.'

147

'We could have Chinese tea, if you're into all that.'

'What for, Frank?'

'Old times' sake.'

'And you think we should drink to that?' She starts to walk away. He follows, keeping up with her stride.

'There were *some* good times, Liz.' It upsets him to hear these words on his own lips. You always know that the hour is going to come when you will have to try to rescue the past in a sentence. You always know that trial waiting for you. Now, at last, he's heard himself say it. Now he really is old.

She is softer, momentarily, than he'd expected her to be. But more final, too. 'There were good times,' she said. 'Some. But that doesn't mean you want the memory of them back.'

So fuck off, Frank. Shut the fuck up and get the fuck out.

'How are your children?' he asks.

'My children,' she says, 'are fine. But since when were you curious about my children?'

Since meeting Hamish? No, it's too soon for Hamish.

'How's Kurt?' he asks instead, as he pursues her down a flight of steps leading, he is alarmed to notice, to Sinai Hill.

'Ask him yourself, Frank.'

'The last time I spoke to Kurt he told me never to speak to him, or have truck with anything that appertained to him, ever again.'

'If you're wondering whether he's softened his attitude, he hasn't. Neither have I softened mine. It's been good to see you, Frank. Go home.'

He wants to kiss her. It seems an interminable time since he's kissed anyone. He's kissed Josh Green, of course, but he's not counting what he does with men. Even before he was booted out he hadn't kissed Mel in months. Months! — years rather, if we're talking about kiss with the whole of the mouth, a kiss kiss which is different from a peck kiss. He may have had his dick out in the presence of a couple of whores in the not too distant past, but you don't get into kissing with whores. It is with whores as it is with wives and lovers – the kiss is the first thing to go.

But even if he'd kissed half of creation that very morning he would still want to kiss Liz now. Her face has begun to reassemble itself retrospectively; he can now recognise the creases he was once able to turn into channels for laughter to escape by. He feels affection for her, and, sentimentally, for himself through her. He could mourn his own youth in her face. But he can also celebrate his age in it. He wants to put his hand on her cheeks like a father. Yes, he likes it that she's no longer young. Now young's gone, who wants young any more? In a general way, he likes the blur that you see in mature faces, the suffusion of warm furry weariness; but it moves and stirs him especially to see that Liz is well on the way to looking like an old lion.

But if he's going to kiss her he's going to have to catch her. She is a lot further down Sinai Hill now than he is. He calls after her, but she is gone in a billow of Chinese canvas, in through the door of an end-of-terrace lime-coloured cottage which he is just close enough behind to hear her slam and double-bolt and chain.

Is that in fact a good sign, Frank wonders. Does it mean that Billy isn't home? If Billy were home to protect her she wouldn't need to double-bolt and chain her door, would she. She'd leave it ajar so that Frank could come barging through smack into her husband's ukelele fist.

Ha, ha, ha. Turned out nice again.

He bangs at the brass door knocker. A yacht. Poor Liz, to have thrown herself away on a Yuill. He puts his nose to the ridged and frosted pane of glass. A common front door to a common little cottage. What's the point in having a holiday place by the sea if you can't see the sea? Was it his fault? Did he ruin it for her with Kurt, and by confiding their subterfuge to Billy Yuill did he leave her only Billy Yuill to run to? Poor Liz. He can't see or hear anything. He puts his eye to the letter box and is just able to make out four matching green wellingtons on a sanded floor. Nothing is easier to imagine than the life of a couple. One inanimate object, the spousal equivalent to a stool or a thimbleful of urine – that's all you need to tell you everything there is to know. A single green wellington would have been plenty. But four! The odour of cohabitational hell wafts through the letter box. So is Billy Yuill at home or isn't he? Frank doesn't care now. He feels as if he's been drinking. 'Liz,' he shouts through the letter box. 'Liz, let me in!'

Apart from the sound of water running, the cottage remains silent.

He goes around to the side of the house where a lime-yellow gate gives access to a small yard. No garden in which to enjoy the Gulf-stream clemency of the climate. Poor, poor Liz. He hasn't told himself what he's actually about, but it appears that he means to rescue her. He climbs the lime-yellow gate. Not difficult. It's no more than four feet high and has cross-beams that help him with his footing. When did he last climb a gate? His heart is thumping with the irresponsibility of his actions. It could be forty years since he last climbed a gate, that's if he has ever climbed a gate at all.

There is a broom in the yard, leaning up against a wall. And a pile of logs, axed to go into an Aga. So there's an axe about. He tries the latch of a small brick lean-to. Locked. Of course locked. Billy Yuill wouldn't leave an axe where anyone could find it. Precise husbands always know to lock all sharp and pointed implements away. They live with women who would separate their heads from their shoulders given half a chance.

He sees hot sudsy water coming out of the down-pipe.

Someone's taking a bath. He steps back and looks up. It's a low cottage. If he had a footstool he could just about see into the upper storey windows. He calls out again. 'Liz! It's Frank. Let me in. We have to talk.' Again there is no answer. Only an increase in speed and volume and soapiness, he reckons, in the water coming out of the down-pipe. So she isn't taking a bath, she's taking a shower. There's hope in that.

He locates what has to be the bathroom window. He scours the unlittered yard for something to throw against the pane, but can find only fine slivers of masonry. If he could lay his hands on the axe he'd be able to chip away whole corners of bricks. Alternatively he could throw the axe. He gathers up what he can find, throws underarm, misses, throws again, but the best he can achieve is a feeble pattering, like light rain on the canvas roof of his Saab. No one showering would hear that.

What he needs is a ladder. He tests the down-pipe to see if it will take his weight but he knows he isn't serious. Even supposing he gets to the steamed-up bathroom window, he is not going to be able to climb through it. He could get her attention perhaps, but he wouldn't be well situated to press his suit. And he isn't looking for a conversation. He's looking to help her out of the shower, take her in his arms, and dry her. And mustn't that, in some corner of her consciousness, be what she's looking to happen as well? Why else the shower? A showering woman is commiting her flesh to flux. A showering woman is consigning her anterior life to the plughole, inviting the waters of change to have their way with her.

It's while he is peering into the kitchen, looking for a ladder, that he notices that one of the windows is not locked. He applies only the slightest pressure to the frame and it opens. Easy. Easy, even for a drunk. Easy, too, to wriggle in, climb over the sink, and land lightly on his feet like a cat burglar. He isn't sure what's exciting him more, his recklessness or his athleticism. Either way, he's in new territory. Liz might be an old flame, but there's nothing old about his ardour, or about the risks he's taking. Nor is he, in the old stale way, merely submitting to the caprices of his pancreatic juices. Yes, he feels as though the lining has come away from his stomach, but it's not the usual negative obverse of morality lurch that motivates him to hunt whores. This is more what is meant by heroism. His heart is engaged. He has a lump in his throat. It's only an hour ago that he was up on the cliffs grieving for Mel. Well, just as a man grieves for all women in the single woman, so he redeems all women when he redeems one. In that sense, what he's doing he's doing for Mel. He hasn't been able to order her a memorial bench yet. So he's stealing Liz for her instead.

Sit on a bench and cry, sit on Liz and cry – it's all one to a man with a breaking heart.

It's so distressingly uplifting all round, that by the time he has climbed the stairs and pushed open the bathroom door he is weeping again.

At that very same moment a figure steps out of the shower. It is not Liz. Nor is it Billy Yuill. Nor is it some mysteriously unidentified third party. Unexpected, certainly. Unidentifiable, no. Would that it were. The person who steps out of the shower is Kurt.

Kurt!

Frank!

Only that's not how it is. Not how it ever is. Not how it ever will be. Not ever ever ever.

Perhaps because he is naked, perhaps because his face and hair are wet and there is water glissading down his chest, glossing his skin, washing every sort of advancement off him, Kurt looks the same to Frank today as he has looked in his memory throughout the last twenty years. A boy still. Sallow and self-sufficient, like an Indian brave. An Indian indian too. Sabu, that's who he has always looked like. The boychick on the magic carpet.

And perhaps because Frank is always pestiferously with him, Kurt is not as surprised as Frank would have imagined him to be, to see him standing there in the steam, caught out again. Sad for Frank to face, that Kurt will never be astounded by any infamous act of violation he commits, will never expect anything else of him but trespass and treachery. And fake tears.

'I'm not going to ask what you're doing here,' Kurt says. His mouth is unsteady – this is to be Frank's only consolation. That Kurt, too, was upset. That Kurt, too, couldn't keep it together. 'I don't want to know. I'm just asking you to go. Don't say anything to me. I won't listen. I don't want to fight you. I'm not angry with you. I don't have any feelings towards you. I just want you to go.'

No swearing. No shouting. No shut the fuck up and get the fuck out. Just the grave consideration of an old friend who wants only to wipe you from his life. Just go. Just vanish.

And Frank goes, vanishes, his leaping heart shot down as though by a deadly hunter. His eyes gushing tears the colour of plonk.

EIGHT

'So you reckon that Hamish told you Kurt was in
America in order to get you to leave Cheltenham?'

'No. I think Hamish believed Kurt was in America. Yes,
he wanted me to leave Cheltenham; no, he was not party to
any deception.'

'Deception in relation to you?'

'Deception in relation to Billy Yuill.'

'Remind me who Billy Yuill is.'

'Billy Yuill is the person to whom Liz is now married.'

'Hamish told you that?'

'Hamish told me that his mother has remarried. I made the
connection.'

'So how do you know you are right?'

'If she isn't with Billy Yuill what was she doing in Billy
Yuill's cottage?'

'And you know for sure it was Billy Yuill's cottage?'

'A bit of a coincidence if it wasn't. Billy Yuill has a cottage
in Lynton or Lynmouth. I go to Lynton or Lynmouth. I run
into Liz. She runs into a cottage. Who else's cottage is it
going to be?'

'It could be Billy Yuill's cottage without Liz being married
to Billy Yuill. She could be borrowing Billy Yuill's cottage.'

'So what was Kurt doing there?'

'Kurt is her husband.'

'Not according to Hamish.'

'But according to Hamish, Kurt wasn't in the country. It's looking to me as though Hamish can't be trusted. You didn't trust him when you first clapped eyes on him.'

The speaker remembers when Frank Ritz first clapped eyes on the boy they call Hamish. The speaker is D, the fat comedian, and she was there in a wine bar in Montpellier at the time. Tonight she is in a hotel in Torquay, sitting up in bed, eating black chocolate and drinking brown ale. She is on a black chocolate and brown ale diet. If she eats and drinks nothing else for the next twelve months she will be thin. It's a combination diet. Together, the black chocolate and brown ale will adequately nourish her while at the same time eating her fat away from the inside. The combination works only so long as it is not intruded upon. Swallow so much as a grain of rice and the black chocolate and brown ale immediately fall out. They are like a couple of newlyweds sequestered in the country; the marriage works fine so long as no one calls in on them. The trouble D is having with this diet is that as soon as she has finished the black chocolate she rings down for a hamburger and chips.

Frank too is sitting up in bed eating black chocolate and drinking brown ale. He doesn't need to lose weight. He is acting companionably. He is sitting up in the same bed as D but he is not her lover. D has no lovers. D is a celibate on principle and Frank respects her principles. Shortly he will go back to his own bed in an adjoining room. They don't lie together. They merely sit up at the far ends of the same bed to watch television and go on D's diet and discuss whatever is on their minds. The arrangement suits Frank down to the ground. A period of protocolic celibacy is exactly what he needs. But just in case nature suddenly tries to get the better of protocol, a bolster runs the length of the bed between them.

At D's insistence, they wear night-shirts and pyjamas (severally) and dressing gowns.

Frank, who has never owned pyjamas, has had to go out and buy himself a pair.

He is being brave about it. So OK, it's happened, he's old, he wears pyjamas, and a plaited cord now swings where his dick once would have. Change, too, is part of life.

D also wears bedsocks.

Frank has explained that he cannot go so far as that himself. But he will be careful to keep his feet in his half of the bed.

The fiction is that the bed is like a bomb – one inadvertent touch and it will go up. The truth is that Frank's powder is wet. And D wouldn't go off if you dropped her out of an aeroplane.

Frank agrees that it is inconsistent to trust Hamish given that he has jewelry through his face. But he can't see what would be in it for Hamish to lie so comprehensively about his parents.

'Parents?' D leans ironically on the final syllable of that word. Paren*tz*? 'I thought the theory is that Hamish is your*z*. And that's why you're having so much trouble believing that what you got from him was a cock and bull story. No son of Frank Ritz would tell a lie! Isn't that the sort of bollocks that's going on in your head?'

Frank waves away the insulting imputation of gooey fatherliness. That the shivering morose kid with punctured skin might turn out to be a child of his – the fruit of what he pumped into Liz Bryll before he filled her full of hair brush (and who's to say that that early trauma wouldn't account for the kid's moroseness: who's to say how soon a sperm begins to feel?) – he does indeed fear. But the dread is more general than particular. This is about the age it always happens. You're fifty, minding your business, of course distraught, of course charging fast towards the cliff-edge, but at least knowing who you are, and who, if anybody, is yours, when wham! bam! out of the blue some reprehensible little cunt in a backwards baseball hat flings himself into your arms: 'Hi, dad, I'm the splat of jism you jerked into your best friend's wife. Call me Hamish.' Now's the time for all the Hamishes to come crawling out of the wordwork. To be absolutely truthful, Frank has wondered why they haven't made themselves known to him sooner. When you've chucked as much spunk around as he has, you expect some of it to stick. You even start worrying why it hasn't. None stuck in Mel. None was meant to stick in Mel. She wasn't the adhesive type. But even she has been bracing herself over the last few years to reject the inevitable army of foundlings whose undeniable facial resemblance to Frank Ritz, the poor bastards, will do nothing for her but enumerate instances of his infidelity. Some of them will predate her, right enough. But they've been together long enough now, Mel and Frank, for others to be coming along who originated in sperm that was rightly hers. Hers to kill, maybe, hers to suffocate in spermicidal jelly, hers to entrammel and garrotte in loops and coils, hers to have scraped out of herself along with sundry impurities of the colon, but still hers. None of this, though – least of all what Mel has been bracing herself for – has any bearing on the present conversation. He isn't suffering precautionary paternal pride. *No son of his would tell a lie!* Come off it. Maybe he *is* suffering precautionary paternal pride: of course any son of his would tell a lie. Not the point either way. The point, as he explains to D, is 'Why would Hamish be in on the fact that his father – Kurt, I'm talking about – is having an affair with his mother? Do parents tell their kids that sort of stuff? Hey, Hamish – remember your mother, the woman I acrimoniously divorced? Well I'm shtupping her again on the side. Be pleased for us, but keep it to yourself.'

'And that's what you think was happening when you shimmied up the drainpipe? You interrupted a man in a shower who was about to give his ex-wife a seeing to?'

'I know Kurt. I grew up with him. He only ever showers before a shag.'

(That's for her. Shag is her word. Shtup is what Kurt does. Kurt only ever showers before a shtup.)

'And where, in this scenario, is the current husband?'

'How can I know that? Away. Fishing. In America. Standing at a lamppost. Not around – that's all. Out of the way.'

'Out of the way just long enough for a how's your father?' She pops a chocolate, then folds her arms on her chest. 'Shag shag shag.'

That's the thanks he gets. 'What do you mean, shag shag shag?'

'You're a pervy little bastard, Frank. You think all dealings between men and women are depraved. You *hope*! What's wrong with the simple explanation? Why can't your friends still be married? Why can't they be borrowing this Billy person's cottage in the country? Why can't Hamish be their child? Why can't he be lying to you about his parents because he knows they get upset whenever your name crops up (you being such a shit) and he wants to spare them that? Why has everybody got to be shagging someone they shouldn't be shagging?'

'Happy families – is that what you're telling me they're all playing out there! Is that the only game in town suddenly – happy families? Everyone else is shuffling the happy family deck and there's just me, Frank Ritz, playing snakes and ladders. So how come you can still *buy* snakes and ladders?'

'What's snakes and ladders got to do with anything, Frank? I'm just asking you why everything has to have a warped sexual explanation?'

'What's warped? Where's that word come from? I haven't described anything warped. What's warped about shtupping your first wife? Myself, I think that's rather a nice thing to do. Myself, I think Billy Yuill should hurry back home and join in. I'd have, if they'd let me. If Kurt had been any kind of a friend he'd have been only too pleased that I once shtupped his wife, and if Billy Yuill were any kind of husband he'd be only too pleased that Kurt wants to shtup her again. And they both should be only too pleased that I'd still be only too pleased to join them. It confirms your judgment when another man wants what you've got . . .'

'Oh yeah? I saw your face, Frank, when I suggested that you'd been booted out to make room for another man. I saw how confirmed in your judgment you felt.'

'I'm talking about ideal behaviour, D, not the accidents of the hour. Can't we have some philosophy around here? It's a compliment when someone wants what's yours, that's what I'm saying. Sure, it may take a little time to see it that way, but when you do, gey gesunterhait, is what you should say. Be my guest, enjoy yourself, go in good health. Here, look, I'll even hold her legs apart so you can enter her in comfort. That's how much I love you. That's how much I love her. Kuk the knish – go on, get an eyeful of the cunt. You'll never see a finer. And while you're down there you should listen to it as well. Looks like a shell, sounds like a shell. Splash, splish – the music of the knish. Beautiful, *n'est-ce pas*? I'll hold it open while you put your ear to it. And you call that warped? I call it devotion. Devotion, D. Friendship. You want to know what warped is? I'll tell you what warped is – ' He bangs the bed, sending the squares of black chocolate flying in all directions. 'Warped is going to bed in your socks.' He rips at his pyjama cord. 'Warped is dressing up to go to sleep. This is what I call warped' – he punches the duvet – 'this fucking bolster!'

Woman – mouth – talk.

Man – forehead – bang.

He is dismayed by his own violence. Anyone would think he resents the territorial integrity which her bolster and her bedsocks stand guard over. Whereas he doesn't in the least. See her diaphanously bagged in her flouncing pig-out night attire, reader; see how ill the crocheted cuffs of those same woolly bedsocks set off her jammy limbs, and you will believe Frank when he swears he has only celibacy in his heart. Now, though, it is open to her to accuse him of regretting and even resenting the undertaking he has given her – not exactly a vow of chastity on his own part, but decidedly a vow to respect whatever she's vowed.

She'd laid her cards on the table three nights before in a factitious boutique bottle-drinker's pub in Exeter – The Hole in Gertie O'Reilly's Bucket, or something like – where he'd persuaded her to meet him after her show to hear the apology owing from Cheltenham and to receive again his offer to be her chauffeur if a chauffeur she still required. Ella Fitzgerald was singing on the factitious nostalgia juke box. All the dreamiest, most aching urban stuff. 'Stars Fell on Alabamba'. 'Moonlight in Vermont'. 'A Foggy Day in London Town'. D loved Ella Fitzgerald. Ella Fitzgerald found her soft side. Frank too. Frank had smooched his first ever smooch to Ella Fitzgerald, not knowing what she looked like. He was surprised, later, to discover that it was a fat woman in glasses who had stirred him to such smoky city-lights eroticism on the floor of the Plaza ballroom on Oxford Road in Manchester, moved his heart and his manhood to dance in that perfect accord. Fancy a fat woman having the power to synchronise him. He was also surprised to discover, later, that the girl he had smooched with had lifted his wallet while they were cheek to cheek. In memory, the lost wallet only increased the ache. A hotel room with a balcony high above the lights of the city, the smell of expensive perfume and guttering candle, neon flashing, a sax playing, champagne in a silver bucket on a silver tray, yourself in a tuxedo, an unfamiliar golden head on your shoulder – petty larceny too belonged to the experience. And why stop at larceny? Let the golden top go ahead and plug you with the pearl-handled forty-five she's got concealed in her Gucci evening purse, the night can only get better. So powerfully does it come back to him – not anything he's ever had, but everything he's always wanted to have – that he takes D by her pleated wrists and pulls her up from the beery table and puts his arms as far around her as he is able. It may only be The Hole in Gertie O'Reilly's Bucket in downtown Exeter, but music speaks to all time and all places, does it not? D wouldn't disagree with that. Ella Fitzgerald awakens tawdry new world longings in her as well. There is no room to move, but then who's moving? Cheek to cheek's hard; nose to nose, though, they can just do. 'I behold your adorable face,' the fat woman in the glasses croons, and as long as the song lasts D and Frank agree to behold the adorable in each other.

It was immediately after this, back down among the brown ales, and returned to her loud laconic stage-shagger's intonations, that D took him into her confidence.

'I'm not,' she told him, 'on the best of terms with my cunt.'

Frank was man enough not to look around. 'Who's to blame for that?' he asked. 'Or is it six of one and half a dozen of the other?'

'We're just not in comunication. If you want to know,

I've seen neither hide nor hair of my genitals since I was a sixteen-year-old comprehensive schoolgirl.'

'Is that so?' Frank said. He hadn't wanted to appear too inquisitive. Like the cunt-fearing devil in fairy stories, he wondered if she bore some terrible deformity between her legs.

'I have an apron of fat,' she told him (there you are, he was right), 'which covers my genitals completely. I can't see myself.'

'Well I could always lift it for you,' Frank had ventured philanthropically, 'while you look . . .'

She showed him her tongue.

'Alternatively – '

'It isn't funny to me, Frank,' she'd said, despite the sacred responsibility she owed, as a professional comedian, to find everything funny.

She didn't like herself, surprise surprise, that was what it came to. She told fat slag shagger stories on the stage which were of practical help, surprise surprise, to everyone but herself. She reconciled two thousand women a night to the grossness of their bodies, but she hated her own too much ever to trust it to a single act of love.

'It's like being the captain of a sinking ship,' Frank said, understandingly, 'or a member of the priesthood. You're expected to save every soul but your own. Telly critics are the same. You expiate every other fucker's sins of time-wasting and triviality, but there's no one to square things up for you. They're back on dry land, sleeping the sleep of the righteous, and you're still stuck on the burning deck, having to watch crap on the box all day.'

Having said which, he sat back in his round-armed bar chair with the look of a man who had revived a corpse. That was the cunt problem solved. Next.

But she didn't want her cunt problem solved. She was

relieved not to be on good terms with it. There was a bright side to not having to see it, not having to be reminded of it, every day. She was liberated. She could have friendships with men. An ulterior motive was at a stroke removed.

OK by Frank. He'd read about friendship with women. And he wasn't doing anything else.

As captains of their separately sinking ships they should help each other, because no one helped them – that was the deal. They could keep each other company on the road. Frank was wrong about how light she travelled. There was more loot on that stage than he thought there was. She had a van to take care of all that, but who wants to be shaken around in a van? So yes, Frank could drive her, unencumbered, and in a spirit of non-ulterior-motive friendship, across Dartmoor to her next gig at Torquay. After Torquay she was down to have a few days lazing in the sun, which really meant sitting up in bed noshing chocolates, and he could join her in that. Then, if things were still working out, he could drive her to St Austell, which was not that many blind Cornish miles (not that he was counting) from Little Cleverley. And she, for her part, could be around late at night, as a sort of surrogate anchoring device, to stop him taking his dick out in public places and otherwise losing sight of his own best interests. That there was to be absolutely no fucking or anything in the slightest bit preparatory to fucking – unless you call black chocolate and brown ale a preparative to fucking – suited him fine. After what happened to him in Lynton or Lynmouth he has come to a new understanding of what it means to be fifty. Instead of wanting to fuck, you want to blubber. The day he left Mel he had cried, and he has cried on just about every day since. Sperm or tears, where's the difference? One way or the other it's the same profligacy with liquids and emotions. One way or another you're still jerking off. So what you have to do is stay away from temptation in regard to spillage of either sort. And as far as any such temptation goes, D does indeed seem to have the requisite quality – the effects of Ella Fitzgerald's intercession notwithstanding, she no more wants any of Frank's liquids than any of Frank's liquids want her.

Except that now he is shouting and banging the bolster.

If that were Mel at the far end of the bed, he would at this point expect to be banished to an inferior room and a lower storey. But then if that *were* Mel at the far end of the bed he would never have got to finish his speech. Because he doesn't love D he is free to admire her, and one of the things he admires about her professionally (and no one is admirable *except* professionally) is her confidence to allow hecklers to have their say. Patience is a potent comic weapon in her hands; she stands still as a mantis on the stage, her arms folded across her chest, exactly as they are now, her lips puréed into a parody of infinite forbearance, and just waits and waits, assured that the trouble maker will at last choke on his own too much. This is an advantage she enjoys over Mel as a companion – she gives Frank leave to expatiate. Thereafter, mind you, the opinions of the two women quickly converge. And that's another reason he's glad he's not fucking any more. There is now so little ideological or cognitive disparity between women – between the ones Frank meets, anyway – that there is a sense in which once you have fucked one, you have fucked all. See how time has changed him from the boy who thought he would be pulling at the Kardomah till he was a hundred, so peculiar in every particular, so infinitessi-mally herself and not another, was every girl he met. He was a cunt collector then, and to a trained eye no doubt cunts are still as various as they ever were. But as befits a man at the end of his sexual usefulness, he notices only the intelligences of women today, and it's those intelligences he doesn't mind he isn't fucking, since he's fucked them all already.

A long and heavy silence has prevailed since he banged the bolster, broken only by the sound of D knocking back what's left of the ale.

'I think sorry is the word you're searching for,' she says finally.

He agrees with her. 'I am sorry,' he says. 'I've been a bit shaken up over the last few days.'

She allows a light yeasty belch to part her lips. It's not quite a snort, though it's on a snort's errand.

'Do you know what I'd do if I were you?' she asks, but without waiting, as Mel would have waited, for an answer. 'I'd go and see a therapist.'

'To what end?'

'To get help, Frank. You need counselling. Did you hear yourself just now? *The* cunt. *The* knish. You talk about women as if they're nothing but parts. *The* bit of what you fancy.'

'It's the definite article you object to, is it? Would you be all right about it if I went indefinite. *A* cunt? *A* knish?'

'Who's talking about grammar?'

'You are, D. You think the definite article is degrading to your sex. You think it objectifies them. But that's not what the definite article does. Think of the the in *The* Holy Ghost, or *The* Lord, or *The* Ten Commandments. It gives them definition, doesn't it, it confers the distinction of specificity on them. And *the* Lord (and no other) said unto *the* Israelites (and to no one else), gey gesunterhait, go forth and multiply and honour *the* knish − meaning *the* knish and nothing but *the* knish.'

'A cunt belongs to someone, Frank.'

'Does it? I'm not sure it does. A cunt is leased to someone, I'll accept that. I think a cunt belongs to nature, and a woman is but the steward of it. But anyway I thought we were talking about *the* cunt, not *a* cunt − '

'There is no *the* cunt. Just as there is no *the* shag, or *the* wife, or *the* bit on the side. You have to start again every time.'

Frank thinks about that. 'You mean every shag is a new shag.'

'It's not a shag. It's not *a* shag or *the* shag, it's someone.'

'So we are talking grammar after all. It's the impersonal pronoun you really don't like. It's the *it*. What you're actually against is that when our sex looks at your sex we think of giving it one. It's the impersonal mirth you don't like.'

'Mirth!'

'Dead right. Mirth. When we were kids we used to go on ynaf hunt. You won't know what a ynaf is. You're a London girl and London slang begins and ends with apple and pears. Where I come from, ynaf's backward chat for fanny. Great name for a vagina, wouldn't you agree? Ynaf. Wonderful to get your tongue around. Philosophical, to boot. It's got why in it – the big question – and wine in it and naff in it, but mostly it's got laugh in it.'

'The laugh being *mostly* on whom, Frank?'

'The laugh being mostly on us, D, we little Ahabs obsessively stumping over the great sperm-filled oceans of Wythenshawe and Droylsden. We knew what we were about. We knew the ynaf was making clowns of us.'

'Oh, yeah? Well I've seen blokes on ynaf hunt, and none of them ever struck me as having a particularly sophisticated sense of the ridiculous. Speaking as a steward of the ynaf, I have to tell you that I don't remember any masterful jokes made in pursuit of mine – unless you call "Show us your cunt" a masterful joke.'

'It could be, depending on the context. Bluntness is its own fun, as you know perfectly well. You're on stage five nights a week shoving bits of bloke into every orifice – you don't need me to tell you about the mirthfulness of brutality.'

'Parody, Frank. I'm up there taking the piss out of you lot. It's called redressing the balance.'

'The fuck it is. That's not why those fat birds are sitting there in their thousands with their tits shaking, because you're redressing the balance. They're into the violence of it, D. They're into the ancient fucking needling antagonism of sex.'

'Wrong, Frank. Those fat birds, as you so nicely call them, are laughing with the relief of being able to get their own back at last. They've been the objects of your antagonism for however many thousands of years, now they're enjoying being able to express their own.'

'So we're not arguing. It's great to slag off the other sex. There's nothing in the world like it, I agree with you. I don't give a shit about the history of it. If you've allowed yourselves to forget where the pleasure lies, that's your fault. I'm glad for you if you've got it back. But don't tell me you're just redressing a balance. Because what's going to happen once you've redressed it? Are you suddenly going to stop finding cock – *the* cock – funny?'

'I don't think we need to worry about that quite yet. I think we've plenty to do.'

'Sure you have. And it's not called therapy, either. I'm surprised at you. If there's one person who oughtn't to believe in therapy it's a comedian. You *are* the therapy.'

'A comedian can't do everything, Frank.'

'Yes, you can. Not for yourself, I grant you. But you're not doing it for yourself. We're already agreed on that. You're the captain of a sinking ship. It's us, the passengers in the lifeboats, you're meant to be thinking about. And we don't want you pretending we're not in trouble. Sing to us of death and drowning. Tell us the one about the cannibal and the shark. That's the shit that keeps us going.'

'That keeps *you* going.'

'OK. But I'm the audience, remember.'

'You're not my audience. If I ever catch you in my audience I'll make you wish you'd never been born.'

'What'll you do? Joke me to death?'

'I'll tell the story of your life, Frank. I'll tell them what's become of you after half a century following the great white ynaf that bit your appendage off. My girls like a good adventure yarn. Especially when it's got a happy ending, like the hero bleeding to death on Exmoor. I'll tell them what you've told me. That you no longer know whether to cry or to come. I'll drag you up on stage. You can weep through your weenie for us – '

'You need therapy, D.'

She throws a chocolate at him.

So everything's all right then. Back to happy families.

'I think that's the only therapy I can allow,' he goes on, 'therapy for comedians. Help for the physicians who cannot help themselves. And I suggest we start by lifting that little apron of fat you've got down there and seeing if we can get a look at the knish.'

'I prefer ynaf.'

'I prefer show us your cunt.'

He makes a lunge in the direction of her deformity. She snorts with fright and laughter, bunching the bed clothes around her, piling on the fortifications. He doesn't, of course, actually touch her. A deal's a deal. And it's its own kind of fun exactly as it is, galumphing with a corrugated dirigible, whose tits hummock about under their protective wrapping like badgers chasing their tails under parkland, and who lets you expatiate, lets you explain her job to her, lets you choke on your own too much, without feeling the need to kick you out of the house. Or in this case, the Five Star hotel.

Could it be that Frank's found the secret of relational contentment? Agreeing from the outset to stay away from the cunt, except in horseplay? Are there to be satisfactions in being fifty after all?

He often thinks he'd like to have been a comedian himself. He would have enjoyed being on stage, making them laugh with that one.

They stay in bed, looking at the sea and the telly and not touching, for three more days. Each night, when there's no more tolerable telly left, Frank goes back to his bed in the room next door, and each morning he returns for bacon, egg and coffee, followed by brown ale and black chocolate, in hers.

It's a life. It's a convalescence, anyway.

When he does put a foot outside the hotel he is surprised to see how bright it is. He rubs his eyes. That golden ball sitting in the sky . . . Could that be the sun? And those long thin things, the colour of salmon, moving about in the glare of the water, not eating . . . Could those be people? He catches sight of his reflection in a shop window. He has to look twice before he's sure it's him. He has put on weight on D's diet. But he looks different in some other way as well. Good and not good; fraughtly placid.

He has banking to do. D has asked him to draw cash out for her on one of her cards, though what she needs cash for, unless it's to tip room service, he can't imagine. And he has to transfer funds from his savings to his cheque account. He's gone through a further couple of thousand since he broke his resolution to stay away from five star hotels. If it goes on like this he's going to have to get another column. It's a thing he's always promised himself – that he will never, *never* allow himself to be reduced to writing about family values or having the builders in, but he has been made a vagrant by his long-term partner and needs must when the devil drives.

She – *she* – has responded promptly but coldly to his faxed request for her to stick his mail in a jiffy bag and forward it to him poste restante, Torquay. She's sent him everything, leaflets, handbills, minicab cards, menus from take-away restaurants, shopping lists from home deliverers, circulars from real estate agents, quotations for double glazing and loft conversions, notices of church fêtes, invitations to car-boot sales, plastic sacks for the blind, electioneering material (including a signed letter from Tony Blair), the local council newsletter, an appeal for information about a missing cat, a free shampoo sample, and of course the domestic bills. All the shit that comes through the letter box she's bunged him. So that he should feel he's still at home? So that he should miss the palpable evidentiality – the dailiness, as sentimentalists of the hearth call it – of their domestic life? Some hope. There is no letter from her. No personal mark, other than a few impatiently scrawled arrows directing his attention to over-due amounts. It could have been worse, he accepts that. She could have thrown up in the bag before she sent it.

The violence of women. The vindictive uses to which they put the postal service. A girlfriend of Frank's once sent what was left of an intimate chicken dinner, registered mail, to another girlfriend of Frank's. Bones, carcass, gristle, giblets, parson's nose, the lot. And that wasn't all the big brown envelope contained. Used toothpicks fell out of it as well, the contents of an ashtray, a couple of lipsticked tissues, a wine cork, a tea bag – all the evidence Frank had stupidly forgotten to clear away (the waste bin isn't *away*) of girlfriend number two's infraction of the rights to exclusivity of girlfriend number one.

Perhaps exclusivity wasn't the only issue. The chicken

dinner in question had taken place while girlfriend number one was out of town. And had been cooked in her kitchen. And consumed on her dining table. And the ashtray had been found on her bedside table. And girlfriend number two had been her best friend.

But the violence of the response, none the less . . .

She rang him up in tears, the recipient of the bones, to solicit his understanding. 'I had to *sign* for them, Frank.'

'It must have been terrible,' he said. But without conviction. He was a sucker for the meticulous ferocity of girlfriend number one. Fancy gathering it all out of the bin, fancy wrapping it all up, fancy quantifying your grievance to the last bone, and fancy, after all that, going down to the post office and filling out a form. It was awesome.

Mel had not put herself to that kind of trouble. Her rage never stooped to precision revenge. She was a blanket bomber. Whatever dropped on the mat and wasn't addressed to her she simply swept into the bag and sent him. He wasn't worth making distinctions over. She hadn't even bothered to stick a stamp on the envelope.

Such ferocity. Such a fury they're all in. D too is a volcano ready to blow. Not because she isn't fucking. Frank wouldn't be so gross as to suppose that a woman who isn't fucking is bound to explode. Who was ever kept calm by fucking, anyway? No, not fucking isn't what's making them all sore, it's a sense of individual injustice. It's as if they've arrived at an idea of self late – later than Frank's sex, certainly, and probably later than the amoebas and the bivalves, come to that – and don't know what to do with it now they've reached it. Take D's objections to being thought of as cunt. Why so sensitive? Frank would love to be thought of as cock. 'I wouldn't mind a piece of that,' he once overhead one woman saying to another in a theatre queue. If he wasn't mistaken he was the that she wouldn't have minded a piece of. He'd never been more complimented in his life. He never has since. If someone were to think of him as a *that* today, and were happy to take any piece of him that was going – *a* piece, she said she would have settled for, any piece – who knows, his garden might bloom again. He's easy about being objectified, that's his point. He's not self-sensitive. Everything in the world is wrong, but its wrongness isn't a personal affront to him. As it is to them. As it is to D who won't look under the apron of fat God gave her; as it was to the one who posted off the giblets; as it was to the Ethiopian whore who would rather suck his car upholstery than his balls; as it is to Mel who has made herself a successful pornographer on the strength of it. She gets a shiver up, the way ladies like it, because every act of sex appals her and shocks her. And why does it do that? Because it somehow takes from her. A fuck committed on her in person takes from the her that doesn't fuck; a fuck committed on another takes from the her that does. Hence she finds it an act of infidelity, a betrayal and a vilification, either way. Hence she writes it filthy. Hence she excites her readers. Frank has seen the instructions which the new publishers of women's filth put out to would-be exponents of the smutchy art – under no circumstances, they all warn, make a joke, for a joke interrupts the erotic trance. Well no joke ever interrupted Frank's erotic trance. But then it was never a trance of the vilified self, was it? When they went on ynaf hunt, he and his china plates, they went in the expectation that they would come first and laugh later. But any other order would have done as well. A man can come when he's laughing or laugh when he's coming, it doesn't matter. The cosmos is a joke to him, not an act of spite directed at his person.

He saunters about in the festive brightness of Torquay like a truant. 'Don't go looking for a knocking shop while you're out,' D had told him. 'Come straight back after banking and we can have an oyster lunch in bed.' He thinks he'll skip the oysters. And maybe bed as well. Not in the mood. It's the maleficent bag of bills from Mel that's done it. And standing waiting at a poste restante counter once again. Too cruel the contrast. No beating heart this time. No has she, hasn't she. When it's Mel you're expecting to hear from, you know the answer to that – she hasn't.

He sits on a bench, the last in a row of old men, and gazes at the masts of sailing ships. The masts clink lightly in time with one another, as do the sagging scrotums of the old men. Chink, chink, chink. Soon he'll be ready to join a bowls club.

It's too sad in the sun. The cosmos is not an act of spite directed at his person, but if it were this would be the means of its perpetration – sunshine. The full mocking glare of sunlight. Frank's lost track of time. He thinks it might not be August any more, but it's still a long way to winter. Roll on the dark days.

Walking away from the sea, he finds himself in a municipal park. Men with remote-controlled power boats are gathered around a pond. They have the look of husbands who have left the house early, like anglers, to escape the violence and pornography of their womenfolks' conversation. Every two or three minutes they haul their craft out of the water, because they've capsized or crashed or gone aground on an island of floating litter. Frank has never seen creatures more engrossed. Or more united in a common purpose. The bottom of one man's boat is the bottom of all their boats. They aren't men as he knows them. They aren't conversationalists or ironists or fuckers. They are an earlier species; perhaps what men would have been like in the garden had heaven not come up with the concept of a helpmeet. Yes, that's what defines them – they aren't helpmet. Which for some reason touches Frank to his heart.

He takes a cab back to the hotel and unthinkingly lets himself into D's room. He's been coming and going from it in the normal way, popping out to clean his teeth, popping back to grab a chocolate. But in the normal way she's expecting him. This time he's been out, and been out longer than he said he was going to be. So this time he should consider himself a formal visitor. He should knock. He should wait to be let in. But he's lost in a world of toy boatmen. He forgets. He puts the key in the lock and turns it. And as a consequence disturbs D, lying on her side with her fingers busy beneath her custodial apron of fat, exciting herself, as though she is both pianist and grand piano, into little ricocheting arpeggios of exquisite pain.

By the time he has identified the cheeping it is too late for him to withdraw.

She is furious with him for bursting in on her like this. She is flushed and shamed and thwarted and angry. 'You were supposed to come back for oysters,' she cries. She rights herself in the bed. 'What was I to do? Sit here twiddling my thumbs until fucking *Newsnight*?'

'It looked to me as though twiddling your thumbs was exactly what you were doing,' Frank says. For the cosmos is a joke to him.

She looks for something to throw at him. The closest thing to hand is the book she's been reading, the paper-pornoback woman's rut-*roman* whose rude romanticism was responsible for rolling her on to her side and turning her thoughts to impurity in the first place. It catches Frank a glancing blow on the forehead. He is not unduly discommoded by that. What unduly discommodes him is the novelette itself. He recognises it even before it hits him. He knows the look of it well. The blatant high-gloss art-work — purple on black, woman in marvel-bra on top, man with bruised eyes and soft mouth under, helpless to resist despite arms that could raise the *Titanic*. There is a stack of them in his house – in what *was* his house – in Dulwich. It is called *Coming Is Too Good For You* and its author is his partner – *was* his partner – Melissa Paul.

So how does he feel, as they ask on the box? What are you meant to feel when the woman with whom you are sharing a bed, albeit chastely, is discovered playing Rachmaninov on her cunt as a consequence of reading what your estranged lover has to say on the subject of fucking and its attendant folderols, which are not matters she has had anything to say to you about for some considerable time? Can there be a sexual advantage to yourself anywhere in this?

If anyone can find it, Frank can.

NINE

OUTSIDE THE PALAZZO *the snow fell in heavy flakes. Before she'd met Lorenzo, before this afternoon, her existence had been as cold as that dead ground, as colourless as that leaden sky. Now everything had meaning. His jutting penis. Her wet clitoris. His savage thrusting. Her gorged vagina. Everything.*

'Carissima.'

'Don't talk,' she said. 'Just go on filling me with meaning.'

But he had to talk. It was her talk he had originally fallen in love with. The way she shaped her lips to make words. The darting movement of her lizard tongue whenever she used a word that began with L. Love. Lick. Liquid. Long. Lorenzo. If he talked to her, Italian custom demanded that she talk back to him. He had to get her to talk to him. He had broken into every other part of her, now he had to break into the maidenhead of her silence.

'Tell me you love me, Sabina.'

'Hush, my darling. I want to listen to the snow fall while you fuck with me.'

But Lorenzo wanted to hear a word that began with L.

'Ask me to lick you, Sabina.'

'I don't need to, my darling. You will when it feels right for you.'

'Describe my cock, Sabina.'

'Wonderful.'

'What about its size?'

'Thick.'

'I mean the other way.'

'Interminable, my darling.'

'Do you know what I am going to fill you with, Sabina?'

'Of course I do.'

'Say it, carissima.'

'Meaning.'

Inside the Palazzo Lorenzo's liquid fell in heavy droplets, lubricating her longing labia.

If only the moron would shut his fucking trap, she thought. If only he'd put a lock on his ludicrous lips.

Or something like that.

Frank will have remembered it, naturally enough, from the man's point of view. Will have disobeyed the publisher's express instructions and slipped mirth into it. Will have missed the intensity of Sabina's struggle to be mistress of her own destiny. If he remembers rightly, Sabina gets control of the Palazzo and Lorenzo ends up being hung from a hook in Sabina's study, a gag in his mouth and a leather strap separating his balls, so that Sabina can choose which of them to flick, at whatever time of the day she chooses to flick it. His penis is attached by two fine gold chains, one to the mouse of her computer, the other to the keyboard – that way it inclines towards her every movement, like a sunflower following the sun, traces every word she writes at the very moment that she writes it. Eventually he will learn to understand, the only way a man can, what it is she is thinking. When she wants him to come – and his coming is entirely at her discretion and bidding – she types the word come on to her screen and he comes. Sometimes she opens her mouth to swallow him while he's coming and she's working, sometimes she doesn't. He, of course, because he is blindfolded as well, has no way of knowing whether her mouth is open or not. But if he guesses wrongly, or misses, he is beaten.

He knows he cannot cry out or otherwise make a sound. If he otherwise makes a sound he knows Sabina will cut his tongue out.

But not even that will give Sabina any real pleasure. Whatever she does to a man, still, in Wittgensteins's words – *Ich kann mich nicht selber aufwecken* – she cannot awaken her true self. Her dream body, her *Traumleib*, moves, but the real her does not stir. *Mein wirklicher rührt sich nicht.*

Something stirs in her panties. Is it real or is it a dream? She puts a hand under her skirt. It is real. She is wet. Thinking of Wittgenstein always causes her to wet her panties.

Perhaps tomorrow she will stab Lorenzo in his heart with the silver knife she uses to open envelopes. Perhaps that will bring her out of her dream body, back to herself.

She will see.

Tomorrow.

The End.

'Where I think it falls down,' Frank says, 'is in the characterisation of Lorenzo.'

Yes, they are talking. Just. But they are not talking in bed. As the scene of the shame and the incursion, bed is out. They are in a gay vegetarian restaurant of D's choosing, overlooking the bay, watching the sun go out. Frank has not told her that the Melissa Paul who wrote *Coming Is Too Good For You* is the same Melissa who booted him out of his house. You can tell too much sometimes. He simply admits to knowing something of the plot, having found the lurid treatise on top of a paper towel dispenser in the lavatory of an inter-city express train.

'How long ago was that?'

'A year or two ago.'

'Where was the train going?'

'Oh, I don't know. Glasgow, or somewhere.'

'I don't believe you. You wouldn't be going to Glasgow. I've heard you on the subject of Glasgow. And if it was a year or two ago you wouldn't have remembered the characters' names. I bet you're a secret porno reader. I bet you've got piles of the stuff at home.'

Too true. He smiles weakly. Is he prim? Why does he hate being implicated in the universal comedy of wanking? It's the breeziness. That's what it is, it's the chirruping. Once she'd got over the shock of being crept in upon and had returned her bedwear to something like its proper order, D had defended stoutly her right to paddle in her snatch since there was nothing on the telly and he was out mooning in the park, watching men playing with their boats. Frank had no attitude to that other than surprise that Melissa Paul's prose could so much as remind her that she had a snatch.

Don't take a tone with me, D had warned him.

A tone, he'd told her, was the last thing he was taking. He was all for making oneself feel sick with porno.

Who, she'd wanted to know, was making themselves sick? She was enjoying her body, that's what she was doing. She was getting to know herself. She was treating herself lovingly. It was a change – and she had Melissa Paul, among others, to thank for that – to read eroticism that had women's parts in view.

Bully for you, he'd told her, but he didn't see why her sex had to go in for all that flowery self-discovery vocabulary when they were in it for the debasement, just as the blokes were.

Debasement! Did he say debasement?

He most certainly did: wanking debases you, that was his

point; wanking debases you, that's why you do it. And pornography – while he's on the subject – degrades you, and that's why you do that. Sex and death, D, sex and death. I'll jump into the flames with you any time, D. I'll lift your apron and describe whereupon I look and we can go to hell together, but don't pretend we're doing it *to get to know our bodies better.*

This is how they have got on to Lorenzo. Frank reckons that he's the one who's getting the most out of this revisionist fantasy – Lorenzo, the man, yet again the man, just as in all those instances of pornography that Ms Paul is meant to be revising. What does it change, hanging him up, dividing his balls, stuffing his mouth, pulling his dick, computerising his come, cutting out his tongue, sticking him with a paper knife? It's just the same old porno in a nutshell. If Melissa Paul thinks she's reversed the formula she's mistaken. Death of the man has always been what it's about.

D shakes her head. She is got up like Jessye Norman doing Madame Butterfly tonight, with chopsticks in her hair. When she shakes her head Frank has to look out for his eyes.

'You're just trying to provoke me,' she says. 'First of all you've made that up about Lorenzo. No one sticks him. She just hangs him where she can get at him. It's a joke. You're always saying you want jokes. Now you've got one. Hang the bloke up where you can get at his dick when *you* need it. A woman's joke, Frank. And for me, whatever you say, a nice change from the usual splayed female. Death of the man is *not* what it's always been about. The carcass is invariably a she, Frank. It's always a woman left shagged on the slab.'

'Yeah, but that leaves out where the man is and what he's doing when he's reading about it.'

'On his knees, with his dick out.'

'Exactly. In the supplicant's position, with his back to danger, with his cheeks red, with his eyes popping, with his self-esteem shot to pieces, with a pain about to arrow through his anus and his testicles, with his heart leaping out of his throat, with hot sperm about to jerk through the hole in his cock and mess up the carpet, and with the knowledge that in thirty seconds from now he'll be wishing he were dead. Tell me about degradation of women, D. Tell me that it's time a man was made to suffer.'

'Who wants a man to suffer? Most of us just want him to give us a decent shag. If he'd get up off his knees for five minutes we'd all be in with a better chance.'

'If you don't want anyone to suffer, what do you want porno for?'

'Pleasure, Frank.'

She isn't serious. He can't get her to be serious.

'Are you telling me that when I burst in upon you this afternoon you were experiencing nothing but pleasure, sheer contextless unassociated free-floating keep-your-nose-out never-met-you-before born-yesterday pleasure?'

'Why do you find that so hard to believe?'

He can't do it. However much she deserves it, he can't give it her between the eyes, he can't ask her why, if she was experiencing nothing but pleasure, she looked so much as though she were in pain, why she lay in the bed like a shot elephant, why she made noises like a dying family of chaffinches, why she was sobbing, why she was hissing, why the pillow was dyed cheese yellow by her perspiration, why there was so much tension in her body that the glass in the hotel windows was shrieking.

She's no use to him. She isn't serious. She isn't like Mel who, although she has resented having to write her crap as much as he's resented having to watch his, has always known that you can't do porno unless it tends to death. Mel's a moralist. That's why she hung Lorenzo. That's why she kicked Frank out. A moralist can't live with another person.

Nor can another person live with a moralist. Least of all if that other person is also a moralist. But of what possible use to you is someone who is so little of a moralist that she thinks she's covered sex when she calls it pleasure – and this in the face of the fact that she doesn't have any sex – and who won't admit that a wank is an act of wilful damage to the self? What's the matter with this D? Is she Dutch, or something?

The arrival of cappuccinos saves him from having to tell her why it's hard to believe anybody who doesn't own up to the universal blackness. D has been to this restaurant before. They do wonderful cappuccinos. Organic.

It feels like a secret. Just something shared by the gay community of Torquay and D. Where to get the best camp cappuccino in the south west.

A waiter with a face pitted like the moon dances the coffee to their table. Mops up the spillage in Frank's saucer. Sugar for her, sugar for him? White, brown, raw, lump? Oh, he's forgotten the mints. Away he goes, back he comes. Mints for him, mints for her. How he laughs when D makes a grab for Frank's. Now, now. How he knows about greed.

It's D who notices what's been done to the cappuccinos. 'If I were you . . .' she warns, using the side of her hand to tip back Frank's chin as it's on its way to the cup.

'What? Is there something in it?'

Frank once belonged to a gentleman's club in W1. Under a high Mediterraneran blue ceiling the waiters spat freely into your coffee. Gay merchant seamen, ex, most of them were. At home only in a world without women. But with an inexplicable grudge against toffs. That was the reason he relinquished his membership in the end. He couldn't justify a thousand a year for the privilege of swallowing marine faggots' spittle.

'Look,' D says. She shows him hers. No chocolate has been sprinkled on hers. 'Now look at yours.' On Frank's a small and quite perfect brown circle, painstakingly, even artistically, formed.

He peers from her cup to his and back again. 'Chocolate.'

'Keep going.'

'Me chocolate yes, you chocolate no.'

'Keep going.'

At the best of times he hates tests. But tonight, after she has failed all his . . . 'What are you showing me?'

'Well, there's no accounting for taste, but I suppose you'd have to call it a mark of their admiration for you.'

He narrows his eyes and stiffens his shoulders, a diver preparing a leap into the foaming ring of chocolate. But he can't jump. He shakes his head. 'I'm sorry, I don't get it. Unless it's supposed to be a bull's eye.'

'Why would they give you a bull's eye?'

'Why would they give me anything?'

She throws him one of her waiting for a heckler to hang himself looks, lips cockled, neck sprung, what are we going to do with someone as slow as you. Wait no longer, is the answer. 'It's an anus, dickhead,' she shows him. 'They've made you a sweet little milk and chocolate anus.'

Have they? He peers in. Is that an anus? How would he know? How would she know, come to that?

Sounds of strangulated manly mirth emanate from the kitchen. Frank looks up in time to see the waiter with the cratered complexion peering through the porthole in the swinging door, gasping for air.

It's an anus.

But that's just for starters, isn't it? The next part of the joke will come when Frank lowers his lips to it. Gets froth on his lips. Browns that nose.

He pushes the cappuccino from him. Spoilsport. 'Did you put them up to this?' he asks.

'Why would I do that?'

'Why would *they* do *that?*'

'Maybe they fancy you, Frank.'

'Poofs don't fancy me. Poofs have never fancied me. They never did when I was young and rangy; why should they bother now I'm old and slack?'

'Maybe you excited them with your description of what you look like tugging at your todger. Maybe they found the picture of you on your knees with your cheeks red irresistible.'

It *was* her. Getting her own back. For being found in bed in the middle of the afternoon cheerfully re-discovering her own body parts. She's paying him out, measure for measure, diddle for diddle. But just in case it wasn't her, or wasn't *only* her, he requests that she sees to the bill. He'll put in his share. He'd rather not be involved in the transaction, that's all. In fact he'll wait for her in the street.

'Fancy you . . . !' she says, as they walk home. 'Fancy you being embarrassed!'

They return to her room to find a tribute to the incomparable Ella Fitzgerald on the telly. They keep the box going twenty-four hours so they can walk in and out of it. Wallpaper. Ella's almost finished, but they just make *Every Time We Say Goodbye*. They smooch. One hand on the small of the back, the other hand grasping a bottle of brown ale by the neck. Frank dodging the Cio-Cio-San chopsticks which protrude dangerously from D's coiffure. Moonlight on Tor Bay. They die, little by little. The fat lady sings and it's all over.

They both know it's all over. Or rather, what they both know is that it's never going to start.

He's too heavy for her. Too touchy, too censorious, too pedantic. She says tomato and he says she's missed the point.

And she's not serious enough for him. Sure, she's a comedian, but a comedian, of all people, you expect to be serious. There's not the whiff of death about her that he needs in a woman. You can't smell the grave when she laughs and you don't fear for your life when you fuck her. Of course he wouldn't know what you feel when you fuck her. But then that too is part of the problem. It's not the fuck he misses, it's the trip to the underworld that accompanies it.

She has to be in St Austell for a show tomorrow night. He'll drop her there and call it quits. He'll have a few days on his own in Cornwall, remembering the time he spent there with Mel, going placid amid the din, then he'll have to think about returning to town, dumping his stuff at the Groucho, going round estate agents, finding an apartment with enough plugs, all that. Charming, to have come to this at his age. Thanks, Mel. Thanks, girls.

And thanks, boys?

Back in his own room – for that's the rule: beddy-bye byes time and he has to tinkle back to his – he frets about the scummy chocolate anus bobbing on the surface of his cappuccino. What if it wasn't D's idea? What if the gay caballeros were whispering him a message on their own say-so? Passing him their calling card because they believed he would not be altogether unreceptive to it?

What he told D was true. He had never been an object of deviant attention. He had so *not* been an object of deviant attention, in fact, that it sometimes hurt him, not where he was hungering or needy, let it be clearly understood, but in the area of cold commodity valuation, in his idea of himself as an aesthetic object. As far as conscious desire went – as far as *his* conscious desire went – he had never come close to understanding what anyone could want with something that didn't have a cunt. He had no principled objection; he just couldn't see the point. But he is a little more than half as old as the century, five per cent of the millennium; lay twenty men his age end to end and there's a wait before William the

Conqueror arrives – you can't go all those years and not occasionally wonder about yourself. As when a pitted waiter sculpts a chocolate anus in your coffee, for example, or when you dream of having someone's penis in your mouth.

He has had the penis dream twice that he knows of. He's prepared to accept that he may have had it more than twice and has wiped the memory. It is always possible, though he thinks unlikely, that he dreams it every night and wipes it every morning. More pertinent to his state of mind is his fear (if fear it really is) that he is about to have it again. This is an entirely rational expectation, quite separate from the cappuccino incident, based on his conviction that the two dreamed penises were in fact the same penis, that they were not fictional penises but strict representations of an actual penis, and that he has seen the actual penis of which they were representations dripping shower water only recently in the bathroom of an undistinguished cottage in Lynton, unless it was Lynmouth, but in a place he had no right to be in either way. When Frank says he dreams of putting someone's penis in his mouth he means he dreams of putting Kurt's penis in his mouth.

There is a very ordinary explanation for this. Though it is based on a most wonderful fact. Referring only to aspect now, and setting everything to do with emission and flavour aside, Frank and Kurt have identical penises. Alike in the challenge presented by their length, in the consideration shown by their thickness, in the divine harmony suggested by their curvature and colouration, the penises of Kurt Bryll and Frank Ritz could have been swapped in the night, whether by a skilled surgeon or a bad fairy, without either party, or any party to either party, being the wiser in the morning. In the parlance of the times when Frank and Kurt routinely had their penises out in company, their own grandmothers wouldn't have known the difference. Speaking ordinarily, then, when Frank dreams of sucking Kurt's penis, he is only dreaming of sucking his own. And there's nothing deviant about that.

What an ordinary explanation fails to honour, though, is the immensity of the grief Frank experienced when he awoke from the dreams and found his mouth empty. The first time, he was sleeping alone. He knew the minute he came out of the dream that he was mistaken, that the bed was cold around him, that he had been on an exciting and unaccustomed journey and would have to lie there a long time to recover from it. He had loved the sensation, he couldn't deny that. He had loved opening his mouth and receiving. The texture of what he had received shocked him, but the experience of recipience itself shocked him even more. This was what was new – opening, waiting, submitting, being filled, taking not giving. Sucking, not pushing. Very interesting. Very. Whatever else he was going to get up to that day, or for the rest of his life come to that, there was no question of him allowing his mouth to be used in quite that fashion again. No sir. Absolument pas. So he'd had a contrary experience – so what? You can't pursue every fugitive bodily whim that seizes you in your sleep. He'd murdered in his dreams on occasions. That too had left him feeling pretty good. Was he to arm himself with an axe and get cracking as a consequence? No. No to the mouth. He was sure about that, but lying there in the penumbral aftermath of the dream, he was sad about it too. Very.

The second flight from conformity was even more turbulent. Mel was with him that night. What had been given him in the dream he never remembered, only what was taken away; so the dream and the waking spilled dangerously into each other. The dream had done with him, wanted to beach him, wanted to spew him out. His desperation to stay in it became the nightmare. There'd been a dick in his mouth and now it was gone. So where was it? He writhed in the bed, scouring Mel's body with his lips. He was bereft, but he was also angry. Where was the bastard thing? His mouth found her belly, coils of snapping hair, the swampy moistness of that bourne from which no traveller wishes to return. It had to be down there, there was no other place it could be. But it was gone. Forever gone. Nothing was down there. Nothing but loss. He hung from the dream like an injured climber clinging to a rock face. If he woke, he fell. If he woke, the person by his side fell with him. For she too had been brought into the shadowland of loss. The dick that was missing was missing between them. Their child. He cried to dream again.

She woke irritably, to find him the wrong way round in the bed, mewling. He lied about the cause. He said he'd been dreaming a death. He would rather not say whose. He preferred not to talk about it.

Hardly surprising. What if he'd been dreaming about the death in his heart of heterosexual love?

For one whole week he sat abstractedly in his office, surrounded by his neutered machines, unable to push out any work that pleased him. Had there been a litmus test for these things he would have braved the doctor's surgery, shown him his tongue, and allowed science to decide. Blue you're straight, pink you're gay. When he finally ventured into the waking world it was with no other intention but to look at men.

But what was he meant to look *for*? He knew what aroused him in a woman. Everything aroused him in a woman. When it came to women he was in the last stages of chronic erotolepsy. Certifiable. For the thoughts he harboured about the tension of a skirt across a woman's buttocks, for the labour he expended discerning the impression of a nipple through a bodice, a blouse, two cardigans and a winter coat, he could be locked away for life. Now his dreams told him he was a lunatic in quite another direction, and yet he didn't have the first idea where to direct his eyes. Muscles? Shoulders? Waists? Loins? Or was it a warm personality he was meant to be winkling out? What did daytime telly girls say they looked for in a man – a sense of humour? a tight bum?

On a blustery November Friday in London he set his senses loose. He strode along Oxford Street, eyeballing policemen, postmen, traffic wardens, bus drivers, cab drivers, van drivers, street-sweepers, builders, newspaper vendors, dispatch riders, delivery men, window cleaners, hot chestnut sellers, mock auctioneers, fly-by-night perfume pedlars, shoppers, husbands, lovers, fathers even; he sauntered through Covent Garden, sticky-beaking street clowns, jugglers, wine-waiters, silversmiths, potters, Africans, vegetarians, cheese-eaters, overdressers jabbering in fashion alleys; he took a cab to the Chelsea Barracks to get a load of dough-faced corporals in berets, knobby-headed privates in weekend civvies, lads with rifles at the ready, inchoate ruffians with hard chests and glistening moustaches of the sort Lawrence liked sitting next to in trains and who might just have given poor unconnected Forster the thick ear he forever craved; then up to Knightsbridge for the moneyed tourists, the Germans in their animal skins, the Iranians with their black-masked trains behind, the easily bruised Frenchmen in their existential scarfs – stereotypes, as D would have called them, but what was he to do? he didn't design or dress them. He didn't want to undress them either, that was the outcome of the exercise. Not with his eyes, not with his heart, not with his dick, was he attracted to a single person of his own sex.

Only to their wives and girlfriends.

Sitting in a cab in a traffic jam in Battersea he watched a

group of the spunk-filled body-built labouring young patch a six-inch hole in the road, one on a drill, another on a shovel, another in the cab of a heavy roller. They jerked and twitched and whistled and grinned and bawled and rattled and drove and shovelled and shook and larked and slipped and yanked and box-kicked and cuffed and goosed and nutted and scratched and yawned and farted and jerked and twitched . . . Sport with them? Might just as well, Frank thought, go skylarking with a colony of mud crabs.

Barely a woman went by whom he did not consider from some angle or imagine in some contortion. Neither decrepitude nor derangement stood in the way of his passing fancy. If she were old he re-conceived her young; if she were disordered he reassembled her. But for the male animal – whatever the age, whatever the colour, whatever the condition – he had no possessive or regenerative instinct. As they were they were. They were no business of his.

And neither, clearly, were his dreams. He read some Edmund White, just to be on the safe side. But the high falutin' squiffiness, all the talk of the beautiful and the brave, and then straight into the old brown crack, only confirmed what he suspected. He wasn't gay. He didn't have what it took.

And now?

Say ah! and he'd still turn the litmus paper blue, he's sure of that. But he has to concede that there's a pattern to his socio-sexual preferences that isn't all it should be. He's too deferential. There's too much docility in him. When he kisses the likes of Josh Green, he lets them make the running. They envelop *him*. When he smooches with D she hoists him up to her level. He allows whores to take liberties with him. He adopts the submissive posture. His recollections of Mel's scarlet prose disturb him. It's all very well laughing at Lorenzo; the truth is he, Frank, wouldn't say no if some

Sabina with a throbbing cunt offered to chain his dick to the mouse of her computer. Not say no! He'd kill for the chance. Better still, *be* killed for the chance. Watching a late-night telly programme sympathetic to perverts, he has learnt that sado-masochists divide themselves into tops and bottoms. He's a bottom. That's what the gay vegetarians had intended by their mooning cappuccino – not that the bottom was his tendency, but that the bottom was him. He'd misread the nature of their gift. They'd presented him with his portrait – that was all.

Now see the advantage of age. Discover a submissive tendency in yourself when you're seventeen and you have plenty to worry about. How will you describe yourself to your future wife? How will you be able to beat your children without wishing it were the other way round? Which clubs will you join? But when you're one-twentieth as old as the millennium you don't have any such anxieties. So you prefer the lower bunk. Who cares? What bearing can that have on the little that's left of your life? Lie where you like! If Frank feared there was any real danger that he'd sink into senility – senility proper – in black stockings and a pinny, doing the dishes for a touch-me-not whore in a brushed nylon housecoat, that'd be another matter; but it would be with the housework as it had been with the ogling of male bodies in Covent Garden – he wouldn't know where to start.

So nothing's wrong, that's where, on the fringes of sleep, on his last night in the next room to the fat comedian, he is content to leave it. He is not in any danger. All's well. Nothing's up. It can't possibly do him anything but good, though, to be reminded of a time when he cracked the whip, when he was indubitably the top, and had the sovereignty not just of one bottom but of two, to prove it.

Little Cleverley it is, then.

TEN

'ʼLO, FRANK. YOU all right?'

He has no sooner parked his Saab in the old familiar ferry car-park, locked, stretched, and once breathed the fishy air, than he is greeted by the owner of The Poldark Inn parking her car. When was he last here? Seven years ago? Eight? Yet she hails him as though she'd pulled him a pint only the night before.

Time moves differently down here.

'You got a room for tonight, Vera?'

She'll check for him. It's a busy weekend coming. The last before the kids go back to school. The last weekend of emmet hell before the better class, freer-spending, childless mob descend.

It all comes flooding back to him, not only how differently time moved down here, but how it was mapped by the temperaments of the tourists. Invasion was always the name of the game, rape and pillage however you cut the deck; but at least when the marauding underclass had gone, in a last explosion of flying pasties and jemmied tills and howling snot-strewn babies, you could lie back and let the middle classes walk all over you in soft-soled cabin-creepers.

Is that why he'd enjoyed it down here — because it was a submissive, masochistic place?

Hang on, though. He hadn't enjoyed it down here. It was Mel who had enjoyed it down here.

Mel who'd found it. Mel who'd wanted it. Mel who'd allowed him to join her only on the understanding that he'd go quietly.

The only part he'd unambiguously enjoyed was Clarice.

But then Mel had found her as well.

It didn't answer to the truth of things, though, to separate Clarice, however she came about, from the place she came about in. Wasn't there a sense in which Clarice *was* Little Cleverley? L'état, c'est moi; Nellie, I am Heathcliffe — that sort of sense. And yet Clarice wasn't in the tiniest bit submissive or masochistic. She had a genius for acquiescence, which is quite different.

It's her acquiescent nature that leads Frank to believe she will still be here. Elkin the slate painter will never leave Little Cleverley, never has left Little Cleverley, not even for a long weekend. He made it to the outskirts of Plymouth once and immediately turned back. Couldn't hack the crowds. Clarice has been acquiescing to Elkin, on a personal as well as on a business level, for too long to think of leaving him now. Only if Elkin's dead is there any chance Clarice won't be here. And even if Elkin's dead she will still go on running the Slate Gallery, because that's what Elkin will have wanted her to do. She will never run out of original Elkins to sell; when Frank was last here it was Elkin's boast that he had two hundred thousand slates painted, in reserve stock, as a safeguard against a sudden loss of limb or inspiration. He was getting on, moving into stroke territory, the country of the blind, arthritisville. He could wake up one morning and just not want to do it any more. Enough with the badgers and the blue tits. Enough with the fucking sailing ships. So while he could, while he still had the stomach for it, he was knocking off one hundred and fifty slates a day, which was a third more than he needed to keep up with what the shop could shift even at the height of the season. In the event of his death, all Clarice would have to do was drill the holes, thread the cords, and hang the art. She was looked after beyond the grave. All this for the small price of acquiescing to a tedious old fart who sat humming in shorts and a smock the whole day, with his brushes pushed into his beard, breaking slates into unusual shapes and colouring them with sufficient skill for the form of a seal or a puffin to disclose itself to the astigmatic crap-watching clamjamphrie from Wolverhampton who trooped through their gallery with neither hope nor purpose for seven months of the wheeling year.

Yes, it is Clarice's fate to be here forever. Like the rocks beneath, the poor bitch.

But where is she? He's been here ten minutes and already he's seen half the village. From the window of the Slate Gallery you have a fair view of the car-park, and an even better one of the Poldark, and wasn't Clarice always at her window? Is she frightened to come out? Is she reluctant to see herself in Frank's ringing armour, for fear the mirror cracks?

Yes, Vera can do him a room, since it's him. No Mel? No Mel with him?

No, Vera. No Mel.

She all right?

Yes, Vera. You know Mel.

She laughs. She does. The bugger!

That's Mel who's the bugger. Not that Vera isn't a bugger herself. The bugger!

They're all incorrigible buggers, those who have anything to do with Little Cleverley. Emmets if they're visiting, buggers if they stay. Frank suddenly feels homesick for the place. Maybe he liked being here more than he's remembered. The embrace of community, that's what he misses. Being a bugger in the eyes of those who know and understand you. Never to be forgotten. Remember that old bugger Frank? *Requiescat in pace*, the bugger!

He should go out on to the cliffs. That's what Mel would insist they do if she were here. And that's what she would want him to do solus. Cliffs first, Frank. Behold the wonder. But he can't face it. What if there's a bench out there with a dead girl's name on it?

If he plunges in, towards the nautical riggers and all the other emmet memorabilia shops, he will pass the Slate Gallery. Then it will look to himself as though he's come on only one errand. And if he should happen to be wrong in his calculations as to Clarice's genius for acquiescence and she is no longer here, will he then turn tail and run? Wouldn't it be better not to know for a while, isn't there a virtue in keeping oneself in suspense?

A light rain has begun to fall. The first Frank has seen since he was expelled from his home. He had forgotten rain. Good to see it again. It cheers him up. Soon it will be dark at four in the afternoon. It brightens the coach parties and crap-watchers up too. There's nothing for them to do in Little Cleverley when the sun shines, other than walk. Now at least they can huddle in the doorways of pasty huts, drip on to postcards, and complain. As though obeying one universal impulse, all at once the rain falls, the holiday gods exhale their watery relief, and every single emmet who was previously in shorts and taupe slip-ons is suddenly anoraked, hooded, zipped, toggled, as though for the Antarctic. Where do they carry these anoraks, Frank wonders. Where do they buy them from in the first place? And are they themselves paid, like sportsmen, to bear the makers' names and logos, the brands of racing cars and running shoes, across their chests? They are such mysteries to him, these creatures of the dreadful towns. That's when they're not standing at street corners in the whoring night, nodding their cunts at his car. *Then*, he has a better understanding of who they are. Or at least what they're for.

This will be a bad hour for Clarice. Come the rain, the gallery fills, slates get knocked off the walls, and Elkin comes out to perform. This particular colour, he tells them, I get from mixing soot with urine. They all retch. Slate of the sort I paint on, he tells them, is half a million years old – so you're not just getting a painting, you're getting a genuine antique. An old master. They all laugh. Clarice retches. They hand her wet money. They don't understand the principle of change. They ask who does the painting, though they've just watched Elkin paint. They huddle round to observe her wrap a slate. Look ma, a woman wrapping a slate! She is a heritage object, a rural craftsperson, a holiday treat, a goody. She is lucky they haven't eaten her.

Frank is lucky because he has.

He retrieves an umbrella from the boot of his car, says 'You all right?' to Adrian the second-hand fruiterer, walks in the direction of the harbour, then shoots up the hill by the side of the church. St Poldark's. This is going to be hard for him, though not as hard as the cliff would have been. This is the terrace in which he and Mel had their holiday cottage. And there *is* their holiday cottage, with someone else's curtains hanging in the window – lace, to add insult to injury – and one of Elkin's slate houseplates on the front door. A fieldmouse with its tail curled into a number 9. Painted in soot and urine.

Frank has no right to think of Number 9 as *their* cottage. It never was *their* cottage. Mel had bought it with her porno-earnings – she was writing and selling faster then, when the porn came softer and had happy endings – as a hole for her to bolt to from their house in London. Not a retreat, but an alternative. Not a holiday cottage either, originally. She meant to live here forever. To get away from him and his noise for all time. She'd quietened him down considerably after the ruse of getting him to fuck her every minute that God sent, but he was still too clamorous in his appetites. And too brutal. Still a man, in short. Little Cleverley was her last throw of the man-free romance dice. She'd been visiting the place for years, drawn to its secret coves and heaving seas, and of course to its Daphne du Maurier associations. 'All that lesbian stuff, you mean,' Frank said. See the problem? He couldn't leave her to her yearnings. She had porno waiting for her on her desk each morning and porno lying next to her in bed each night.

She relented in the end. He could come down with her if he agreed to go quietly.

'Last night I dreamt I went to Little Cleverley again,' he said.

'That's not going quietly,' she warned him.

She packed vases and photo frames and gardening gloves and walking boots and notepads and bottles of ink into the boot of the car. He'd wanted to bring his machines, but she forbade them. He reminded her he couldn't do without a television. Make it small, then, she told him. And silent. He spent two thousand pounds on a television he could wear on his wrist and hold to his ear. It was no way to run a column. But he suffered the inconvenience, for her.

He stands in the rain, looking into the cottage garden, and sees Mel, still warm from the bed, still in her going quietly flesh-pink sarong with never-never Japanese flowers printed on it, still with duck feathers from her pillows in her hair, sitting out in the early morning with her pad on her lap, sucking up the first rays of the sun, marvelling at the light.

On those mornings she *was* the light. Flowers opened to her. Seagulls went quiet in her presence. At the first sound of her tread the worms came up out of the soil and showed her their backs. Stroke us, Mel. And she did.

''Lo, Frank. All right?'

It takes him a moment to realise that the voice is coming from the bedroom window of the cottage next door. Virna's place.

'You still here, Virna?'

'Where'd you think I'd be, Frank?'

'Somewhere wild, Virna.'

'Me?' She laughs. Just dangerously enough to show him she hasn't changed. 'Little Cleverley's wild enough for me. Mel not with you?'

No, Virna. Mel not with me.

'She all right?'

What did she think? She knew Mel, didn't she.

She sure did. The bugger! They'd been pals, briefly, Mel and Virna. Mel had encouraged her, when she was dithering about ditching her husband, to dither no more. They'd met on the cliffs. Mel was sitting on one rock, writing about wet panties; Virna was sitting on another, sketching the sea. They were making each other's art. What struck Mel was how angry Virna's work was. She never felt she had finished a sketch until she had obliterated every memory of white from the page in a fury of charcoal. She seemed to see only black oceans. The other thing that struck Mel was how close to the surface of her skin Virna's blood was. Even on the coolest afternoons, she boiled. Mel could feel the heat coming off her. It wasn't the change of life that was doing it, it was the sameness of life. Virna lived on the edge of Bodmin Moor, washed shirts, made jam, saw to the flowers in her church, and accompanied her husband, a squeaky counter-tenor, when he sang away from home with the St Breward Choral

Society. She claimed she went because she loved the music and enjoyed the coach trips, but Mel deduced that she went because she was suspicious of the contraltos. She had a purple, crumpled face which crumpled further when she addressed the subject of adultery. There was always a lot of talk of adultery in Little Cleverley. Adultery was what they did there. It was a coastal thing. As an inland woman, Virna abominated adultery. Adulterers, she told Mel, as they sat on adjoining rocks and paused from their work, should be flogged . . . And then left to bleed to death . . . And then buried in unmarked graves . . .

'It's only a matter of time,' Mel told Frank. 'All she needs is a cottage.'

Then, quite out of the blue, the cottage next door came up, Mel mentioned it to Virna, Virna moved in her things, and overnight became coastal.

She raised the heels of her shoes but remained in every other aspect of her appearance, including the crumpled face, a shirt-washing, church-going Cornishwoman. The heels were all it took. The heels and a certain way of swinging her abdomen when she walked through the village. Within a week of her moving in, there was not a man in Little Cleverley that wasn't hers for the asking. The illusion was too fascinating. The contrast between what they saw and what they got – like cracking open a crab and finding the flesh of pawpaw – drove them all to madness.

'I suppose you want some now, as well,' Mel said to Frank.

'Virna! Do me a favour.' But he was only human. When a plain woman well past her prime starts swinging her abdomen, of course you want some.

That it's a sort of death dance only intensifies your interest. You want some quick. This was what lay behind Frank's surprise to find her here. Could she still be going? Was she still managing to hang out against age, against the suck of respectability, against re-retirement in Bodmin? Can she still swing that abdomen?

All that's visible of her from her doll's house window is her purple crumpled face.

'You here for long, Frank?'

'I don't know, Virna. A day or two.'

'Be in The Poldark tonight?'

Virna's first lover was a part-time barman at The Poldark. In the daytime an electrician. They'd opened their account in his van on the way back from a darts match in St Austell. 'I could die for you, maid,' he'd told her, as she gave herself to him on a bed of cables in the the back of the van, threw wide her legs at last and to hell with what they did to adulterers. 'And I could die for you, Vernon,' she told him. So determined were they to die for each other that they fell asleep with Vernon's stubby dick still inside her, careless of who might find them, in a lay-by on the A390, right by the Little Cleverley turn-off. 'But you know, Mel,' she declared later, 'in the morning you want to live again!'

Will he be in The Poldark tonight? He'll be staying there, but will he be in the bar, that's what Virna means. Will he be joining in the singing? 'Going Up Camborne Hill Coming Down'? 'Why, why, why, Delilah'? He can't say. That will depend on Clarice.

By the time Mel had finished helping inland women from as far away as Liskeard and Redruth to ditch their no-good husbands and *de facto*s by finding them a coastal cottage close to hers, the entire terrace had become a sanctuary for absconding beldams. Seven fishermen's cottages, all but one of them occupied by rusting matrons looking for their last good time. Or more often, their first good time. The odd one out being Mel herself, who, having got rid of Frank by proxy, as it were, still hadn't got rid of him in the flesh.

'Ironic,' he observed, 'that I should be the only man in residence.'

'Don't count your chickens,' she warned him.

The terrace became a haunted little place. Not only the souls of the originally rejected husbands, but those of subsequently rejected lovers, flitted here, tapped on the window panes, pleaded to be let back in. They would come wandering late at night, in the heart-ache hours, as silent as wraiths. Sometimes, as Mel and Frank were sitting reading by the fire, they would see a face appear at the window, look in distractedly, fragment with pain, and then vanish. Sometimes, the light-sleeping Mel would jump up suddenly in bed, disturbed by the sounds of low male weeping in the street below.

Magic was afoot. One woman going to the bad attracts its own sort of curiosity among the men of a village. But a row of them raised a peculiar ire in the breasts of the jilted. What had happened wasn't private, wasn't individually about them. Someone was casting spells. The finger pointed to the outsider, Melissa Paul. The witch. And the village knew what to do to witches. Rubbish suddenly began to appear in her garden. Suggestive, systematic rubbish. Mel would come out in the early morning to stroke the worms and there it would be – the masticated carcass of a chicken, bones, gristle, parson's nose, the liver and the kidneys still in their plastic bag; a party-pack not unlike the one Frank's girlfriend number one had posted off to Frank's girlfriend number two, only without the registered envelope. Then her cat disappeared. For a while she was frightened to be out late on her own. The village lights went off at twelve. Then the glorious silent starry blackness that stirred her soul became her enemy. A car drove her into a hedge. A can of beer was thrown at her from an unknown window. She was threatened. She was mugged. Once, outside the cottage, a holiday maker walking her dog was punched to the ground and damn-near raped. In the dark the woman resembled her. A day later a card was posted through her letter box — NEXT TIME IT WON'T BE AN EMMET.

'Look on the bright side,' Frank said, forgetting to go quietly. 'They've accepted you.'

There was no point calling the police. The husband she had encouraged Virna to leave behind in Bodmin was a sergeant in the force.

Clarice was not among those Mel enticed to the terrace. Clarice was well established as a woman going to the bad on her own terms long before Mel turned up. And those terms did not include dumping your previous life and running for it. Why so emotional? Why be so either-orish about it? Clarice had no ambition to expire in the back of someone's van in a lay-by on the A390. She wanted to laugh, not die. But then she had Elkin, and as long as Elkin had a pot of paint to piss in, his own tankard waiting for him at The Poldark, and Clarice to stick the price stickers on the slates and man the till, he left her alone. Elkin was the means to her freedom, not an obstacle to it.

The one time Elkin did play up, he delivered Clarice clean into their hands. Mel's and Frank's hands, that is. Hers and his. His and hers. In truth no one knew, the time Elkin did play up and subjected Clarice to either-orishness, whose hands were whose. And no one cared.

Did Elkin blow because he had reached the point where he could take no more, or was it a discrete one-off explosion, caused by the gossip that followed Clarice's interpretation of Molly Bloom at the annual Little Cleverley Dramatic Society summer gala night? Impossible to say. What's jealousy, anyway, if it isn't overheated love? The pan might boil over occasionally, but you can't blame the flame for the soup.

Elkin didn't see Clarice's Molly Bloom with his own eyes. It was his domino night at The Poldark. And he probably wouldn't have gone to see her had he been free. He never particularly liked going anywhere that he had to wash the paint out of his beard for, or change out of his shorts and smock for; but he especially never liked trudging up the hill to the village hall, where he had to sit on uncomfortable seats and listen to something arty. He made his own art. Out of soot, urine and slate. And when you've made art all day you want a break from it at night. For Frank, who watched crap all day, it was of course different. As it was for Mel, who wrote crap all day. For them the trudge up the hill was nothing but pleasure and relief. As was Clarice's Molly Bloom, whether or not she put in twice as many yes's as James Joyce had already given her.

Discussing the performance afterwards, Frank reckoned it was Clarice's Cornishness that made her Molly Bloom unlike any he had seen before. The Cornish talk as though they have shingle in their mouths. You hear the tide pulling at the beach. You hear the whole gravelly content of the ocean bottom stir and shift. In Clarice's Cornish mouth the familiar hopeful lyricism of Molly Bloom's ribaldry was ground into the cold knowingness of the mermaids, more a dare than an affirmation, the shipwreck taunts of the rock-bound sirens, whose yes I said yes I will Yes is a diabolic act of ventriloquism, your words not theirs, yes to their porphyritic breasts, yes to their perpetual seaweed-embrace, yes to death by drowning Yes.

Who was Mel to demur from that? All she cared to add was that she thought Clarice's writhings on the covered snooker table – doubling as the Bloom's lumpy old jingly bed *and* the Alameda gardens – also played their part in making hers a Molly to remember. As did the baby-dolly night attire Clarice wore, to suggest both the drawers into which the cuckolded Leopold would soon come tonguing *and* an Algeciras romper suit for kissing in, under the jasmine moon.

Perhaps she'd overdone it, that was Mel's point. Not an accusation, just a wonder. Perhaps – in the name of dramatic verisimilitude, she didn't doubt – they'd all seen too far down, then too far up, Clarice's shorty nightie.

On this, Frank kept his counsel. He'd always seen the point of Clarice. Enjoyed the sight of her flouncing through the village, her horsey face never not decipherably eye-lined and unequivocally lipsticked, her red hair flying, her small breasts pushed out, her jeans cut tight into her cunt which she bore in front of her the way some men carried their dicks, as though it were an encumbrance not of their own making or desiring, a gift to others no doubt, but a sore trial for them. When he could remember to be envious, he envied the men who were said to have enjoyed her. But she wasn't an erotic necessity to him. She was too the thing she was. Although not exactly a beauty herself, like beauties proper she left you nothing to add or subtract. If she'd suddenly gone deaf or developed a squint he might have gone for her. As she was, he didn't. But the extravagance of her Molly Bloom changed all that. The extravagance of her Molly Bloom was akin to suddenly developing a squint. She'd flung herself full length from pocket to pocket of the snooker table and shown the whole of Little Cleverley – or at least that part of it that had crowded into the village hall – the inside of her thighs, and then she'd hung over the side of the snooker table, and showed them every blue-vein of her pink-tipped conical breasts. This was the flaw that showed him his way. He could, after all, add to her. He could fuck her into better taste.

She'd gone too far, even for coastal Little Cleverley. The Yacht Club with its louche professional membership would have supported her of course, but the Yacht Club was too preoccupied with getting drunk in the evening to think of turning out to applaud James Joyce. All the next day, and all the next, those who had been there described what they had seen to those who hadn't. And then those who hadn't seen but at least had heard, described it to those who hadn't seen or heard. One or two of the older village women hissed when they passed her in the street. Even the rampaging harlots in Mel's terrace felt it behoved them to be censorious. 'I can forgive adultery,' Virna said, in a purple fluster, 'but I can't condone exhibitionism.'

'A flogging, do you think?' Frank wondered.

Virna thought about it. 'No, not a flogging,' she said. 'It would excite the men too much.'

But the men already were excited. Like Frank, there wasn't one of them who didn't see a way of adding to Clarice now. Or subtracting from her.

And Elkin? No one knew what Elkin knew. He had the gift of withdrawing into himself. He could sit smirking into his beard in his corner of The Poldark, sipping his favourite bitter from his special tankard, and not notice that Clarice was sucking off the whole pub. But the morning when Angie, who ran the National Trust Shop, popped her head around the door of the Slate Gallery and called out 'Slut!', Elkin did look up quickly from his painting. He looked up, looked around, pulled his right eyelid, greeted Angie – 'You all right, Angie?' – then looked down again.

What happened subsequently – subsequently being, by Elkin's slow-moving clock, some six hours later – Frank heard from Mel who heard it from Clarice. Mel was out on the cliffs with her notebook. She loved the early evenings of late summer, when she felt she was stealing light from the seasons. Just one more long afternoon. Just one more eked out sunset. Little Cleverley was suiting her. She was getting her quiet. Frank had never seen her look better. She clambered among the rocks in her climbing boots and her no-sexual-nonsense dungarees, the bib unfastened, her arms brown but her chest soft in a faded blue singlet. Workman below, goddess above. A sort of centaur: half brute, half angel. Maybe that was what Clarice thought when she saw her, too. Only it would have been the angel half that attracted her. She'd done with brutes.

The surprising thing from Mel's point of view was not the sight of Clarice sitting on a bench on Deadman's Point holding a handkerchief to her eye, but the sight of Clarice on the cliffs at all. You never saw Clarice up here. She didn't dress for cliff walking. Her frocks were too airy to go anywhere near the sea in. One gust of wind and she'd have been over the side. And her jeans were too tight for climbing. You could cut a deck of cards with her cunt, but you couldn't negotiate a cliff path with it. In fact she was wearing one of her airy frocks today, an ankle-length butterfly print which she'd secured to the bench with a couple of small rocks. Hence Mel's greeting. 'You look like a reluctant kite, Clarice. Is anything the matter?'

She'd thought Clarice might have been weeping. But then that could have been wishful thinking. Who doesn't want to see a slut getting her desserts? Even a pornographer craves justice. But Clarice wasn't weeping. Her eye was bruised but her soul wasn't. What she was doing, sitting weighted down on the bench, showing her long horsey nose to the sea, nursing her injury, was laughing. It was too funny, she told Mel. It was too ridiculous. Elkin angry. Elkin inflamed. You should have seen his face. All pinched like a rodent's arse. No mouth left. Just a scar where a mouth had once been. And his dick so thick. Elkin with his dick out. *In the shop.*

It was a good job she'd secured herself with rocks, else she'd have laughed herself over the edge.

What had happened was this. Elkin had suddenly and without a word of explanation risen raging from his easel, cleared the shop of stunned emmets – 'Out! Out!' he'd yelled, 'Just fuck off out of here!' – switched the OPEN sign to CLOSED, emptied the till ('Emptied the till first, note'), bent her over the counter, pulled up her dress, ripped off her pants, entered her rudely, come inside her with more despatch than he'd shown in ten years, turned her around, belted her in the eye, thrown her out of the shop, and bolted it behind her.

If it wasn't so funny she'd have been annoyed.

'And this was when?' Mel wondered.

'Just now. Half an hour ago. I'm still dripping with him. I've not been able to get back into the flat to have a shower. He's locked that as well.' Then she removed one of the rocks and lifted up her dress. 'Look, he didn't even give me my pants back.'

A high bare thigh, marbelled blue, shaved deep into the trench, then a controlled fringe of sprouting black hair, for Mel to think about.

That's a lot of Clarice, in the last few days, for Mel to think about.

They began to cackle like witches. The life of a woman, eh. The shit you had to endure. The mucoid indignities you were expected to submit to. Mel too had had her pants snatched off her in her time. Been bent over desks and benches and kitchen tables. Been kicked out of her home by crazily jealous lovers whose features had shrunk to the size of a rodent's arse. Been punched in the eye. Been forced to wander the streets unshowered while the unwanted sperm ran like treacle down her legs.

'Frank's?'

'No. Frank's the other kind of bully.'

'What kind's that?'

Did Mel want to be talking to Clarice about Frank? Was that a good idea? 'The receiving end kind.'

'Frank likes you to bully him?'

'Sort of.'

'Do you bend him over the desk?'

'Of course not. It's more mental than that. It's his mind he wants me to damage.'

'And how do you do that?'

'Well I don't do it. That's the trouble. The trouble for Frank, I mean.'

'But what would you be doing if you did do it?'

How? What? Why? Redder than the evening sky, Clarice's avidity. Hungrier than the sea.

How smart was this, Mel wondered. She rose from the bench, turning her eyes from the burn. 'You want to know what Frank wants of me?'

Silly question. Forget Molly Bloom. Molly Bloom had time only for her own itch. Clarice's unpunctuated curiosity embraced the itch of everyone she encountered. When it came to sexual tittle-tattle, she was the Jane Austen of Little Cleverley. One day a sign would be erected on the west bank of the Tamar, welcoming you to Clarice Country. In the meantime, of course Clarice wanted to know what Frank wanted of Mel.

'What I think Frank wants, and has always wanted, is to feel ill. I think he's wanted that with every woman. But I've been privileged – with me he believes he can feel more ill than he's ever felt before.'

'Ill while you're fucking?'

'In a way, yes. Ill around the whole business. Either that, or he's a moron. Only a moron, or someone who thrives on trouble, would do what he does . . .'

Thinking about her life with a moron, or someone who thrives on trouble, Mel allows her voice to drift away into the immensity of the sky, where the first of the evening stars is waiting to swallow it up.

But Clarice's needs are greater than any faraway prick of light's. 'Which is what? What does he do?'

'He invites torment. He comes at me when I'm bound to turn on him. He knows exactly what rubs me up the wrong way but he won't learn from the experience. He would rather lay himself bare to my impatience every time. That can only be because he likes the humiliation of rejection, wouldn't you say? Unless he's a moron.'

'Sounds like you make him very happy.'

Mel thinks about it. But not for long. 'No, I don't make him happy. No one can make Frank happy. It doesn't matter how hard a time I give him, it's never hard enough. I'm still not able to deliver him the final blow he craves. You know how men are always terrified that you're going to show them up in some way, embarrass them or betray them in public, make fools of them before the world? I think Frank wants me to do it once and for all. Hit him with the killer blow. Deliver him from the fear of it.'

Now it's Clarice's turn to have a little think. 'Is that what I've done to Elkin? Hit him with the killer blow?'

'You may have. Though I have to say that Elkin has always struck me as more self-sufficient than Frank. He isn't sitting there waiting for it to happen. He has other preoccupations.'

'Hasn't Frank?'

'Frank? No. Frank has only one preoccupation. Feeling ill and waiting to feel iller. The masochistic little bastard.'

'Frank's a masochist?'

'Oh God, yes.'

'So why don't you just pull out all the stops and give him what he wants?'

'Give a *man* what he wants!'

How they laughed. How they cackled.

But Mel, conscientious Mel, wasn't altogether satisfied with her answer. 'But I guess the real reason is that it isn't what *I* want.'

'Which is what?'

'What do I want? Oh, I suppose I want the same as him. For me, I mean. That's the trouble. I'm a masochist too.'

Clarice opened her eyes wide, then tapped the space on the bench which Mel had vacated. Come back here, Mel. Talk to me. Tell me. Spill all to Clarice.

Under the shower in Mel's cottage Clarice washed away the last of Elkin's impetuous seed.

Frank was out for the afternoon. Faxing his column from St Austell. No machines allowed in the cottage. Mel sat in a rocking-chair by the low leaded window and tried not to look at the steam ghosting out from under the stripped pine bathroom door. She could hear Clarice still laughing in the shower. It reminded Mel of the sound of a school playground. A warm milky odour, reminiscent of a kindergarten, filled the cottage – everyone stretched out on their little beds for a mid-morning nap. Mel fought not to let herself be overwhelmed by any of those mothering instincts she'd painstakingly excluded from her life. She wanted to warm a bottle. No she didn't. She wanted to inhale the smell of brand new life from Clarice's scalp. No she didn't. She wanted to give Clarice pocket money. Yes, she did. Here, a nice bright new-minted one pound coin, now go home.

When Clarice emerged from the bathroom wrapped in a towel like a boiled sweet, pearls of water sitting on her skin like icing sugar, Mel turned away.

'I could kill a gin,' Clarice said.

But there was no gin in the cottage. Not allowed. No machines, no alcohol. Want to fax? Go to St Austell. Want to drink? Go to the pub. Compulsiveness – that was what she was trying to beat. The noise and riot of habituated appetite.

If Clarice wanted a drink it would have to be The Poldark.

No, not The Poldark. Elkin would be in his corner of The Poldark, grinning into his tankard.

She was frightened of Elkin?

Of course not. No one could be frightened of Elkin. She was punishing him, that was all . . . Giving him a hard time.

So they decided they would go, the two witches, to The Frenchman instead. More of an emmet pub. Children's room. Bottled lagers. Scampi in a basket. Just the place to be if you wanted to gossip unheeded.

What impulse was it that made Mel think twice after she had locked the cottage, sent her back inside, told her to leave, at the very least, a terse note for Frank on the scrubbed pine table? – IN THE FRENCHMAN.

A loving impulse.

And what impulse was it that made Mel ask for champagne, in a bucket, and two, no, make that three glasses?

The same.

They sat facing each other across a round brown table, deaf to emmet commotion, and raised their flutes – you didn't get a flute at The Poldark, but then you didn't get champagne at The Poldark either – in a toast to Elkin.

'And to Molly Bloom,' Mel laughed.

'Did I overdo it?' Clarice asked.

'Not if you were happy for the whole of Little Cleverley to see everything you've got.'

Clarice shrugged and swigged. The whole of Little Cleverley already had, that was what her shrug denoted.

She loved flashing herself. She looked at Mel through the bubbles of her champagne, swirling it in the glass to keep it frothing. She just *loved* flashing. Didn't Mel?

No, Mel thought on the whole she didn't. But then Mel acknowledged that she had become a prude. Where her own body was concerned, she meant. She wasn't a prude for Clarice.

What Clarice loved best was showing herself to men when Elkin was there, but just out of eyeline. She flashed in the shop sometimes. She'd select a man she knew she could embarrass, someone wearing badges or mountaineering boots, someone with five kids in tow, someone carrying National Trust literature, and just as Elkin was getting to the bit about the antique value of the slates he painted on, whoosh! up would come the skirt and out would come the cunt. It was terrifically good for business. They would always return, the men she'd flashed at. Next year, on the dot, there they'd be in their badges and their toggles, their eyes soft and pleading like those of a favoured pet. Over time she grew to recognise some of them. And those she recognised she teased the hardest, making them wait for hours before she whipped her skirt up, forcing them to wander round and round the shop like connoisseurs of slate-art, up and down until they knew every particular hair on the head of every particular field-mouse on every particular slate. And then, just as they thought it was not to be and maybe never had been, was nothing but a filthy figment of their fevered imaginations, a Cornish chimera, a vapour, a wispy illusion ... whoosh! there it was again.

She took even greater risks with the local boys, who knew to ring her doorbell between six and seven in the evening, at the time Elkin could be relied upon to be beard down in his supper. Three long rings, followed by one short. Then eyes to her letterbox. Clarice would be standing in the hallway with her skirt ready. The moment the flap trembled, she raised her skirt. Sometimes she would press her body to the hole in the door and give them a close-up. If she was really in the mood she would let them touch her, blow on her, smell her, finger her, make her come.

'What I especially like,' she told Mel, 'is never being certain whose fingers they are. That's what makes me come. Does that shock you?'

No one in Little Cleverley knew how Melissa Paul earned her living. Mel, that was the only name they knew her by. Some sort of a journalist. 'No,' she said, laughing, 'of course it doesn't shock me. I've always thought sex is best with people you don't know. Sex with people you can't see either, sounds better still.'

But she was making mental notes. Lady Serenissima Montefiore, heroine of *Yes, My Lady*, who invites the kitchen hands at Montefiore House to poke their penises through the letterbox of the oak door to the great hall, on the other side of which she waits on her knees with her mouth open, finishing *Tractatus Logico-Philosophicus* inter-fellatio – something to chew on between violations – originated in this conversation.

It wasn't just sex with people you didn't know and couldn't see that Clarice liked. It was coming in places you didn't normally associate with coming. She'd got sick of coming only in bed. The hallway, on the coconut mat, with Elkin obliviously tucking into his supper above, beat bed all ends up.

Mel knew exactly what she meant. Fucking beds. She'd fought this one out with Frank, who thought coming was not only a bed event but a morning event. Preferably prone. Preferably not fully awake.

Oh, yes yes. Men prone in the mornings. Their dicks their only waking part. The sheer uninventive mechanicalness of them. They cackled on. Witches sistered in the conventional domestic come.

Mel called for another bottle of champagne. 'So what it amounts to,' she said, raising her glass, 'is that every boy in the village has seen your cunt.'

Clarice raised hers. 'And every man.'

A pause. Was there a pause? 'Including Frank?'

'Excluding Frank.'

'Poor Frank. What's he done wrong?'

'You're my friend.'

Aha. Mel knew all about friends. 'How can you be sure he hasn't seen your cunt through the letterbox?'

'I'd have recognised his eyes.'

'You know Frank's eyes that well?'

'They're distinct.'

'So Frank misses out . . .'

Another pause. Was that another pause? Hard to tell when you're into champagne bottle number two. 'I could always show it to him,' Clarice offered, 'while you're there.'

Mel thought about that. 'He might not want to see it while I'm there.'

Now there was a pause. Before Clarice found just the right words. 'Who cares what he wants!'

They laughed. Their eyes met through their winking champagne flutes. Danced. Acidified.

Suddenly they were in competition. Who would blink first?

It was at that moment that Frank turned up.

'Go on then,' Mel said. 'Show him.'

And Clarice did.

ELEVEN

CONSIDERING HOW LITTLE he has ever liked pubs, Frank has to concede that they have been good to him over the years.

He checks with Vera that his room is ready for him at The Poldark, collects his stuff from the car, plugs in his batteries, freshens up in the sink – the bathroom is down a flight of stairs and he is all at once too impatient for that kind of palaver – and strides over to the Slate Gallery.

The rain has stopped, but the shop is full anyway. Mid-spiel, Elkin nods his beard at him. Then turns away to expel someone licking an ice-cream. There are more no-eating signs in Elkin's slate shop than there are slates. But the signs never stop them. For signs to work people must have been taught to read.

Clarice is standing behind the till with her arms folded on her chest. Bored. Not impossibly selecting a flash victim. She has not perceptibly aged. The mouth is a little more fixed, otherwise she is as cascading as she was. Her eyes splinter like a shattered windshield when she catches sight of Frank. 'You!' She points at him, as though to inform him who he is. She bursts into laughter, still pointing. 'What are you doing here?'

She is the first person he has met today for whom a year is not a minute, who doesn't think she last spoke to him the day before. Good. Someone has noticed he has been gone.

'Just passing through.'

He knows not to hurry to kiss her. They work to a different social clock down here. He can't do any of that grab and shoulder-swivel stuff he does when he meets a woman he knows in Soho. Nor can he fall into her arms the way he does when he meets a man. Any hairy abrasions will have to come later. There's no middle ground of companionable touching in Little Cleverley. In Little Cleverley you go from icy detachment to clawing each other to death in a single movement.

She comes across the shop floor to him and surreptitiously runs a long bloody finger down his shirtfront. 'Mel with you?'

He shakes his head. Coming from Clarice, the question doesn't carry what it might coming from someone else. His answer, too, is free of the usual opportunistic algebra – Mel no equals dick yes. That's not how things compute with Clarice. Really, Mel ought to be here. Really, he ought to ring Mel on his mobile and put Clarice on. But he's not sure he even remembers the number.

'Is she well?' Meaning, he detects, has she forgiven me.

Something else Frank has forgotten. There was no fond leave-taking between the women. They went from clawing each other to death to icy detachment in a single movement. That's if you can call three days and three nights a single movement.

'Mel? Well? No, not well.'

Clarice scrutinises his face to be sure what sort of not well he is reporting. Then, having cleared it for serious ailments of the body, she says, 'She always took things hard.'

Which is a bit soon for Frank.

He leaps to correct a false impression, to restore Mel to vigorous good health in the eyes of Clarice. 'Mel takes things the way Mel takes things,' he says. 'When I say she's not well I should add that she's well enough to have booted me out of the house.'

But there's no shaking Clarice's complicity. 'I bet you deserved to be booted out,' she laughs. 'Knowing you.'

Meaning, you bugger! Not meaning, poor Mel.

But what does he want? He's turned up out of the blue on Clarice's shop floor, Mel-less, you could say flaunting his Mel-lessness, with a face full of bad intentions – has he any right to expect Clarice, for whom this is a busy emmet-watching day, to launch immediately into an itemisation of Mel's virtues? And what impossible standard of probity is he demanding of himself? Is he Mel's little soldier suddenly, sent out into the world, fully-armed, to fight for her good name?

Funnily enough, as his nostrils progressively fill with Clarice, that's exactly how he does see himself. Mel's little warrior.

Clarice has to leave him for a minute. Elkin is beckoning. An emmet family needs help deciding between a medium seal on a rock and a large field mouse in a field. They prefer the medium seal *qua* seal, but aesthetically favour the colour of the cord from which the large field mouse hangs. Easy. Clarice changes the cord for them while they watch in a stupefied hush. Unties the knots, re-threads the cord. Look, ma, a woman re-threading a cord! Frank sees how showing customers her cunt was the logical next step for Clarice.

He, too, watches in a stupefied hush. She is, after all, now he can see more of her, showing signs of wear. She flaunts a shorter skirt than she used to – the regulation callisthenics tunic of the new woman – but her flesh is not as confidently in charge of itself as it was. The wrong sort of dimpling is at work. There is vein activity afoot. She is being undermined, from the inside. Tick-tock. Tick-tock. Soon she'll be asking for just five more years. Maybe she's already started the negotiations.

Smelling her death on her, Frank is aroused. It isn't morbidity that does it, it's pathos.

Frank has always possessed the gift of seeing all women in the one woman. In Clarice, bent over the counter wrapping slate, her skirt tight across her flesh, but her flesh no longer tight across the bone, he re-acquaints himself with all the mortally sad girls of his life. His grandmother, who was scarcely older than he is now when she died, though she seemed an aged and worn-out woman; his mother, whose fate it is to be nudged forever gravewards by him – here I come, mother, treading on your heels, faster, come on, faster; all the fat nebbishy keife he lifted off the streets of Droylesden in the days of the great white ynaf hunt; all those hysterical foreign students with their St Vitus cunts; poor poor self-depilating Mel. Can any of them look to him for recompense? Is there any way he can make amends? Yes. Tonight he will give himself to Clarice as a way of saying sorry to the lot of them. All for one and one for all. If one cunt is every cunt, then he has it in his power to kiss that long continuum of sad girls better, doesn't he? – down on your knees, Frank, tongue out, for one last all-embracing act of lingual expiation.

'Look, I can see you're busy,' he whispers to Clarice. 'Is there any chance I can see you tonight?'

'Where are you staying?'

'The Poldark.'

She whistles through her teeth. The Poldark's always difficult because Elkin's always there. Stupid of Frank. He should have remembered. And besides, everyone knows her at The Poldark. She can't just slip upstairs and slip back down again, fatter by however much Frank pumps into her, not in The Poldark.

Obstacles. But only *obstacles*. It comes back to Frank, on a warm tide of fond and forgotten pleasure, how wonderful it is to be in the company of a woman for whom there are only obstacles, never compunctions.

Compunctions lead invariably to a power struggle. Argument. Persuasion. Rhetoric. Whereas an obstacle is a partnership thing. A mere hindrance you can overcome together. Which they do. She will slip out of the flat. Late. After twelve. Elkin won't hear a thing. He'll be out cold, snoring through his beard. Height of the season fatigue compounded by extreme emmet exasperation. But she won't risk The Poldark. She'll meet him up on Deadman's Point. Say, twelve-thirty. By the bench. Just watch your step. There'll be a moon, but watch your step anyway.

Frank knows better than to ring Mel on his mobile and say, 'Guess where I'm off to tonight.'

But it crosses his mind.

Now he understands what Mel means when she complains about the noise he makes. If there were anyone he could complain to, *he*'d be complaining about the noise he makes. He can't hear himself scheme or regret, he can't hear his own counsel, he can't even hear himself think twice, above the boom of his agitation.

How to get through to midnight plus thirty? See the sea? No, the sea must not be pre-empted; the sea is for tonight. Lunch? Crap on a paper plate. Crap with chips. No again. If he eats he will drink, and what if drink affects his enthusiasm for Clarice? Fortunately he has some crap-watching obligations to attend to. They'll take care of the afternoon at least. Where would a man be without his work?

He returns to his room, stretches out on the Iron Maiden,

which is what The Poldark means by a single bed, and surfs the daytime telly. On every channel a twenty-two-stone woman is being reunited with the child she abandoned at birth. The child too is now a twenty-two stoner. So it's true what they say: it's in the genes.

The cameras go gloating over the ruined features of the studio audience. Not a mouth that's still. Not a chap that hasn't fallen. Faces like messed-up jigsaw puzzles, every one of them. Frank's too. He'd like to dry his tears but he is afraid that if he puts his hand to his face he'll find his oesophagus where his eyes should be.

He can't go on watching. He is overcome with grief and guilt, and therefore self-disgust. He is supposed to be a critic not a person. But he knows that if he switches off he'll only be swapping one sort of agitation for another. And at least what's on the box is impersonal. Species-shlock. The mess we're all in together. As opposed to the mess he's individually cooking up for himself. In about ... how many hours ... ?

Why *is* he so tense? What is he doing indulging such agonies of anticipation. It's only Clarice, for God's sake. An old family friend.

Treachery, is that it? Going behind Mel's back?

No. He's done treachery. Besides which, he's a free agent. You can't go behind the back of someone who's denied you her front. (*And* might be granting it to someone else, newer, younger, nicer, quieter.)

Going solo then, is *that* it? Going solo where previously he'd gone *à deux*?

No. He's done solo, too. Slipped in while Mel had her face averted. Only the once, but he's done it.

That only leaves the dick. Following the dictates of the dick, one last time?

Forget it. The dick no longer dictates to him. In so far as the dick is in the picture, he dictates to it.

So why the breathlessness?

Why?

He falls asleep with the crap still churning. Out like a baby; one minute taking no shit, the next taking whatever his unconscious throws at him. He'll be lucky, the state he's in, not to be sucking off Kurt again. When he awakes it is evening. He can hear the bar going. The laughter of locals. Virna expostulating. A Ceilidh band.

He carries his soap and towel down the passage, showers, shaves, sighs, and goes downstairs. Elkin is nodding in his corner, snapping the hinged lid of his pewter tankard in time to the music. He enjoys a Ceilidh band. Virna less so. A band – any band – takes from the attention she is here to receive. She is wearing a purple satin shimmer suit to go with her complexion and raises one leg behind whenever a man kisses her. Strictly according to the Miss Manners Book for Wayward Bodmin Matrons. Mel would be proud to see her still going strong. It's all about when you time your run. Mel and her friends tore the field apart in their early days. Now they sit dried out in the knacker's yard, extruding their colons, preparing to become dog meat. While Virna, who kept her ankles together until she was fifty, is moist and full of running.

She espies Frank and calls him over. Frank's here. 'Lo Frank. All right? A drink for Frank. He hesitates. Does drink improve him or deplete him? He can't remember. That's how long it's been since he had a midnight cliff date to keep.

He asks for water but doesn't drink it. He doesn't want to be peeing into the sea all night.

The Ceilidh band is the usual baffling mix of pixie men in frayed cardigans and woolly hats, and beautiful strong-jawed women with perfect teeth. The men thump timbrels with knobbly sticks. The women raise faerie pipes to their lips. And blow. Back in their caravans the beautiful strong-jawed women submit to the unwashed knobbly men and have their babies. Why?

One of the tympanists reminds Frank of Hamish. Cheltenham Hamish. His maybe son. He has a similar way of hugging his chest, between tunes. And is studded and padlocked in all the same places. Funny how quickly that adventure in paternity came and went. D's fault, strictly speaking. It was she who put the case, from the available information, for everything being domestically *comme il faut* with the Brylls. Kurt, Liz, Hamish — and they all lived happily ever after. Very well, then. Who is Frank to worry, one way or another? Obviously, he is not the fathering kind. If he was the fathering kind he'd have fathered above board ages ago. He sees it now. There's an Einsteinian dimension to it. It is all about the way you regard your dick in time. Fatherers choose to have the dick over and done with. Been and gone. Dick — seed — child. Job finished. Non-fatherers, amongst whom Frank must from this day hence number himself, are more forward looking. They are not ready yet for consequences. Time is curved, so they may yet fuck themselves back into their own boyhood, never mind Hamish's. Now's then and then's now. The game is still afoot.

See what the promise of a night on a bare mountain can do.

Which reminds him. Time to go. It may only be ten-thirty, but what if Clarice decides to make an early run for it herself? He has learnt from Mel that women have a far lower patience threshhold than men. How many street corners has he lingered on until three, four in the morning, until the dawn breaks, on the off-chance that his date for seven o'clock the night before had missed a bus or got the time confused? You gave a woman every chance. You gave your dick every chance. But in the days when he was meeting Mel at corners she'd be gone if he wasn't at least thirty minutes early. She wouldn't even look up and down the street. No Frank? Get fucked, then. I've got better things to do. And she was off. What if Clarice is the same?

A cold, ironical bitch of a moon surveys him as he clambers up to Deadman's Point. Fireflies flash in the gorse. Adders slither out of his way. The sea holds its breath. No Clarice. Good. She can't have come and gone already. He stretches himself out on the bench and stares back at the moon. They know each other well, Frank and Selene. She's seen him through many a humiliation. Fifty years' worth. Though she might be said to be carrying her years better than he is carrying his. She stares him out. He blinks first. Then blinks again. Then nods off. Old guys need a lot of rest.

He half-wakes to a pain in his chest. Oh no. Not that. Not now. Not here.

But it isn't that sort of pain. It's more exquisite. More precisely located. A pectoral pain. A mammary torment. A burning of the nipple. And what's this 'a'? It's two burnings – a fire in each nipple. Excruciating. As though he's giving suck to twins.

But twin what? Twin adders?

Fanged, whatever they are.

When he opens his eyes he sees that Clarice is on her knees before him, an expression of intense comic concentration on her face, her fingers in his shirt, squeezing. A vein twitches in her neck. Moonlight elongates and Egyptifies her nose.

'Hurt?'

(What does she know?)

'Yes.'

223

'Good.'

(*What* does she know?)

'Why good?'

'Your punishment for taking so long to come back and see me.'

(She is at play. She doesn't know anything.)

He tries to sit up, to kiss her, but she uses her weight to keep him down.

'Uh, uh,' she says. 'Mel wouldn't like.'

Fancy her remembering that. Coming out of the cottage bathroom, half way through day two of their indecorous spree, Mel had found them on the floor playing conventional missionaries and savages, conventionally blowing down each other's throats. Given the unconventional journey they had been on together, the three of them – losing souls, not saving them – this spectacle had struck Mel as a betrayal. 'If you're going to start that,' she'd complained, 'I'm out of here.'

Frank had immediately snatched his mouth from Clarice's mouth and returned it to her cunt, where it gave no offence.

At a level below the pleasure of the pain, Frank is irked by Clarice. Twice now, in the course of the few sentences they've been able to exchange, she's invited him to join her in scorn for Mel's queer rectitude. As though there's a freemasonry of insouciance that Clarice believes they share, as though she's addressing a fellow free spirit. As though she can assume that when it comes to a shoot out, Frank is on Clarice's side against Melissa.

But by God it's something to have a sharp-nailed woman tear your nipples off beneath a sneery moon.

She unbuckles his belt and slides one hand inside his trousers. A promissory gesture. Right this minute she wants a cigarette. Even Clarice knows that there's something to be said for a build-up.

'What do you look like,' she laughs.

224

'Well? What do I look like?'

'Like a cat that's got the cream.'

She's referring to his abandonment on the bench, his shirt open, his nipples red as roses, his dick magnetised by the moon – a pasha on an ottoman.

'I sure have missed the cream,' he says.

She pulls an oh yeah face. But there are no real problems of that sort between them. They were never a pair. They were always part of something larger.

But he would still like to pay her an individual compliment. 'I often think about it,' he lies.

'Me too,' she says. Then, after a long drag on a cigarette, 'Does Mel?'

'I don't know. She doesn't allude.'

'Never?'

'Never.'

'You know she came to see me again.'

'You're joking.'

'You didn't know? I thought you'd cooked it up together. I thought you were waiting in the car to hear all about it.'

'No. Absolutely not. I'm astounded. When was it she came?'

'I don't know. Three years ago. Maybe more.'

'And what happened?'

Clarice laughs. Tell me, tell me. 'Nothing happened. She came into the shop, just like you did. Asked me to meet her, just like you did. Asked me to fuck her, actually. You know Mel, no beating about the bush. She said I owed her one. I agreed to meet her up here. But she didn't show.'

'You weren't late? Mel doesn't wait.'

'No, I wasn't late. And the state she was in you'd have thought she'd have waited till Doomsday.'

The state she was in. Frank looks at Clarice in her faded jeans and baby-blue cardigan, takes in her streaming hair, her handsome but shallow face, and feels deeply insulted on Mel's behalf. Could Mel ever have been *in a state* for her? Never mind could Mel, *should* Mel?

Curiosity, though – gross, indiscriminating curiosity – gets the better of him. 'And then what?'

'There was no then. She just didn't show. I sat up here for an hour. Got cold and went home. That was that. She never came back. Never left a message. Never apologised. I suppose she got cold feet.'

'Not like Mel.'

'To get cold feet?'

'To get cold feet or to ask for a fuck. Mel isn't an asker.'

'Not true. She asked me for all sorts of things that time. She woke me up while you were still sleeping and begged me to let her suck me. Begged me to tie her up and fist-fuck her.'

Frank's stomach lurches. Floods with pancreatic juices. This is what he has come to hear. No point fighting it. No point being insulted on Mel's behalf. Insult is where the thrills are. Insult is what he's returned to Little Cleverley to confront, suffer, make friends with.

'And I know how much you love being begged,' he says. His voice is wheedling. Like Little Red Ridinghood's making up to the big bad wolf. Little Red Frank. They knew, the vegetarian waiters who sculpted his portrait on the cappuccino, they knew what whipped importunings his voice was capable of. Disgusted, the moon allows a gauzy kirtle of cloud to cover her gaze.

Clarice responds with a further promissory squeeze. Yes, she'll submit to his submissions. But first she has a fag to finish. And a few more discommendations of Mel to deliver.

'What I love is having fun,' she says. 'You two take everything too hard. Especially Mel. She was so overwrought. Everything mattered too much to her. She took it all too seriously.'

Too seriously? So it was light, was it? Light, twining his fingers with hers and together making love-knots inside Mel's cunt? Is there something wrong with him? Is he wrong to think that that was not an especially frothy thing to be doing, not an everyday occurrence, even for country folk, shaking hands with a third party inside your affianced's cunt? And what about when Clarice inserted the fingers of her other hand into Mel's anus so that she could make membraneous contact, feel through the wall how she and Frank were doing in the chamber next door – would it be altogether too heavy of him to say that that, too, was worthy of remark, an experience to treasure, one to tell the grandchildren?

And what about – ? His memory tails off. If he is going to lie here going through it all, squaring his sense of it with Clarice's, balancing his indignation as to then with his desire as to now, he'll be here when the dawn comes up.

They'd gone back to the cottage, the three of them, hard on the heels of Clarice flashing him her fur. They hadn't waited for Frank to catch up with their champagne intake, hadn't lingered long enough for him to get even the teensiest drunk. He was a man. He was being offered cunt in more combinations than he had any right to hope for. What need had he of alcohol? As an estimate of a man's erotic subtlety this was low, but who was he to say it wasn't accurate.

The two women left the pub with their arms around each other's shoulders. To hell with what anyone thought. Out into the grey slate street they'd rolled, a pair of drunken sailors, indifferent to the gawping emmets, careless of who they met, loudly derisive of the broken men weeping at Virna's gate. What, weep for love? Frank followed behind them, his eyes on fire.

The finger twining was just the beginning of it. It was Clarice's idea to start that way. Her cunt had been out, been turned this way and that in conversation, now it was Mel's shift.

'Let's see it, then,' Clarice said, as soon as they were inside.

'I'll clear the bed,' Frank chimed in.

Mel looked at Clarice. 'See?' If they were going to have the kind of good time they wanted it would be in spite of a man, not because of him.

They threw cushions on the floor and Mel, undressed and tipsy, flung herself wide upon them. She was meatier then, and hairier. These were the pre-colon-hoovering, pre-Hitler moustache years. A journey up Mel's Weimar cunt in those days still had an element of jungle risk to it, even if you did have a friend's hand to hold.

The first two or three hours skipped to Clarice's orchestration. She opened Mel up, played with her like a rag doll, rolled her on to her side, then on to her stomach, then on to her back again, grabbing handfuls of her hair, squeezing two tits into one tit, dividing one tit into two tits, plucking at her inflamed nipples, biting her, making her come with an ease that caused Frank to simultaneously grieve and marvel. Mel, who normally stood on such erotic dignity, acceding to this rough treatment! Mel, who kept one silver orgasm in her revolver as a last resort, exploding in all directions like a blunderbuss! As for him, he simply went where Clarice told him. He was there to help her expose and pry into Mel, not to help himself. He held Mel's legs open so that Clarice could go to work unhindered. He separated her labia one from the other – splish, splosh – so that Clarice should not miss any of the far rippling effects of her labours, not one convulsion of the deep romantic chasm, not a single crimson cavernous pulse. He covered Mel's mouth to stifle her cries. He covered her eyes to protect her innocence.

He might have been Clarice's factotum – Figaro, not Frank – so busy did her curiosity keep him. First she wanted to see what Mel looked like with a dick going in and out of her cunt. Frank! You're needed.

Then with a dick in her mouth. Frank! Over here.

And now with sperm running down her chin? Frank! Frank! Come on, Frank!

But if sperm was going to be running down Mel's chin then Mel considered it was time she had a say in the matter. Yes, let's do it, but let's do it properly. No conventional kitchen come, thank you. A drizzle of Frank she could have any old time.

'You two fuck on my face, then,' she said. 'It's my turn to have something to look at.'

So Frank at last got to enter Clarice, like a dog entering a bitch, Mel's eyes open beneath them, and Mel's mouth open too, waiting to catch whatever spilled from either of them. And in time – in short time, to tell the truth, but that's not so surprising is it, considering? – Mel got to see what sperm looked like, leaking out of Clarice's cunt, and Clarice got to see what sperm looked like, running down Mel's chin.

Satisfied, Clarice?

Frank too, by rearing up over Clarice's extended neck and parting her mane, managed a look down. It sometimes happens, in the course of a long life, that a man beholds a sight he knows he was born to see, perhaps had seen before in an earlier, better existence. Mel bearded by Clarice was just such a sight. Frank had tumbled with women in numbers before, made the beast of as many backs as you could squeeze onto a Wythenshawe floor, but this was different. This time one of the women was someone he cared for. And as practioners of the arts of interpersonal healing are forever telling you, the caring is everything.

Mel was the first to tire mentally. Frank felt the air around her begin to chill. Enough. He could tell that she wanted Clarice to go now. Time for sleep, and in the morning time for normal service to resume. She'd been visiting hell on a champagne quickie, that was all. She'd merely popped her head around the gates. She wasn't intending to stay.

But Clarice was in no hurry to beat a retreat. She'd bunk down in the spare room if that was what Mel preferred. But she couldn't go back to Elkin, not tonight. Elkin was going to have to worry about her for a little longer than that. Elkin was going to have suffer.

An hour later, sleeping the sleep of fallen angels in the spare bed, Clarice was woken by a tongue tracing circles on her thigh. 'Mmm,' she murmured. 'That's good, Frank.'

In the sense that Frank and Mel had been together long enough to be married in the eyes of God, and in so far as man and wife are one flesh, Clarice was right to suppose that the tongue which was tracing hot circles on her thigh was Frank's. Applying less spiritual criteria of ownership, though, the tongue in question in fact belonged to Mel.

Clarice had not been telling Frank anything he didn't already know when she confided Mel's secret visits to her bed. Frank's eyes may have been closed but he wasn't himself sleeping when Mel slipped out of their room. Sleep! He didn't expect ever to sleep again. And the filthy adventure Mel was now embarked upon only proved why he *must* never sleep again. Close an eye for a second and you might miss perdition. He sat up and pricked his ears. In the normal way of things sounds carried preternaturally in the silence of a Little Cleverley night. You could hear a wave crashing half a mile away. You could be up on the cliffs and hear a husband sobbing into his hands outside Mel's row of wayward matrons' cottages. But tonight was no ordinary night. And why was this night different from all others? Because on this night Frank had fucked another woman –

noisily! – on Mel's face and not been punished for it. No post-facto bitterness. No recriminations. No shut the fuck up and get the fuck out. Such a miraculous event did wonders for his hearing.

'You have to let me,' he heard Mel say. 'You owe me.' Her words couldn't have been clearer had she been lying by his side. Except that lying by his side she never said you have to let me.

There was the awesomeness of it. Mel, his Mel, asking. Mel, his Mel, going begging.

He didn't hear Clarice's answer. Who cared about Clarice? In the course of the next few days Clarice took a sort of fairy tale control of their domestic arrangements, going about the cottage stark naked, her muff fluffed pugnaciously up, her conical tits pushed pantomimically out, sometimes with just a leather belt pulled in tight around her waist, sometimes with just a tie from Frank's wardrobe knotted loosely round her neck, all the while muttering stuff about making a slave of Mel, locking her into handcuffs, putting her into a dog collar, burning her nipples with candle wax, all that soft gartery sadism which there was every chance she'd found originally in one of Melissa Paul's own soft gartery sado-romances. But none of it cut much ice with Frank. Of course he was aroused. But when wasn't he aroused? A flea in a brassiere would have aroused Frank. The thing that put a torch to his innards, heated his blood to twice its normal temperature, was not what Clarice did but what Mel didn't. She didn't put a stop to it, that was what was so extraordinary. She didn't say hold. She didn't say enough. No sooner did the the air around her begin to chill than it began to thaw again. She turned aside, fell asleep, then an hour later was on her knees to Clarice, asking for more. Of course it was disgusting, that was what refuelled her. She couldn't disgust herself enough. She got them to fuck on her face again. She got them to fuck on the old spring mattress in the spare room while she lay underneath clawing at her own cunt, shouting 'This is disgusting,' and laughing and grunting and crying and coming all at once as the springs crashed about her.

He'd have understood it better had it been him under the springs. He and his old pal ignominy. They had grown up together. Together, their sperm had failed to pass muster in a public gardens in Harrogate. Together, they'd come home from a shtuppenhaus in Wythenshawe and found a pair of fat girl's knickers in their pocket. Under the springs was just the place for them. He was a man. Ignominy was his middle name. But in Mel it was shocking. Blinding. It was as though she was his idol, and had fallen.

In the end, of course, she threw the spell off. Enough. Enough. And this time she meant it.

But how were they, Clarice and Frank, mere babes in the woods of Mel's measured degradation, how were they to know that this time she really really really meant it? They climbed back on to the spring mattress and began bouncing. Come on, Mel, get under!

Enough, she said.

Clarice went over to her and held her chin. Any more trouble and she would slap her face. Under the mattress, Mel.

Enough, Mel said.

Lick my cunt, Clarice told her. You and Frank. Together. Now!

Ten minutes later Mel was dressed, waiting for a taxi to take her to the railway station. Four hours after that she was back in London.

That was how Frank and Clarice got to spend one conventional night together, fucking like ordinary sublunary lovers, without having to worry about Mel's special needs. But the following morning, early, Frank too was in a taxi.

And that, effectively, was the finish of Mel's bolt hole, the place she'd bought to enjoy peace and quiet in, her last throw of the man-free romance-of-nature dice. An estate agent's sign went up soon afterwards.

Poor Mel. No wonder she'd demanded silence. It wasn't only him she needed to shut up. It was herself. Enough now. Enough with all the noisy importunings of desire.

You can't go on listening, that was her point. You can't afford to go on listening.

But there's no getting rid of the noise in his brain tonight. Poor Mel twice over. An idol doubly fallen. Fancy her having returned on her knees to Little Cleverley. Fancy her having come all this way to get another lick of Clarice. And never telling him. That's if she had. But what if Clarice was lying? What if Mel had never come back that second time? What if they'd cooked this up in bed all those years ago, calculated that he'd come back one day, wouldn't be able not to come back, and when he did, what fun for Clarice to concoct some cock and bull story about Mel having been back before him? He didn't know what Mel was capable of, that was what it amounted to. D the fat comedian had seasoned his imagination with jealousies of the conventional sort. Another man ... men ... Mel sprouting hair again. Now Clarice was dropping still deeper deviancies into the boiling pot of his uncertainty. There was pain in it for him whatever the truth was. Mel actually coming back to Clarice, or Mel fainting in Clarice's arms, plotting the deception. Disgusting, either way.

Just how disgusting are you, Mel? Tell me, tell me.

'Keep out of my head,' she had warned him back in London, when he'd tried to get her to whisper to him in the night, tried to incorporate her shame into his. For a fallen idol is a mightily voluptuous concept.

The conventional lovers' night he'd passed with Clarice

was a wasted opportunity. It hadn't answered to any of the needs released by the preceding three days. Sure, sure, she was nice to fuck. But what's one more fuck in a long life of fucking? The needs he hadn't honoured, and should have honoured, were essentially conjugal in nature. They were to do with Mel. You could say he wanted to *be* Mel now. It worked like this: considering that Mel had submitted to the erotic will of Clarice, willingly made herself her vassal, and considering that Frank had always accepted the primacy of Mel's will in most things, didn't it then follow that Frank was a beggar's beggar, a bottom's bottom, and considering that, didn't it also follow that he was doubly in thrall to Clarice? That Clarice herself would not have been able to follow him through all his upside down reasoning only added to the perverse excitement. If a subtle man desires the thrill of throwing himself away, who but a shallow woman should he throw himself away on? That, anyway, was how he ought to have presented himself to Clarice on that last night – as a supplicant's supplicant, the lowest of the low.

But he knew less then, didn't he? He wasn't fifty then. And no one had yet painted his portrait in cappuccino froth.

Tonight, though, he knows everything. Tonight, with only the moon as his witness, he will get Clarice to treat him like the filth he is.

For Mel's sake.

TWELVE

'HAPPY THE PERSON,' wrote the fifth-century monk
Evagrios – Evagrios the Solitary, to his friends, except
that he had no friends – 'Happy the person who thinks
himself no better than dirt.'

So Frank must be delirious, must he not? The nonpareil,
the shape and form, the very looking-glass of happiness?

He is a monk himself now. In a manner of speaking. By a
man's company ye shall know him, and Frank is keeping
company with monks. He sleeps in a bare but comfortable
cell in a new wing of the Abbey, sharing facilities with fifteen
other retreatants from the howling world of fleshly sin. He
eats his meals, in silence, with the monks. Crap still – there is
to be no escape from crap, on the box or in the belly: for a
man must toil and a man must eat – but at least sanctified
crap. A plain sufficiency. Sprouts, sausages, black pudding,
blackened potatoes, gravy, rhubarb and redcurrant compote.
He gives thanks for it in Latin before, and after folds his
napkin and leaves the refectory with his eyes lowered.

On some mornings he rises with the monks for vigils and
lauds. An electric buzzer goes off in the corridor beside his
room, telling him it is 3.30 a.m., but it's up to him whether
he rises or not. Free choice. He has not taken orders. He has

seriously considered it, but the monks have made it plain they would not seriously consider him. He is too old. Too set in his ways. Pope Gregory, whom we have to thank for what we know of St Benedict, the founder of Frank's adopted order, set great store by men of Frank's years. 'Temptations of the flesh are violent during youth,' he wrote, 'whereas after the age of fifty concupiscence dies down.' Frank can vouch for that. Were it not for habit, inadequate preparation for old age, and an incapacity to think of anything else to do with himself once he reached it, Frank would have willingly kissed goodbye to concupiscence the moment it kissed goodbye to him. Well, the old horse is dead now, right enough. Not all the whippings in self-chastising Christendom can ever bring that beast back to life. So why don't the monks consider him good monastic material? There's a flaw in the order. It isn't enough that a man has a broken back; they want to be the ones that do the breaking. Benedict himself broke his own, won a victory over temptation by rolling naked in sharp thorns and stinging nettles, tore his own poor sinful flesh to shreds. But that was before there was a Benedictine order to do it for him.

Frank finds vigils and lauds harder to get up for the further the year advances. It can get cold in the North-East of Scotland at three-thirty in the morning in November. Yes, he's seen the last of the summer off up here, and most of autumn, and now means to do the same to winter. And maybe, after that, to spring. And then, who knows? He's taking it a season at a time.

The monkish life is growing on him. He rises, or doesn't, to the pre-dawn torture buzzer. He prepares himself a simple breakfast in the retreatants' kitchen, white toast, Summer County margarine, and orange marmalade made by the monks. Sometimes he greets his fellow fugitives, like Gordon who has been here even longer than he has, and who acknowledges Frank's greeting with sad heroic eyes, as though unable to decide whether he's pleased or not to have made it through one more night. 'Yes indeed,' he says, when Frank comments on the beauty of the day. Yes indeed. It's that or burst into tears. Otherwise it's brave good mornings, and little else, all round. But that's fine and dandy by Frank. He doesn't want conversation. He's said all he needs to say for one lifetime. And heard all he needs to hear. By the beauty of the day he means the imminent withdrawal of all signs of life. The earth is already half dead up here. The begrudging light is slow to show itself and quick to go. Dawn will soon be ten a.m. and twilight fifteen minutes later. Get into the pine forest that rises up behind the Abbey, protecting its rear, and you can forget you ever knew what light looked like. That too suits Frank. He wants the day over and done with. He may be skipping vigils regularly now, but he never misses compline, the peace before sleep, the calm that ushers in the Greater Silence.

Noctem quietam et finem perfectum concedat nobis dominus omnipotens.

The Lord Almighty grant us a quiet night and a perfect end.

Mel should be up here, whoever Mel is.

For Frank, compline is the high point of his day, a pure moment of monastic theatricality that vindicates the nothingness that precedes and follows it. All lights go out. A solitary monk enters the medieval church and puts a taper to the candles. The crepuscular vaults flicker. Are we inside or out? The monks arrive in a blur of white. White is not the usual colour for Benedictines, but these Benedictines have been Cistercianised somewhere along the way. So much the better. Their whiteness etherialises them. They are angels. Sitting in his pew, watching Gordon's heaving back, Frank has also become angelic. He lowers his elbows on to his knees, makes a cup of his hands, and drops his chin into it. If he were an item of church furniture he could not be more inanimate. Or more hushed.

The monks take their places in the choir stall. Their voices are not the voices of men. There is nothing of earth in them. They are starry, crystalline, composed of elements entirely foreign to Frank's understanding. It is quickly over. The Greater Silence descends. The Abbot, who has a small neat unravaged face, is the first to leave. He swings his censer in Frank's direction, blessing him, preparing him for the night. Be sober, be watchful. Your adversary the devil prowls around like a roaring lion, seeking someone to devour. Be sure it is not you, Frank. Resist him. Be firm in your faith.

The monks wait for the Abbot to quit the church, then they leave their stalls and drop to their knees in stray patterns, like sheep on a field. First they bow to the altar, then they prostrate themselves before the Virgin, in front of whose portrait two high white candles burn. Nothing the monks do in Frank's sight is more demonstrative or more passionate than this. Some stay on their knees, wringing their hands, a long time. Regimented all day, this is their hour of pure individuation. They choose their own moment to rise and depart, regretfully, like lovers, now one, now another, followed at last by Frank Ritz, into the Silence.

According to Pope Gregory:

One day while Saint Benedict was alone, the tempter came in the form of a little blackbird, which began to flutter in front of his face. It kept so close that he could easily have caught it in his hand. Instead, he made the sign of the Cross and the bird flew away. The moment it left, he was seized with an unusually violent temptation. The evil spirit recalled to his mind a woman he had once seen, and before he realised it his emotions were carrying him away. Almost overcome in the struggle, he was on the point of abandoning the lonely wilderness, when suddenly with the help of God's grace he came to himself.

It was in order to see to it that the blackbird did not call on him again that Benedict rolled naked in those thorns and nettles.

Frank too, on only his second night in the Abbey, was visited by the fluttering blackbird of lewdness. Only in Frank's case it visited him in his sleep. And the woman that was recalled to his mind was not one he knew or had ever seen, unless she was the abstract and précis of all the women he had desired.

She was suddenly there, whoever she was, on his arm. Not young. A woman in her late thirties, say, with close cropped dark hair, apparently a famous memoirist. He was walking up a hill with her, into a cul de sac, peopled with labouring masses, chimneys all around, a factory at the end of the cul de sac, wire fencing, and a forbidding gate. They were separate from their surroundings and not going anywhere. Ambling, arm in arm. He could feel her breasts moving against his shoulder, her dress was loose fitting and flapped against her thighs. Her considered her to be beyond him, despite their proximity; out of his league, not on account of her beauty but her worldliness and intelligence. What could such a woman see in him, a mere monk? Everything! – that was what was so wonderful. Everything! She leaned into him and blew into his neck. 'This could be it for me,' she said. 'Curtains.' She smiled. He was on fire. Every touch burnt him. This was it for him too. He had never been happier. But he was troubled by one thing: he wasn't free. How was he to tell her, and yet not scare her away, that he was accounted for, that he had taken vows and would only be able to fit her into the canonical interstices of his life, between prime and terce, between sext and vespers? And then, as her dress flapped, revealing her thighs, another thought occurred. *He could make himself free.* He trembled, in his dream, with the audacity of what he was thinking, but she melted into him, vanished inside him, leaving him no choice . . .

And then the buzzer went off outside his room, calling him to vigils and lauds.

Even as a boy, when the roaring lion could do what it liked with him, Frank had never dreamed such sleek insinuations. Was it the Abbey, just as it had been the wilderness for Benedict, that gave the dream its treacherous tactility? Does renunciation turn on you, tempting you with visions far more voluptuous than any you have to deal with in the ordinary sublunary world of regulation sin?

Those poor monks, in that case.

Small wonder, compline over, that they are reluctant to get up off their knees to face the Greater Silence. Knowing their adversary, the silky tempter, will soon be slithering in beside them . . .

They'd be safer from corruption down on the floor of a shtuppenhaus in Wythenshawe.

Poor monks, but not piteous, nor pitiable. Frank watches them going about their business in the fields, dressed in jeans and wellingtons, carrying buckets, tending to the bees, chasing chickens, laughing amongst themselves. Benedict warned against merriment – 'Only a fool raises his voice in laughter' – in deference to which, Brother Ritz the Obedient bears himself most gravely in the precincts of the monastery. Humourless little prick, is how the monks must think of him. Sometimes he feels he spoils their mealtimes, so conscientiously does he interpret the rule and spirit of silence. He lowers his head during grace, averts his eyes, eats sparingly. It's just food, Frank. But he may as well be at a repast for the dead. Funereal, that's what he has become. The other retreatants are the same. They are all or nothing men, every one of them. And now that all has failed them, they are making themselves over religiously to nothingness. The monks, meanwhile, are rollicking. They tuck their napkins into the necks of their habits, they scoop out mountains of yellow cream from their individual containers of Summer County, rub breadcrumbs into their soup bowls, laugh to themselves when the Brother who reads to them throughout the meal comes upon something salacious in *The Tablet* – 'The Pontiff was later said to have hit it off particularly well with Mrs Carey' – and then, when they have finished eating, zip themselves still smiling back into their hoods, like demonic pixies.

Without exchanging a word or a glance with one another they have succeeded in dining communally.

For a sperm-throwing, socially penetrative man like Frank Ritz, there is a lesson here as to singleness and community, if only he knew how to learn it.

'Wednesday!' Brother Cyprian says to him if they happen to run into each other on a Wednesday.

'Wednesday?'

'Lunch . . .'

'Lunch?'

'Fish and chips. Wednesdays. Yum!'

In the past, Frank had always felt superior to people who made a present of themselves to a religious order. Taking the easy way out, was how he thought of it. (Not battling hardships, the way Frank did.) Refusing to face up to life's responsibilities. (Not engaging with them full on, the way Frank did.) And most importantly, making freaks and eunuchs of themselves. But now he is beginning to look at it differently. Freakish? What does their life lack? Fucking.

Nothing else. Only fucking. That was his real objection to the way they lived. They didn't fuck. Ugh! How vile! They didn't fuck. But now Frank doesn't fuck either. So what divides them? Nothing divides them. Might he not as well become a monk, then? It's pleasant up here. Ordered. Quiet. Cold. Dead. What about it?

He can still do his column. He is still doing his column. He wanders Schubertianly in the pine forests in the afternoons, listening to the kuk-kukkings of the wood pigeons. Returns to his little cell on the final squeezing out of light, leaving his muddy boots with all the other muddy boots in the hall below. Washes in the wash basin. Puts on something seemly for compline. A tie. A pullover. Warm but not too — a shiver is in order. Walks over to the church. Drops into his seat where he sits as quiet as a font. Receives the Abbot's blessing. Watches and wonders as the monks collapse before the Virgin. Enters the Greater Silence. Then returns to his room and switches on his Hitachi portable which he listens to, out of respect for the rule of St Benedict, through headphones.

It's all there where it always was and always will be. The crap. Leaking out of the sockets even this far north. The soaps. The sitcoms. The scunge. The classics. Oh, worst of all, the classics. Mel's alter ego, the little fool of Manderley, showing her pink-tipped tits to Maximilian de Winter. Dorothea in her nightie. Nostromo in stereorama. The Three Tenors. Placido, Pavarotti and the little one, still in a sperm-hurling competition at their age. Wouldn't they be better in a monastery? Isn't it time, boys?

Frank props up his machine on a little kitchen chair and sits on the edge of his bed in his headphones, looking slightly down at the screen. Anyone catching him in this position would take him to be a spy, unaware that the war is over, still tracking Allied submarine movements in the North Sea.

There is something of the *Thirty-Nine Steps* about him. As there is about this part of the country. Out on his walks, Frank sees men meeting in fields with dogs at their feet and rifles on their shoulders. They wear tweed jackets and deerstalkers and drive away from their assignations in BMWs and Audis. Need one say more? Meanwhile the monks innocently collect the honey from the hives. Ignorant of what goes on. Ignorant of the machinations in the fields and the crap-watching in Frank's room. Every evening when he's finished he packs the Hitachi into his travelling bag and pushes it under the bed. Just in case he passes away in the night and they find it in the morning. Just in case they wouldn't like it.

Slowly, Frank is coming to realise that he is far more censorious of the world than they are. He's the real monk. They're not in flight, he is. When they get to see telly they quite like it. They could never understand what he finds in it that makes him so violently angry. One Sunday morning the Father Abbot prays for it, prays for the media that they may be channels of enlightenment and discernment. What about fire and brimstone, Father? Remember Sodom? The monks lower their heads and pray. For the telly. For the radio. And for the morning papers. But then they aren't spiritual. Spiritual men fuck away the first half of their lives and then expend the second in an illumination of fine discriminations and loathing. Which isn't at all how monks apportion their time.

It was not knowing that he was of necessity already more spiritual than any unexercised eremite could ever be that brought him up here in the first place. He'd lit upon a metapsychic atlas in a New Age bookshop in Bodmin the morning after his final act of abnegation on the cliffs of Little Cleverley – a guide to establishments offering nourishment of the soul – and had picked the Abbey as the place for him. It did no harm that it was at the other end of the country, at the other end of another country if one was to be strict about it. The drive would have its own significance as pilgrimage. He was off, heading north, Saabing into the cold, silencing the beast. Such indulgent times he lived in. Do it, do it, said the box. If you're a shagger, shag. If you're a poofter, poof. Who, anywhere, was for silencing the beast? The monks, obviously. Obviously, the monks. He was heading north for a silencing and a clean-out. Mel periodically had her colon removed and rinsed. He'd do the same with his mind. Cranial irrigation.

It was what Mel had been asking him to do for years. But now he was doing it for himself.

'Use something,' he'd begged Clarice that night. 'Hurt me. Abuse me. Draw blood.' And Clarice, being Clarice, had hurt him, abused him, drawn blood. Being Clarice, she'd gone further, too. She'd got him to wear her pants. And put lipstick on his mouth. Now who's the girl, Frank? And he'd gone along with it, taken it like a man, taken it like a girl, because he owed them all, didn't he – Mel, D, Liz . . .

But now he had to do something for himself.

'I'd appreciate some spiritual counselling,' he said to Brother Cyprian, the Guest Master, somewhere between the third and the fourth week of his stay. He hadn't wanted to be pushy.

The monks had all been through the hands of Brother Maurus, the monastery hairdresser, that morning. There was a frisky youthful look about them, embarrassed too, self-consciously naked, like shorn rams. Brother Cyprian, particularly, looked shame-faced and schoolboyish. His ears stuck out. His brow went a long way back. 'Spiritual counselling?' He appeared to be alarmed by Frank's request.

Frank wondered if he'd used the wrong phrase. 'You do do that?'

'*I* don't.' Now Brother Cyprian was truly startled. 'But I can find you someone wise.'

'Wise would be good,' Frank said.

Later that day the monk caught up with Frank as he was coming back from a turn around the cemetery. When it was too wet to walk in the woods Frank would put up his umbrella and go to pay his respects to the dead. It was secluded and squelchy here. A good place for a memorial bench, had Frank still been thinking of memorial benches. *This bench is dedicated to the memory of Frank Ritz. Though not a monk himself, he was a friend to monks.* Kuk-kuk, went the wood pigeons. Fatting themselves up for the slaughter, the pheasants pecked at the nearby fields. No one else was here. Just Frank, the birds, and the dead. He wandered between the wooden crosses. Here a mendicant, there a prior. All that simplicity and wisdom rotting away. A whole meadow of it. And not a fuck between them.

'I've dealt with that,' Brother Cyprian said, catching him at the cemetery gate.

This time it was Frank's turn to be startled. He was lost in thought, hidden away under his umbrella.

'Your counselling . . .'

'Ah, yes. Thank you.'

'Father Lawrence has agreed to talk to you. He used to be our Father Abbot. But he's retired now. I'll bring him to your room tomorrow morning at eleven.'

His room! Not a perforated wooden whispering box in a dark corner of the church. His room!

Frank spent the preceding night in an agitated condition. An abbot was surely the highest holder of ecclesiastical office he had ever entertained. And a retired abbot was surely more reverend still. It was like being back in his little room in Oxford preparing tea for his tutor. But there were no entertainment facilities in this room. No kettle, no gas fire, no toasting fork. In a monastery a toasting fork had other connotations. He could drive to Inverness and buy wine, but which wine? Wine too meant something different here. Ditto biscuits. Nothing, was his final decision. Honour his abstemiousness, and give him nothing. What he could do, though, was make sure his room was impeccable. Sweep the floor. Scrub the sink. Tidy the small library of religious works that had been waiting for him on the desk when he first arrived. And of course make sure his adversary the devil was not allowed into his bed that night.

That he watched no crap on his Hitachi goes without saying.

The following morning at eleven sharp, terce over, Brother Cyprian knocked on his door. He had an old man with him, a disapproving-looking monk with a noble profile whom Frank had observed during Mass and meals but had never spoken to. Without really thinking about it, Frank had assumed that this monk above all the others knew about his life and condemned it.

'This is Father Lawrence,' Brother Cyprian said. 'He'll talk to you. He is the wisest man in our community.'

'Oh, I don't know about wise,' said Father Lawrence, lowering his eyes, recalling to Frank's mind Benedict's seventh step of humility – 'that a man not only admits with his tongue but is also convinced in his heart that he is inferior to all and of less value, humbling himself and saying with the Prophet, "I am truly a worm, not a man."'

Frank hoped not. He could do the worm stuff himself. Wisdom was what he was after.

It was a struggle to get the old man to accept the more comfortable seat. Frank wished now that he had something to give him. If not wine or biscuits, a container of Summer County at the least. He looked ill at ease and a touch cold, his hood down, a Viyella shirt under his prickly cassock, his feet in sandals and heavy white socks of the sort Frank remembered otherwise naked boys wearing in those gay porno magazines he dutifully leafed through the time he was dreaming about sucking off Kurt. He sat looking at Frank incuriously, sometimes rubbing his head, passing his fingers lightly over a tumor the size of an egg, the single disfigurement to his smooth baldness. The egg of wisdom, Frank hoped. The cyst of spirituality.

'This isn't easy for me,' Frank confessed, sitting forward on the kitchen chair he normally used as a support for his portable television. 'I've never sought counsel before. And of course I'm not a Christian. But then I've never appealed to a rabbi either. Quite what I want from you I don't know. Quite what the trouble is I don't know. Too much mind perhaps.'

The ex-abbot pointed to his chest. 'There must be love,' he said. 'But then the mind can be a good thing too.'

You don't say, Frank thought.

It struck him that Father Lawrence was ready to go now. But Frank hadn't even started yet. 'I am,' he conceded, 'a disputatious man. I earn my living disputatiously. Criticism is everything to me. It is perhaps the only activity in which I am truly happy. It is certainly the only activity I unreservedly value. For myself, you understand. I grasp what Benedict means when he advises against grumbling and speaking ill of others. But given the opportunity to unsay any of the cruel or dismissive things I have said over the years I doubt if I would withdraw more than half a dozen of them. They have not been gratuitous. I hope I am not a gratuitous man. I hope that a disinterested play of mind is what has governed me in all my asseverations. I hope so. But I cannot deny that to be in possession of a relentlessly critical mind is to be frequently wearied. It begins to affect the heart. When I listen to my heart sometimes I hear it begging to be let off. Deposit something kind in my vicinity, I hear it saying. Do warmth for a bit. Do forgivingness. I've heard it said that a bad heart can be as much a moral as a physiological condition. It would seem that you can literally cruel your own heart. I feel that I have cruelled mine. But in a cause in which I wholeheartedly – ha, whole*heartedly* – believe. There's the catch. Where, without also damaging myself spiritually and intellectually, am I supposed to find the forgivingness my heart seems to want? It's as if my several parts, my heart and my mind – my spirit and my intellect, if you like – are at war with one another. How to heal their feud? I am interested in that term you Christian philosophers employ: hesychia. Perhaps I'm pronouncing it wrong. *Hes*ychia? Hesych*ia*? I'm not at all sure I understand it fully either. Tranquility, I think it means. Is that right? A sort of still, seated harmony among the parts. But how to achieve hesychia – there's the question . . .'

So he spoke.

He paused, not because he'd finished – oh no, he'd nothing like finished – but because he assumed it was spiritual good manners, during counselling, to allow the counsellor the time to counsel.

He waited.

Father Lawrence massaged the tumor on his head. He seemed taken aback by the expression of expectancy on Frank's face.

At last he said, 'I had a wonderful holiday in Israel last year. I went for about six weeks. In a group. All Benedictines, of course. I'd never been before, though it had always been my ambition to go. Everyone was very nice to us. And surprisingly knowledgeable. Our driver particularly. *He* was an Israeli. Yet he knew all the holy sites. And their meaning for us. He even knew the Franciscan Fathers on the Mount of Beatitudes and was able to arrange for us to have an outdoor Mass there. It was very moving.'

Was this wisdom of the very highest order, Frank wondered. Was this wisdom and then some?

The eleventh step of humility is that a monk speaks gently and without laughter, seriously and with becoming modesty, briefly and reasonably and without raising his voice . . .

Did the ex-Father Abbot's seriousness and reasonableness, his economic spiritual maturity, reside in this: that he knew how to counsel without apparently counselling at all? That he only *appeared* to be talking about his hols; that he was in fact presenting Frank with a working model of the very calm he sought?

But in that case, why didn't Frank feel calm?

'Let me put it another way,' Frank said. 'The problem for me seems to be one of ascendancy – that's to say, how do I get it. When you are used to mental turbulence, and even come to love the noise it makes, come to recognise it as a sign that you are intellectually alive, how do you go about silencing it without feeling that you have immured or even damaged your best self. Your own St Benedict says that the wise man is known by the fewness of his words. But words are my profession . . .'

He looked across at the old man whose hands were folded now, as though deliberately, as an act of refusal, in his lap. Was Frank pleading? Maybe not pleading, but asking certainly. Seeking. Shut the fuck up and get the fuck out, Mel had ordered. He was halfway there. He'd got the fuck out. But how to shut the fuck up?

Seek and ye shall find.

Well, Father? Well?

'Next year,' Father Lawrence said, but this time without recourse to his cyst, 'I'm hoping I will be well enough to make it to Italy. I haven't been to Rome for twenty years, could be more. And there have been many changes . . .'

He has no appetite for it, Frank thought. He has no gift for abstraction and no flair for solace. He has the face of a philosopher but the imagination of a commuter. But he felt he owed it to Brother Cyprian at least to give it one last go. 'So how do you quieten the roar of *your* passions?' he asked. Keeping it simple now, keeping it short. 'What do *you* do when jealousy or anger smites your heart?'

'Oh, you have to see how silly that is, and try to think of something else.'

Frank waited. Was that it? Silly! Had they been sitting there discussing *silliness* for an hour?

Yes, that was it. The old man turned his face to the window, looked out into the vegetable garden where Gordon, all tears, was pulling down an unwanted woodshed. Then he consulted the alarm clock by Frank's bed. Time to be going.

Frank rose and thanked him. 'It's most kind of you,' he said. 'I'm most grateful to you. I'll think about what you have said to me.'

But he knew what he was going to think. He was going to think that he had more spirituality in his dick . . .

. . . and he didn't want to be thinking about his dick.

It's enough to make him miss Mel. He can't find anybody to be serious with.

'Day by day remind yourself,' Benedict advised, 'that you are going to die.' No sign that the monks have taken any heed of that. They laugh uproariously and eat like pigs. And the wisest and oldest one among them is planning his next overseas trip. Only Frank has death daily in his eyes.

And of course Gordon. Though Gordon, strictly speaking, doesn't count. Benedict's words are not intended to drive you to suicide. Day by day remind yourself is an injunction to morbid longevity, whereas Gordon is increasingly looking to Frank like a man meaning to end it all. 'So there it is,' he says one morning in the guests' kitchen. Apropos nothing in particular. So there it is. Frank sees a subtly fatalistic progression here from Gordon's usual 'Yes indeed'. So there it is. So there it was. It'll be over for him before the day's out, Frank thinks. They'll find him face down in the stream. But the following morning Frank runs into him in the kitchen early, buttering toast and loading it with marmalade. 'Lovely day,' Frank says. 'Yes indeed,' Gordon replies. So *he* isn't really serious either.

As for the other retreatants, those Frank cannot avoid speaking to are here only because yoga and meditation and marriage counselling have failed. Next week they'll be Hare Krishnas. 'I've just been reading a book about losing yourself through drugs, the way Mexicans do,' one of them says to him, as they're feeling their way back from vespers in the dark. 'By someone called Audrey Huxley.'

'I think I know a book a bit like that,' Frank says. 'Except that the one I know is by *Aldous* Huxley.'

'That's her. That's the one. Good book.'

And sitting reading quietly in the common room later that same afternoon, waiting to enter the hush of compline, he is accosted by a precociously grey grasshopper of a man with glacial green eyes and two sets of pupils, one not quite aligned behind the other, who has a desire to talk to him about himself. 'I've succumbed to most things in life,' he tells Frank. 'Women, alcohol, meat, drugs. But they're wrong. I've always known they were wrong, but now I know *why* they're wrong . . .'

He waits for Frank to ask him to put flesh upon that why, but Frank has been here too long to ask anyone anything.

'And I'll tell you why,' the man says at last. 'Because it's in the Book. Whatever you need is in that Book. My name's Fletcher, by the way, what's yours? OK – it's out there,

Frank. It's waiting for you to find it. Seek and ye shall find. Knock and ye shall enter.'

'Aha,' Frank says. He knows all about seeking and knocking.

'You might not think it to look at me,' Fletcher continues, 'but I've been everywhere. I've been entertainments manager on the QE2. I've flown Concorde. I've climbed the pyramids. I've dived off the cliffs at Acapulco. I've walked along the Chinese Wall. I've roller-skated on Venice beach. And I can still do all these things. But I know I've got to decide now between a life with love or a life without love. I've got to come down on one side or another. That's why I'm here.'

Aha, Frank thinks. His wife's sent him.

'I know another good book on that subject,' Frank says, getting up to go to prayers. 'It's by Audrey Huxley.'

They aren't serious. They aren't fit to fasten a real recluse's sandals. They don't acknowledge they're dirt. They don't day by day remind themselves they've had it. They're all five more years men. They've all got the gimmies.

Frank doesn't want anyone to give him anything. It's good simply to be alive, watching the year die. Sitting in the cold, in a world without women, losing himself in plainsong. He knows he can't stay with the monks forever. But whether he'll get his own place up here in the dark, or go on a monastery crawl, six weeks here, two months there, he hasn't yet decided. In the meantime, depletion grows on him. One wash basin, one narrow wardrobe, one single bed (and not a thought of the pity of it, oh the pity of it Iago, he and his dick going begging on a mattress, night after night), one electric socket, a single kitchen chair for his portable television and laptop computer — how much else does a man need?

He's come full circle, from the first grand hotel room he

slept in as a boy, marvelling at the teeming future that disclosed itself in every empty lavender-scented drawer, to this last lowly nutshell with its intimations only of the grave.

He's so battened down that even his adversary the tempter doesn't call on him any more. He's safe from grandiosity – no one reads his column in this place, no one recognises him. He's safe from the past – no ghosts of runny girls crook their fingers to him in the cloisters. No one sculpts his likeness in cappuccino froth. He's an impregnable fortress. He's so close to the ground no wind can blow him over.

And then Mel writes to him.

Once a week he's been going into town to fax his copy and collect his mail. Mel is still sending him whatever comes through her letterbox that isn't addressed solely to her. The bills and the takeaway pizza menus and the washing-powder samples all stuffed into a brown padded bag and addressed in love-me-not handwriting to Ritz, Poste Restante, Inverness, Scotland. She is in possession of no other information about his whereabouts. The monastery is his secret. He's damned if he's going to give her the satisfaction of thinking that he's finally taken her advice. Isn't this what she's always wanted him to be – a fucking monk?

So what makes her write suddenly? What makes her enliven the usual anonymous litter with a personal enclosure, the briefest of notes on her Melissa Paul, pornographer, notepaper, but a note nonetheless – *If you think you can be quiet now, you can come home* – ?

Does she know, or is it an inspired guess?

Has her new lover dumped her? Have they all?

And how can she be so sure that this scrap of insolent presumption is all it will take to get him to renounce every vow, kiss goodbye to compline and come charging down the motorway at a hundred miles an hour with his pancreas

pumping poisons and his stomach plastered across the
dashboard like seaweed on a rock?

Don't make us laugh, Frank.

THIRTEEN

So what's the drill? Does he ring the bell or does he let himself in with his key?

You can come home, she wrote. *Home*. That entitles him to use his key, surely. But he's been a monk for the past however many months. A guest in the house of God, not a homeowner. He doesn't know whether he any longer has what it takes just to let himself in. Besides, his hands are shaking. He doubts if he could fit the key into the keyhole. Nerves? No. Yes. And the long drive. And the palsy of old age. His hands have been in the world for fifty years – of course they're shaking.

He rings.

There is no answer.

There are lights on in the house. She could be in the back garden. It's a chilly evening, but that wouldn't deter her. She likes the cold and the dark. She likes sitting out under the stars in one of his cardigans. Submitting to the moon's magnetic pull. If the moon could draw her colon out and clean it, she'd let it.

The garden was always the place she fled to escape him. He watched her sometimes, after they had fought, sitting out there as though she meant never to come inside again, sorrowful and lonely, her back turned on him and on the house, her gaze fixed on nothing. No matter what he had said to her, no matter what she had said to him, the sight of her absorbed into nature, wheeled around like an icy star herself, always broke his heart.

How many times had he gone out to her, to say he was sorry, to see if he could pluck her from the planetary pull, coax her back into the human world, the only world he comprehended. But it always fell out the same way. 'What now?' she would say, oppressed by the long shadow he cast, even in the dark.

'I thought you might want to talk.'

'Talk! What's the matter with you? Are you mad? Are you completely mad? Aren't you getting enough trouble?'

And she would get up, leave the garden, leave him standing there with the hand he meant to soothe her with still raised. Another crime on his conscience. That he had ruined her garden for her as well. Ruptured her union with the flower fairies.

But while it's up there, what about that raised hand . . . ? Had he never been tempted, once in a while, to bring it down upon his lover's refusing neck? Of course he had. There may always have been a monk in him, but he was never a saint. After the heartbreak the hatred. Like everybody else. Love and murderousness – in their early days, of course, these were never in serious conflict. You fucked, you loved, you killed. At one and the same time. This is what fucking's for. The reconciliation of opposites. Tearing with rough strife, thorough the iron gates of life. But once you're not fucking every hour that God sends, you're at the mercy of the violent contrarieties again.

Will there be any tearing tonight?

Unlikely. He cannot say what's in her but there's no violence in him tonight. He's been driving since dawn, or what would have been dawn in a place more accessible to light. He rose with the buzzer, attended his last vigils and was packed and on the road before six. He was glad to be going and sad to be glad. Nothing stuck. Everything hung by a thread. One good gust of wind and it would all be gone. Hence the success of the rule of St Benedict. Expect nothing. Just day by day remind yourself you're going to die. Holding on to the wheel of his Saab in the early cold, Frank bled for the poor transient motorway humanity he sped past. The lumpen lorry drivers with their cargoes of crap, pulling out and pulling in, winking and flashing their lives away. The salesmen on the phone, the chauffeurs in their caps, the kids with their faces full of steel, wired up to their sound systems like the dying on a drip. Even the idiot crap-watchers of the summer, still queuing for all-day breakfasts and scratch-cards in the service stations. Back in their winter clothes, shut down for the season, they took hold again on his pity. You can grieve for people so long as they don't show you their bodies. You can grieve for their immortal souls.

He rings again.

Still there is no answer. This time he tries the door with his key. It opens. Home. He steps inside, knowing she will not be hiding under the stairs, waiting to fling her arms around him, waiting to be swept off her feet and swung around by Daddy, as women who have love in their hearts do on the box with the silver smirk.

He sniffs the hallway. Shaming, but that's what he does. He sniffs the house for newer, nicer, younger man. Then he notices a large packet on the hall table, a bulging brown envelope, not unlike those she's been using to send him bills and washing powder samples. Except that this envelope isn't addressed to Ritz, Poste Restante, Inverness, Scotland. This envelope is addressed to Aphrodite Press, Ladbroke Crescent, London W10. So this is why she's allowed him back; not because she's polished off a lover, but because she's polished off a book. He isn't sure whether he's relieved. What's worse, being in competition with the rest of your sex, or being in competition with literature?

He feels excluded, either way. Something has been happening in this house – his house, his *home* – that couldn't have been happening with him in it. And just in case the significance of that should be lost on him, the door to his study is closed. Not ajar, not pushed to, but shut tight.

He opens it, gently. His study! He'd forgotten all about his study. Its winking red and green lights, its digitised all-knowingness, like the cabin of a jumbo jet. Seeing it again, listening to it crackle and purr with pleasure at his return – at least someone has missed him – he cannot imagine how he ever survived without it. He counts his electric sockets. Fancy that. Already he is rehearsing the argument for having more. And once upon a time, in another life, he got by with only one.

He goes to his window, and yes, there she is, just as he thought, just as he remembers her, sitting in the garden with her back to the house, not quite looking up at the sky, and because of the blackness of the clothes she is wearing – always black, interminably black – not fully distinguishable from the night. He watches her in silence for a while. She doesn't move. But he knows that she is aware he is there, at his window, having gone to his machines before he went to her, playing back the messages on his answerphone, all three-and-a-half months of them.

Frank wonders why she holds herself so gravely, so inexpectantly, given that she has had her way, been rid of him and all his noise for so long, and has effortlessly got him to return on her terms. *If you think you can be quiet . . .* She is mistress of all sound now, she is sole queen of the night. So why isn't she rampant with happiness?

Of course he may not have her right. She may only look like a woman grieving to *him*. This is a discredited act of the imagination, he knows. Anthropomorphism, it is called. Attributing the thoughts and feelings of a man to what is not a man. It is held to be unscientific, emotional, and presumptuous. But what can he do? Anthropos is all he is. He can only feel as a man. And what he feels is that she is sorrowing and sad.

But that's what Frank thinks about all women – isn't it? – that they are sorrowing and sad. That they exist for him to pity. Once, to fuck and pity. Now, to pity full stop.

He goes downstairs and steps out into the garden. And shivers.

She doesn't turn around. Doesn't move. He is so sorry for her. She is so frightened of what he will do. Try a joke. Attempt a justification. Essay something sexual. He knows how little of a threat he is to her. So her fear smites his heart.

There are no candles or garden torches burning. He cannot see how she is, or what she has done to herself while he's been away. How she is wearing her hair. Whether she even has hair. No Castro's beard, he is confident of that. She's been writing, not sprouting. He would love to put his hand out to touch her, to coax her up out of the soil, straighten her rounded back. But what if she were to say, 'What now? Are you mad?' Could he take it? Would he be able to bear it? Never mind on her account, would he be able to bear it for *himself*?

He must risk it. He has no choice. He drops his fingers lightly on her shoulders, as on a keyboard. Pianissimo. *Con amore lamentabile*. Tell a butterfly to land more considerately and it couldn't do it. But the cold in her bones still rises up to him.

How thin she is, he thinks. Is it possible she hasn't eaten since he left? Or has she upped the number of hours she spends hanging over the bath? She doesn't return his touch, but she receives it. He feels her take it in, collect it, as a debt that's owing to her.

Is she right? Is this her due? Or is what he believes right – that his touch is a gift, freely given?

Not a word has been spoken but they are arguing already.

There's a fox out. Screaming for sex. When a fox screams for sex you think its being killed. You can smell the blood. Foxes do it in reverse order – murderousness *then* love. Frank isn't screaming for sex. Frank isn't screaming for anything. Frank's going quietly. He would just like what's given freely as a gift to be accepted as a gift. That's all. And while he's on the subject of going quietly, since the game is Mel's, since she has won, since he's back emptied of all noise, and since there is a fat envelope oozing juicy pornoscript on the hall table, why this continuing tragedy? Why the grief? Why the garden of fucking desolation, Mel?

If he had a free hand he'd be smiting the side of his head with it. Woman – mouth – droop; man – forehead – bang. For two pins, if there were somewhere worth going, if there were some other war worth fighting, if this field of blood were not the most transfixingly interesting place on earth to him, he'd be gone.